About the Author

Elfrida enjoyed a short but interesting career in the theatre as an actress and dancer, where she had many amusing contacts with stars of stage and screen. Her training in ballet enabled her to run her own schools in Australia, Hong Kong and the UK. Her years as a dance teacher allowed her scope for writing and she created many ballets for her pupils. She is also a guest speaker at clubs and institutions.

Her first book of short stories, *Box Set*, was published by Austin Macauley in early 2020.

Elfrida is married and lives in West Sussex.

Elfrida Eden Fallowfield

ANOTHER BOX SET

AUSTIN MACAULEY PUBLISHERS™

LONDON • CAMBRIDGE • NEW YORK • SHARJAH

A CIP catalogue record for this title is available from the British Library.

ISBN 9781398445543 (Paperback)
ISBN 9781398445550 (ePub e-book)

www.austinmacauley.com

First Published 2021
Austin Macauley Publishers Ltd
1 Canada Square
Canary Wharf
London E14 5AA

Dedication

for

Jean Bird
for producing such creative illustrations

and

Oliver Richard William Eynon
who missed out the first time.

Acknowledgements

My thanks again to Walter Stephenson
at Austin Macauley for all his help

Contents

THE JACK-IN-THE-BOX

MARK AND ANGELA were living their dream. Married just over a year and with no commitments, they decided this was the perfect time for their hiking holiday in Wales. They had been told the countryside around Snowdonia National Park was spectacular, and so it had proved. On top of that, the locals had been so friendly and welcoming that they decided when they could they would return, and extend their explorations.

On their fourth day, the young couple left their B&B in Mynydd Bach after breakfast to spend the day hiking in the area before driving towards Llanfaehreth, where they had chosen a delightful-looking guest house for the following two nights.

The weather was perfect and the scenery spectacular. They were so enjoying themselves, but Mark checked the time and said they really should be heading back to the car.

"Don't you think we might just have time to whip up that last hill over there?" said Angela. "I bet the views from the top will be brilliant."

Mark agreed, somewhat reluctantly, but insisted they cracked on with no dawdling.

Angela was right. The views were breathtaking. They took photos with their mobile telephones of the scenery and selfies of them together. The way back to their car was longer than they remembered, and Mark said he just hoped they would arrive before dark. Once they had left the wooded area they were in Mark keyed in the postcode into the satnav that had come with the car. No signal. He then tried another app on his mobile, but still no signal.

"Just have to rely on your skilful map reading, darling," he said to Angela as he concentrated on negotiating the rather rough route.

All went well at first, and they felt they were making good progress until they came to a crossroads, and all the signs were in Welsh! Looking at their map, Angela felt sure they should turn left, and so they did.

They drove on, but as they did so the road became smaller and more twisted, with no sign of life in any direction.

"I must have made a mistake at that crossroads," Angela said. "So sorry darling, but I think we must retrace our steps and try again."

Annoyingly, after the lovely day they had just enjoyed, there was a distinct change in the weather. A wind was getting up and dark clouds were gathering. The normally light early evening in August was becoming increasingly darker by the time they reached the crossroads again. On this occasion they drove straight on. Once again the road twisted this way and that, and then began a slow descent into a valley. Darkness was really upon them by now and, to add to their misery, it had begun to rain.

Angela was beginning to fret. She kept on trying to get a signal on her phone but no luck. She could see Mark was also concerned, and she was only too aware how often he kept glancing at their petrol indicator.

"I don't think we should turn back again," said Mark. "This road is bound to lead somewhere. We will surely come to a village, a hamlet, or even a house, any minute now."

Mark was trying to keep cheerful, but he was seriously worried at the state of the petrol. He silently cursed himself for not filling up the jerry can that was sitting empty in the boot of the car. He had meant to, as he always prided himself on 'being well prepared' – but on this occasion it had entirely slipped his mind.

Adding to their anxiety were the first gnawing pangs of hunger. The guest house had promised them a substantial evening meal, and they could certainly do justice to it, as all they had had during the day were some high-protein biscuits, chocolate and water.

The weather worsened. The wind picked up and over the noise of the engine they could hear the wild moaning it made as it circled and buffeted the small car.

The red warning light came on. 'Fill up immediately' was the indication. Fill up – but where? Oh for a petrol station! Mark, though, knew they were unlikely to find one conveniently just around the next corner.

The road had reached the bottom of the valley by now, and steep banks rose on either side, with at first shrubs and small trees growing. The small trees grew in height, and they realised they were driving through dense wood.

"Look," said Angela, "there on the left. There is a light. Oh hurrah – civilization."

However, the light, such as it was, was deep in the wood. There was no impression of a cheerfully lit house to offer them refuge, unfortunately, and no sign of any other dwelling.

"Surely we must be on the outskirts of a village by now. I vote we crack on. I don't much like the look of that place," Mark said.

Maybe his idea was correct, but after the best part of a mile, with a good deal of coughing and stuttering, their car ground to a halt, completely void of petrol.

Angela tried to contain herself but she was quite close to tears.

"There's nothing for it," said Mark, doing his best to be decisive and not show his own anxiety, "we will just have to walk back to the cottage in the woods. Maybe they can call for some help, or at least give us some shelter for a while."

Grabbing their rucksacks out of the boot, they removed their wet weather gear for the first time on this trip. Mark was pleased with himself that he had at least remembered to put a decent torch in the car. So, each taking the other by the hand, and with heads bent against the driving rain, they retraced their steps until once again they saw the light through the trees.

The cottage appeared to be a solid structure built of Welsh stone. They could just make out the shapes of a couple of small outbuildings.

The light was coming from one ground floor window only. The curtains were closed so they could not see the interior. There appeared to be no knocker or bell on the weather-beaten front door, so Mark rapped with his knuckles. Immediately another light, presumably in the hall, was switched on, and a cheerful sing-song voice with a distinct Welsh lilt called out.

"Just a minute – just a minute. I am on my way. These old legs aren't as quick as they used to be."

With that, the door opened, and they were faced with a little old woman, who appeared to have rosy apples instead of cheeks, smiling at them. She said, "Now *there* you are! I wondered where you had gone to. You're late – and on top of that, you are soaking wet. Come in, come in and make yourselves warm by the kitchen range. The soup is all ready and the bread has not been long out of the oven."

Mark and Angela looked at each other in amazement. Angela tried to clarify the situation by saying, "Excuse me Mrs – um – whoever you are, I am so sorry but you appear to be mistaking us for some other people. We have never met you before, and we are only asking for a little shelter, and hopefully the use of your telephone?"

"Nonsense, my dear. I have been waiting for you for a long time, and I knew you would come today. Go into the kitchen and sit at the table. The soup is nice and hot." Then, laughingly: "Of course, we do not have a telephone here. We are miles away from anyone else. It worried me when you took that wrong turn – but you are here at last. At last."

How on earth did this old woman know about their wrong turn? The young couple were both feeling mystified and decidedly uncomfortable. However, they were also hungry and the soup smelled delicious and homely.

"What is your name?" Angela asked.

"I am Mrs Thomas" the old woman replied, "though you of course know me by the proper name. Now here you are – drink your soup and enjoy it."

All the while they were eating, Mrs Thomas never took her eyes off them, especially Angela. She gazed at her with an expression – Angela was quite perturbed thinking this way – almost of 'love'.

"That was delicious, Mrs Thomas," said Mark after they had finished. "Now, we really must not detain you any longer. Perhaps you could direct us to the nearest village and as the rain is easing, I am sure we could walk there? Also please allow us to give you something for the food."

"Oh, you silly young man!" Mrs Thomas replied, sounding almost irritated. "Neither of you are going anywhere. As I told you before, we are miles from anyone here. Besides, I have been waiting for you for a long time. You cannot venture out again tonight. You would only get lost. You will stay here. Now, before you go to bed, I will make you a cup of my very special hot chocolate."

Mark and Angela exchanged puzzled glances. Whilst Mrs Thomas had her back turned, Mark whispered, "I don't think we have much choice. She is obviously a bit batty, probably due to living here all by herself. In the morning we will set off early…"

Angela nodded in agreement, but she was unnerved by Mrs Thomas insisting she had been 'waiting' for them. Other than that, she seemed a friendly and harmless old woman, and the thought of venturing out into the dark on such an unpleasant night was not inviting, whereas a good sleep was far more preferable.

"That's very kind of you," said Mark, and then he asked, "is there a Mr Thomas?"

"Long since gone," was the somewhat abrupt reply. The cups of steaming chocolate were put in front of them and Mrs Thomas sat down at the table opposite her guests. "The chocolate I use is slightly bitter on its own, so I have put plenty of sugar in the mix. I do hope you like it."

Was Angela being fanciful? She felt Mrs Thomas put an unusual emphasis on the word 'do'.

"Now let me look at you properly, my dear," she said to Angela. "Just as I thought. In fact even prettier than I imagined. You are a lucky young man."

"Oh I know I am" Mark replied. "Very lucky indeed."

"Mrs Thomas, before I drink my chocolate may I use your toilet please?"

"Of course dear – down the hall and it is the last door on the left. Be sure you remember – the *last* door."

"Thank you," said Angela as she left the kitchen.

The hall was dimly lit. There were two doors on the left, and a small door Angela assumed was a cupboard on the right. She opened the last door on the left and groped for a light. The cloakroom was small. An old-fashioned WC with a cistern above and the handle hanging from a chain was opposite a rather cracked hand basin. As she sat down Angela looked at the walls which were covered in black and white photographs, some faded with age, all in simple wooden frames.

One young girl featured in every image. In most of them she must have been in her early teens, and the rest were obviously her as a small child. A young Mrs Thomas appeared in a couple. Other than that no other person featured at all.

As Angela studied these photos she became increasingly disturbed. Looking at the photographs of the older girl, Angela felt she could have been looking at photos of herself! The coincidence was certainly unnerving. She would tell Mark that they must leave this house first thing in the morning.

Angela's instinct was to hurry back to Mark, but as she passed the first door, now on her right, she wondered why Mrs Thomas had stressed so clearly she should only open the last door.

Quickly she opened the door and peered into a room so dimly lit she could barely make out what was in it. She was aware of a cluttered room with a huge closet, a bed, a table and an armchair.

At first she didn't see him, but as her eyes adjusted she was shocked to see a figure of a very tiny old man, who seemed to be asleep. All of a sudden he awoke, and stared at Angela with eyes that seemed to glint, despite the gloom.

"Oh so you did come," he croaked in a frail but urgent voice. "The old crone was right. You must get away – get away. You're not safe. Quick – leave this room before she sees you."

Angela didn't need any persuasion. She swiftly left, and as she softly closed the door a sharp voice said – "Do *not* go into that room. That is *not* the room I told you to go in. Come back here, at once."

"I wasn't going in," lied Angela, "but I thought I heard a strange noise."

"There is nothing in there," still quite sharp, then back to her sweet voice: "Come and have your drink, my dear, and then I will take you to your room."

Mark was more than a little concerned when he saw the expression on Angela's face as she returned to the kitchen and sat as close to her husband as possible. Mark started to inform her that Mrs Thomas had been telling him about her daughter, Meghan. She was born in this cottage and was a beautiful girl. Tragically, one day, when she was 15 years old, she went out for a walk and was never seen again.

While Mark was relating this to Angela, his wife noticed he kept on rubbing his eyes, and shaking his head, as if he was trying to stay awake. "I expect he is very tired after this long day," she thought, "and I admit I am too."

Mrs Thomas pushed the mug of chocolate over to her, and told her to "drink up while it's nice and hot." Angela did so to please her, but she had to agree, even with the sugar it was seriously bitter.

"How dreadful for you Mrs Thomas, I am so sorry," she said. "Did you ever... I mean was she ever...? Um, sorry, where was I? Did you find out what happened?"

Mrs Thomas appeared to swim before her.

"She was taken by the fairies, my dear. They needed her. She was so beautiful and such a darling girl. So they took her, but they promised they would bring her back to me when I needed her." And here she dropped the bombshell. "And so they have. Right now. You have come home to me, my darling. I wasn't expecting *you* as well," she continued to Mark, "but I am sure we can fit you in and you can make yourself useful. It's just so wonderful you are here at last – and you are here to *stay*."

"Mrs Thomas," Mark tried hard to sound firm and calm, "I am afraid there is some mistake. Angela is not your long-lost daughter. She has two very healthy parents living in Wiltshire. Angela is my wife, and I am afraid we are not here to stay."

As he was saying that Mark was conscious that he was finding it hard to speak. His words seemed to come so slowly, and his tongue felt thick in his mouth.

"Oh dear, dear, dear," said Mrs Thomas. "You don't understand, do you? It was your destiny to come here tonight. It was planned. I was expecting you, and now you will stay. Right now you will both be feeling very tired after your energetic day. It is time for me to show you to your rooms. Come along, my dears."

Angela reached for Mark's hand. She stumbled as she rose from the table, and her head seemed somehow detached from her body. She leaned into Mark and tried to whisper. "Shere's a man in the room. He shays we mun leave. Photos – lots – in loo. Shay all look like me. Am frightened."

"Stop whispering, you two. It won't do any good. You need to be in bed *very* soon."

Mrs Thomas led the way upstairs where there was a small landing. "Here is the bathroom," she pointed to a door at the end, "and this is your room," she said to Angela, as she somewhat roughly steered her inside. Mark visited the bathroom while Angela took stock of her bedroom.

It was a small room with a simple single bed pushed against the wall. The walls were covered in a floral wallpaper that was so faded it was almost white in parts. Damp patches were apparent and the edges of the paper were peeling away from the walls. A pair of tattered curtains hung limply at the window, which looked firmly locked. A ragged doll sat on a minute chair, and on the bed was a somewhat grotesque stuffed pink pig, with only one eye and one ear. Angela did not want to stay in this room.

"Where will Mark shleep?" she asked.

"He has his own room. This is *your* room and you are home at last."

With that the old woman gave Angela a push, so that she fell onto the bed. As Mrs Thomas said, "Sleep well, my dear."

Angela knew she had to give in. She sat on the bed feeling frightened but powerless. She heard a key being turned in the lock of her door, but there was no way she could ward off the heavy sleep that immediately engulfed her.

Mark emerged from the bathroom and asked. "Where's my wife?"

"Safely tucked up in her old bed," was the reply. "This room is mine so you have to sleep in the box room."

As she was saying this Mrs Thomas was half-pushing, half-dragging Mark to the other end of the passage. Mark made a half-hearted attempt to resist, but he realised it was no use.

Mrs Thomas opened the door and turned on the single light bulb that hung suspended in the middle room. "There's a divan there," indicated the old woman. "You will be fine." Then, with no more words, she turned and left the room, firmly shutting and locking the door behind her.

Mark did his best to clear his head. He tried to evaluate his surroundings. The light, such as it was, only illuminated a small area in the centre.

The box room was accurately named. There were piles of boxes of all shapes and sizes haphazardly stacked in every conceivable space. Wedged between two piles of larger boxes was a distinctly suspect-looking divan, with a moth-eaten rug thrown over it.

Mark realised the old woman must have put something in their drinks. Although he was fitter and stronger than Angela and therefore not so badly affected, he knew he could not muster any clear thoughts or actions while he was in this state.

"Sleep," he thought, "sleep is what I must have, and when I wake up I will tackle that old woman and get Angela away."

Sensible thoughts; and the only action he was capable of was to stumble over to the divan and collapse on top of it. Despite his worries and fears for Angela and himself, Mark instantly fell into a deep sleep.

———————————

Mrs Thomas bustled downstairs once she had 'shown' her two guests their rooms.

Tidying up in the kitchen, she happily sang to herself. A strange little smile lingered on her face as she then prepared a small tray with a bowl of soup, a slice of bread and a glass of water.

Picking up the tray, and still humming to herself, Mrs Thomas went down the passage and opened the first door on the left.

The old man did not stir from his chair. It turned out he could not even if he had wanted to. He was firmly tied to the chair by his waist and ankles with leather straps.

"I need to go," he wailed. "I've needed to go for a long time. Get me up – get me up."

"I don't know why I bother with you, I really don't," grumbled Mrs Thomas as she undid the straps and roughly helped the old man to his feet. While she propelled him towards a commode she continued, "You're nothing but a nuisance, you are. I could finish you off tomorrow if I wanted."

"Well why don't you, you evil old bat? Why do you keep me like this? You will rot in hell for the sins you have committed. Who else is in the house? I heard the sounds of visitors."

"Nothing to do with you, old man. Just you keep your nose out of things. But I will tell you this. Our daughter has come back to us! There – I can see I have surprised you. You never believed me, but I knew one day she would return. Now she is here, but the silly girl has a husband in tow, so I'll have to sort that one out."

"She cannot be our daughter, whoever this young woman is. You know as well as I do that our daughter is dead. You must let them go. This couple do not belong to us."

"Oh but they do," beamed Mrs Thomas. "My Meghan has come home and I will make sure she never leaves us again. Now – drink your soup and then go to bed. I don't want any trouble from you. Tomorrow will be a busy day."

The knocking was quite gentle – but persistent. Gradually the sound penetrated Mark's still somewhat befuddled brain. *Rat-a-tat, rat-a-tat, rat-a-tat.* As he opened his eyes Mark tried to remember what had happened the night before. The inside of his mouth felt thick and clumsy. He would give his right arm for a drink of water.

Still he heard the noise. *Rat-a-tat, rat-a-tat.* Where was it coming from?

As his eyes adjusted to the dim light, Mark attempted to look more clearly at his surroundings.

Along with the boxes of various shapes and sizes were two old chairs, with damaged cane seats, a small table with one leg missing and a large, old-fashioned wicker laundry basket. Abutting this basket was a tall square box with once bright decorations on its sides, and a hook lock near the top.

The knocking seemed to be coming from that direction. Mark went over to the hamper which was secured by two short leather straps. As he struggled to undo them, the knocking appeared to be even more insistent. Mark had never had an over-active imagination, but somehow he felt the knocking was meant for him. Was there something mysterious inside the old laundry basket?

Gingerly he lifted the lid and was immediately aware the knocking had stopped.

It was almost a disappointment to discover there appeared to be nothing more unusual than a pile of old clothes stashed inside the basket. With a brain that was at last clearing, Mark remembered his torch in his backpack. At least Mrs Thomas had allowed them to take their bags into their rooms with them. By the light of the torch Mark examined the clothes. They were mainly children's clothes for a little girl, and then some for an older girl as well. Packed amongst them were some moth-eaten soft toys and a collection of Noah's Ark animals. Obviously these had all belonged to the long-lost daughter, and Mark allowed himself to feel sorry for the batty old woman.

Rather ashamed of his rapidly beating heart, Mark repacked the hamper and secured the lid.

Almost immediately the knocking started again.

"So," thought Mark, "it's not coming from the hamper. Perhaps it is in this box? Maybe some animal trying to escape?"

He knew that was a somewhat far-fetched scenario, but if truth be told, Mark was decidedly nervous about releasing the small catch to open the box.

Tentatively he pushed the catch to the right, when with a suddenness that caused him to shout in surprise, the lid burst open and up jumped a figure of a clown about 12 inches long, with long floppy arms which waved madly about. The head was clad in a crazy, lopsided hat and wild orange hair surrounded a grotesque face dominated by a garish painted smile and a bright red bulbous nose. But it was the eyes that were mesmerising. They were large and startling in their brightness. The eyes did not keep still. They darted from side to side, as the arms continued their frantic waving.

Not only had he shouted in surprise when the box opened, Mark had also jumped backwards. His heart was beating fast, and his first thought was: "What a horrible present to give to a child. Enough to give anyone nightmares."

Feeling a bit calmer, he returned to the box and attempted to push the clown back inside. However, not only could he not manage this, despite his best efforts – and he was no weakling – he found himself staring at the eyes of the puppet which were now firmly fixed on Mark's face. So he returned to the divan and sat down.

Mark knew he should have a plan to get Angela and himself out of this unpleasant situation they were in. The problem was that they were both locked in their rooms with no visible means of escape. He was deeply worried about Angela, and hoped she wasn't too scared. All the while he was thinking these thoughts, Mark was aware the clown was staring at him.

"It's almost as if it's trying to tell me something. But that is just totally ridiculous, I know. Yet there is something decidedly weird about all this. I cannot really believe it is happening in this day and age."

Out of desperation he tried his mobile again. No signal. He was trying not to, but he found himself looking at the clown again. It appeared to be encouraging Mark to look at a small chest of drawers just by the door. Feeling ridiculous, Mark went over to the chest and opened the top drawer. The contents were the usual paraphernalia of objects that didn't have a proper home: old pencils, bits of string, elastic bands, etc. Nothing of any interest. Mark looked at the clown, and the eyes were still fixed on him. He opened the second drawer which was much the same, but in the third drawer was a rusty ring with a bunch of keys attached to it.

The clown suddenly started moving again. His ungainly arms met together in front of him and parodied a silent clap.

Suddenly Mark heard voices from the other side of the door. He heard Angela crying out for him. He heard Mrs Thomas telling her in no uncertain terms that she needed to behave before she could leave her room. If necessary, she would be made to drink another mug of Mrs Thomas' special hot chocolate.

For some reason Mark made the decision not to call out. The clown at this time was dancing like a mad thing – seemingly beckoning Mark to go closer. Mark did so, and very gently tapped its head. Immediately the clown disappeared once more into the box which Mark shut and locked before darting back to the divan and feigning sleep, just as Mrs Thomas opened the door and entered the room.

"Mark," she called loudly. "Mark – wake up."

Mark groggily opened his eyes and faked a slurry voice as he asked, "Where am I? What's happening?"

"Oh good" said the old woman. "I obviously gave you a wee bit more than intended. Never mind – it'll keep you quiet. I'll leave some bread and water for you. Don't say I am not considerate. You just stay there and don't be a nuisance."

The water was welcome, but Mark had no appetite for the bread. He waited until he could discern Mrs Thomas's footsteps retreating down the stairs. Mark retrieved the ring with the keys from under his backpack where he had shoved them in haste. He looked at them without much hope. They were all decidedly old and somewhat rusty.

"Why did the clown direct me to find these keys?" he asked himself. "Is it possible that one or even two of this bunch might unlock our doors? There is only one way to find out."

Altogether there were eight keys on the ring. Mark tried each in turn, but after the fourth one he began to seriously doubt any one would work. Therefore, when the fifth key slipped effortlessly into the lock, and with only a little pressure from Mark unlocked his door, he was truly amazed.

Tentatively Mark carefully opened the door of the box room, and made a quick check to ensure Mrs Thomas was nowhere in sight. He tiptoed down the passage to Angela's door. Very gently he tapped as he whispered as loudly as he dared, "Angela – it's me. Are you all right?"

"Oh Mark," sobbed his wife from the other side of the door, "what on earth is happening? How can we escape?"

"Listen darling," said Mark quickly, "I have found a bunch of keys one of which unlocked my door, and I am sure one will unlock yours as well. However, I dare not try now as she will be up any minute again. We will have to wait until tonight. In the meantime, just go along with her. She is obviously totally off her marbles, but I also think she is dangerous. Keep calm darling. I will get us out of here tonight. Wait – I hear her coming. Until later..."

Mark hurried back to the box room and softly closed the door. Looking at the bunch of keys he cursed himself for not somehow marking the key he had used. No time now to go through them all again, so as quickly as he could, he hid the keys in a nearby box, and returned to the divan where he lay down just as Mrs Thomas was heard fumbling with a key in the door.

Flinging the door open in anxiety on discovering it was not locked, Mrs Thomas was relieved to see Mark lying quite peacefully on the divan.

"Have you been up?" she asked sharply.

"Well yes – I fetched the water. But I am not hungry, so I don't want the bread." Then sitting up with his feet on the floor, Mark tried to assert himself. "Now look here, Mrs Thomas, I have no idea what your game is, but you have absolutely no right to keep me and my wife here against our will. I demand right now that you let us both go. We shall just walk away, and say nothing about it."

The old woman laughed merrily. "You 'demand', do you? Well there's no chance of that, I am afraid. I have waited years for Meghan to come back to us, and no way will I let her go again. You see – she *belongs* here. You don't of course, but I think you can be useful. For a while. Meghan will stay in her room until she learns to behave. I need to find her some proper clothes to wear. Those shorts are quite unseemly." And with that Mrs Thomas walked over to the hamper which she opened. "Ah yes," she said, "this frock was one of her favourites. I made it myself."

The frock in question was a shapeless dull green dress with a matching tie belt. It had a round neck and slightly puffy sleeves. It looked to Mark like something his mother might have worn when she was young.

"I will take this to Meghan and then I will be back for you." So saying, Mrs Thomas left the room and Mark heard her muttering to herself, "Be sure and lock the door this time you silly old thing."

Once she had gone, Mark made a more thorough examination of the box room. There was no window, although he felt ventilation was coming from somewhere. He shifted some of the lighter boxes to one side, and there he saw a small opening in what must have been the chimney breast. The opening was above a metal grille about the size of an iPad. Mark pulled at it, and after several minutes of trying it came away in his hands. Mark realised he was looking down the chimney flu. It was then he became aware of voices. Despite being rather indistinct Mark easily recognised the voice of Mrs Thomas. The other voice was much fainter, but obviously came from an old man. What was it Angela had said last night? Something about an old man telling her to leave at once?

It was hard to hear exactly what was being said, but the old man was definitely fractious, and "Let them go" was clear enough. Mrs Thomas was sounding mean and bad-tempered. In the end she shouted, "You leave them to me. They are nothing to do with you." This was followed by the sound of a door banging shut.

Carefully Mark replaced the boxes, and then his eye lit on a very useful object. A large old fashioned chamber pot! With no compunctions Mark relieved himself and felt much better having done so.

Mark took his mobile out of his rucksack. Maybe by some miracle there would be a signal. Sadly, no such luck. Curiously he had an urge to see the clown again. He went over to the Jack-in-the-Box and this time prepared himself for the creature to spring out at him.

Mark undid the clasp, and waited. Nothing happened. He tapped on the lid – still nothing. He then had to prise the lid open, and when he did, he looked inside the box and saw the crumpled and forlorn figure of the clown. Try as he might, Mark could not get him to jump out. His arms were all askew, but it was his face that gave Mark the worst shock. While vestiges of the garish smile remained, it was the eyes that filled Mark with a sense of terror. For those eyes that had danced so wildly from one side to the other before directing him to the chest of drawers – those eyes were the eyes of death.

———————————

The door to the box room opened and Mrs Thomas told Mark to follow him to the kitchen. "Don't try to be too clever," she said to him and Mark felt she must have read his thoughts as it would be so easy for him to push her down the stairs. "If anything happens to me, dear little Meghan will suffer."

Angela was sitting at the table looking as white as a ghost, with tear stains marking her cheeks. Her husband felt so inadequate. How was it he had not been able to have protected his wife and even now, when he ought to be able to over power a little old woman, what made his limbs feel so ungainly and useless? How could he have been so careless in forgetting to fill the jerry cans with petrol – and so slapdash in not properly planning the route? Mark felt ashamed.

"Angela – darling – I'm so sorry…" he began to say.

"Be quiet!" came the sharp voice of Mrs Thomas. "Meghan is staying here and has a job to do."

Mark looked at Angela again. She was dressed in the shapeless green dress. Her shoulder-length, soft brown hair had been roughly cut short, and she had been given a severe fringe. She certainly did not resemble his pretty wife of the day before.

Mark went over to her expecting her to stand up. He wanted to present a united front, and without doubt the two of them could force their way out of the house.

Angela did not stand up. She could not. Her ankles were firmly strapped to the legs of the chair she was sitting on. Before her on the table was a jumble of various bits of material that had been roughly cut into squares. Also on the table were a spool of thread, a needle and a minute pair of scissors.

"Meghan began making a patchwork quilt some years ago. Now she must finish it. Not until it is quite finished will I consider allowing her more freedom. She was a naughty girl to run away. Now she must be punished."

"I can't sew," sobbed Angela. "I was never any good. Oh please, Mrs Thomas – just let us go."

"Silly girl," was the retort. "Get on with it and stop making a fuss. You were always making a fuss about things and I see that hasn't changed. It is time to teach you a lesson."

Turning to Mark she continued, "As for you young man, I have a special job for you. Come with me." Mrs Thomas led the way towards the front door.

The rain from the previous night had stopped. The earth smelt damp and musky. Mark stood on the doorstep and listened. There was no sight nor sound of life. No voices – no sounds of cars or tractors even – nor even any birdsong.

Again Mrs Thomas was able to read his thoughts. "We are quite alone here. Miles and miles from anyone else. You could shout at the top of your voice and no one would hear you. So – don't waste your breath. Now – here we are" - and so saying Mrs Thomas undid the padlock which was attached to the bolt of the door to one of the outbuildings he had noticed the night before.

Whilst the barn looked quite derelict from the outside, it appeared as if inside it had been well repaired. To Mark's dismay it looked very secure. Piled into one corner was a heap of logs of all shapes and sizes. Some of them had been there long enough to be covered by cobwebs, and no doubt become a home to a variety of insects.

Mrs Thomas handed Mark a ridiculously tiny axe. "I want this pile chopped into small pieces for kindling," she said. "If I am satisfied, you will get your evening meal. If not – then you get nothing, and nor will your soppy little wife. Don't even *think* about trying to get away. There is no way you can."

After Mrs Thomas had left Mark looked at the stupid little axe and the huge pile of wood, and felt despair.

Mark had always considered himself to be a fit man. He worked out in the local gym at least twice a week. He played tennis on a regular basis, and he and Angela would meet up with like-minded friends to do long walks any weekends they could. They also enjoyed cycling. But this? This looked virtually impossible.

Mark tried to remember the last time he had chopped wood. He had been about seven or eight and he and his family were staying with friends who owned a farm in Devon. Mark had admired the way the boy who helped out on the farm had so effortlessly split logs. "Can I have a go at axing?" he had asked, and to give him his due, he had stuck at it for a long time. The boy had shown him the correct way to wield the axe after he had found him a smaller one to use. Mark tried to recall that technique now.

It did not happen easily. He bashed this way and that, severely bruising the toes on one foot in the process. The silly little axe kept on getting stuck, and he wasted huge amounts of energy freeing it. Amazingly, though, he was making headway, and in a perverse sort of way, enjoying doing so. Every blow of the axe he imagined was for Mrs Thomas. Not that even in these difficult circumstances he could visualise killing her. Just hurting her enough to allow them to escape. That would be sufficient.

It seemed hours before Mrs Thomas returned and by the time she did he was covered with sweat and extremely thirsty, not to mention hungry. The old woman was, thankfully, satisfied. She told him to return to the kitchen.

"Wait," she called out sharply. Mark waited, and Mrs Thomas then proceeded to search him roughly. "Just in case you had any silly ideas." On finding nothing incriminating she told him to "Go on."

What Mrs Thomas did not find was a couple of long, rather rusty nails that been embedded in a log. Mark had secreted them in his shoes. He wasn't really sure why. It at least made him feel he was *trying* to do something.

Angela was still in the kitchen and by this time there was a growing pile of patchwork squares in front of her.

"What was this piece taken from?" Mrs Thomas asked.
"I – I don't know," whispered Angela.

"Yes you do. You silly ignorant girl. It was from the beautiful dress I made for your tenth birthday."

"But it wasn't *me*!" wailed Angela, and with that Mrs Thomas lost her temper and slapped Angela twice across her face.

"Mrs Thomas – how *dare* you!" said Mark as he attempted to rush to his wife's side.

"*Sit down*!" shouted the old woman, "or I will confine you tonight to the barn."

This Mark did not want. He needed to retrieve the bunch of keys. He sat down and looked at Angela and mouthed, "Sorry".

Once again a bowl of soup was placed before them, with bread and water. They felt the soup was quite safe as Mrs Thomas had some herself.

"How long do you plan to keep us like this, Mrs Thomas?" asked Mark, "Only, very soon our families will begin to wonder where we are."

"You have no families. I have seen to that. You will stay here as long as I want. Now then," she continued, "time for your nightcap to make sure you have a good night's sleep." Two mugs of contaminated hot chocolate were put in front of the young couple, and just as Mrs Thomas was sitting down to watch them drink it, they were all startled to hear a loud banging on the front door.

"Now who on earth could that be at this hour?" the old woman muttered to herself as she rose from her chair, and then at the kitchen door she turned and glowered at them both as she said, "If I hear a sound from either of you I will make sure you *pay*." She then firmly shut the door before making her way down the passage to the front door.

The second she had gone Mark leapt up.

"Quick Angela – give me your mug."

As fast as he could Mark emptied most of the contents of both mugs down the sink that he then rapidly washed away. Sitting down again he smeared a bit of chocolate round Angela's mouth and whispered, "Pretend you have drunk it but don't want any more. Don't let her see how little is left. Pretend to drain it, and keep your mouth shut."

Mrs Thomas tentatively opened the front door. She was not pleased to see who it was who had knocked.

"Good evening Mrs Thomas. I trust you are well?"

"Good evening Officer. To what do I owe this pleasure?"

"We have found a car abandoned just over a mile from here and wonder if by any chance anyone had made their way here?"

"Oh no indeed," said the sweet, cherubic, old woman. "Now, when might that have been? Last night, you say? Well, last night was such a fearsome night, if any young couple had turned up at my door I would have been only too happy to have given them shelter. If I see them, I will do my best to set them back on the right track."

"I am sure you would, Mrs Thomas, I am sure you would. So sorry to have troubled you. So – you've not seen or noticed anyone then?"

"I said that, didn't I?" rather sharply, and then in her sweet voice again, "no not a soul."

Mark was on the point of calling out, when Mrs Thomas without a sound, was suddenly standing behind him. She witnessed Angela seemingly draining her mug, whilst Mark's stood empty beside him.

"Who was that, Mrs Thomas?" Mark enquired.

"Not that it's any of your business to know, but it was just a traveller asking for directions."

Mark and Angela had been unable to hear the conversation that had taken place, but despite this, they both suspected Mrs Thomas was lying.

Angela and Mark tried to react as they had the night before when they had previously been drugged.

"I need to go to the bathroom, Miz Thomas," said Angela, "and my feet hurt and my eyes are very tired from sewing."

"Time for bed anyway, my girl. So Meghan – not too bad for a first day. There is quite a lot of training to do, and another task for tomorrow. I will soon have you well and truly established in this household."

"Does that mean you will let *me* go?" Asked Mark, a bit too brightly, momentarily forgetting he was meant to be drugged.

"Well yes – in a way – I will let you go," but then she added in a worryingly sinister voice, "but perhaps not quite the way you mean."

The straps round Angela's ankles were freed, and the poor girl did not have to feign unsteadiness as slowly and painfully she staggered to her feet.

Suddenly the three of them heard a noise which startled them all. It was a loud crash and this was followed by a dreadful cry of pain.

"What on earth was that?" asked Mark.

For once Mrs Thomas looked somewhat flustered. This was not in the plan, and coming so soon after the visit from the police she realised she would have to move things along a bit more quickly than she would have liked.

"I'm sure it is nothing," she retorted sharply. "You two stay here and do not move." With that Mrs Thomas went out and shut the kitchen door behind her.

"Mark – shall we make a run for it? I know we can outrun her." But Mark knew Mrs Thomas kept the front door locked at all times and the key was in her pocket.

"No. I think we will wait until she is well asleep, and I will come to your door. Keep listening for me. I expect we will have to climb out of a window."

The door to the kitchen burst open and a distinctly flushed-looking Mrs Thomas stood in the frame.

"Come along *now*," she said. "Upstairs with the both of you."

Angela did some suitable stumbles, and Mark began to slightly slur his words.

"We muz go to the bathroom first, please…"

"Oh very well – but hurry up."

In the bathroom Mark checked the window, but it appeared to be sealed shut. There was nothing useful in the cabinet either. As he passed Angela on the landing he gave her a meaningful look before he was none too gently thrust back into the box room. As soon as the old woman had locked the door Mark made sure the keys were where he had left them. Thankfully they were, but he waited a good hour before he tried all the keys again until he found the right one. With some difficulty he managed to separate it from the others and put it in his right pocket. He then lay on the divan, with the keys secreted under his body, as he suspected, quite rightly, that Mrs Thomas would check up on him.

Mark heard his door being unlocked and opened, and was conscious the old woman was standing there, checking that all was in order. Quietly she left and re-locked the door. Mark then heard her do the same at Angela's door.

Mark was genuinely tired after all that chopping, and virtually no food. He set the timer on his phone for four hours, and made sure it was in silent mode before he drifted off to sleep.

Meanwhile, Angela changed out of the ghastly dress she had been forced to wear, and put on a pair of jeans, T-shirt and jumper. She was so thankful the old witch had let them keep their backpacks in their rooms. She put on her hiking boots, and checked her phone. It still had some juice, even if no signal. She too set the timer for four hours and allowed herself some sleep.

After she had safely put the couple out of the way Mrs Thomas returned to the room from whence the noise had emanated.

Old Mr Thomas had tried to stand up. In his weakened state, and with his feet tied as well, he unfortunately lost his balance, and as he fell, bringing his chair with him, he hit his head hard on the table beside him.

Mrs Thomas had made no effort to help him, nor to stem the flow of blood from his wound. Instead she had grabbed a bit of cloth and stuffed it in his mouth to stop his cries.

By the time Mrs Thomas returned to assess the situation, Mr Thomas was dead.

"Stupid old man," she grumbled to herself. "He should have behaved himself and then this wouldn't have happened. Now what can I do? He'll be too heavy for me to move him by myself, and if I leave him he will just smell. I suppose I will have to get that Mark man to take him out to the woods. Oh how inconvenient this all is!"

Without a vestige of pity or regret, Mrs Thomas took one more look at her dead husband lying on the floor – stifled a yawn, and took herself up to bed.

———————————

1.45 am: the mobile beside Mark's head reverberated into life. He was awake at once and immediately turned it off. Unlike Angela he had no reason to change, except he removed the nails from his shoes and put them in his right pocket, whilst at the same time removing the key. He hoped and prayed Angela would be ready, as slowly he turned the key in the lock and opened his door.

Creeping down the passage he stopped and listened outside Mrs Thomas's door. He was sure he could hear sounds of snoring.

Trying very hard not to jangle the bunch of keys in his hand Mark tried one key after another in Angela's door. Surely one of them must fit? He was becoming anxious – as was his wife willing him from inside the room.

The very last key was in his hand. Carefully Mark inserted it into the lock and prayed silently, "Please let this one work." It did. It was stiff – but it worked.

Hardly darling to breathe, the two of them tiptoed their way down the stairs.

"I think a window might be our only hope" whispered Mark, "as the front door lock looks newer and I fear none of these would work."

"Well, no good in the kitchen or downstairs loo" said Angela. "We will just have to look in the old man's room, and take our chances that we don't wake him up and startle him." Little did she know what they were soon to discover in this room.

As quietly as they could Mark and Angela crept down the passage to the first door on the left. They were relieved to find it unlocked and quietly they went inside.

Complete silence and utter darkness. No sound of breathing. "We don't want to startle him," said Angela, "but we must see where we are going or we may crash into something and wake *her* up."

Mark turned on his mobile torch. He shone it down on the floor. In an instant he recoiled in horror as the light shone directly onto the face of Mr Thomas, with a cloth stuffed in his mouth and staring dead eyes that Mark knew he had seen before. Not only were they the exact replica of the clown's eyes, but even the old man's arms were positioned in such a way they almost looked as if they had been folded.

"Oh, the poor old man," whispered Angela. "This was obviously the cause of the noise we had heard. How could she just have left him like that?"

Mark was suddenly conscious of the noise they must have made. "Quick," he said, "we must find a window. We can't help the poor man now."

So saying, he manoeuvred himself by the light of his torch to a wall where he could just make out a pair of curtains. He pulled them aside, and as he reached forward to try and open the window the light was suddenly switched on, and a voice shrieked "*Stop!*"

Mrs Thomas stood in the doorway wearing a heavy dressing gown. Her hair, which had been released from its bun, was dishevelled and wildly hanging down to her shoulders. Mrs Thomas's eyes were glinting in fury. In her hands, she held a shotgun.

"Mark," called Angela, "do as she says. She has a gun!"

"Sensible Meghan" said Mrs Thomas. "You and I will be just fine together without these tiresome men around. So – you thought you could get the better of me. did you? Stupid, stupid boy," this to Mark. "However, as it turns out I need you to do one more job for me, then *poof* – you can go too."

Angela was sobbing loudly now. "Please Mrs Thomas, let us go. We just want to go home."

Mrs Thomas turned to look at Meghan in amazement. "You are very slow to learn, my dear, which I confess is a disappointment. You *are* home, Meghan. Home to stay. Now –" more business-like, "you," pointing the gun towards Mark, "untie his feet, and then lift him up. Meghan dear – in the pocket of my dressing gown you will find the key to the front door. Don't even think of trying anything silly, as if you do Mark will find he has a very sore leg."

With trembling fingers Angela felt in the pocket and found the key. Mark had untied Mr Thomas's feet, and trying hard not to look at the old man's face, and conscious there was a good deal of blood still seeping from his head wound, he struggled to lift the old man up.

"I... I will have to put him over my shoulder," said Mark.

"Anyway you like," was the response, "but get on with it. Meghan – go and unlock the front door."

Angela did as she was bid, and then stepped outside into the cool night air. A slight wind in the trees caused a low rustling sound, and in the distance she heard the barking of foxes. A startled owl flew close to her head and made her cry out – and then she thought she saw a low light way off in the trees, but when she looked again there was nothing there.

Mark struggled out of the door with Mr Thomas over his shoulder. "So this is a dead weight," he thought – but at the same time he was wondering how they could escape without either or both of them being shot by the old woman.

"Where shall I go?" Mark asked Mrs Thomas.

"Behind that shed there is an old trough once used for pig swill. No pigs now, otherwise they would have been useful. However, the trough is very deep. Lots of room for a miserable little body – so chuck him in there."

"We can't do that, Mrs Thomas. You will need to report his death and give him a decent burial."

"Are you mad?" shouted the old woman at the top of her voice. "No one need know he is dead as no one knew he was even alive. Now – *do as I say*!" and with that she moved right up to Mark and prodded him viciously in the backside.

As he was stumbling and trying to find his way Mark thought that now would be a good time for Angela to try and escape. He ensured Mrs Thomas was concentrating on him, and then he shouted, "Angela – *run now* – run and hide as fast and as quickly as you can. *Go…*"

Angela hesitated for a moment, then she turned and ran into the woods.

"Oh no you don't," called out the old woman, and with that she fired the gun not once but twice, and with a sinking heart Mark heard Angela cry out in pain.

Completely forgetting poor Mr Thomas, Mark dropped his body on the ground. He reached into his pocket for the two nails which he held in his hand with the sharp ends sticking out.

Not caring for himself in any way, Mark could only think of Angela lying hurt somewhere, and he lunged at Mrs Thomas and hit her hard on her arms and chest. Despite her thick dressing gown, Mark occasionally struck flesh. Mrs Thomas cried out in fury but still held on to the gun which she was desperately trying to turn on Mark.

Mark went on hitting until at the very moment the old woman collapsed in a heap at his feet, a pair of strong arms were put around him, and a voice said, "That's enough now, son. She wont hurt you any more. It's probably better if you don't kill her."

Mark could not fathom what was happening. Suddenly the woods seemed to be full of people. The people were police. One of them walked towards him with Angela who was limping slightly and clinging to his arm.

Mrs Thomas regained consciousness and she glowered at Mark and Angela, cursing them for ruining her plans.

Although the thought of returning to the cottage filled Mark and Angela with horror, they had nowhere else to go. They both needed to sit down. Angela's ankle was luckily no worse than a flesh wound.

"Why were you here?" she asked. "It was so lucky for us that you were."

The older officer replied, "When we were here yesterday we asked if Mrs Thomas knew who might have been in the abandoned car we had found. The old woman denied all knowledge, except she let slip she knew we were talking about a young couple. We decided to discreetly keep an eye on her. There has always been a mystery concerning the disappearance of her daughter. Rumours abounded that she had killed her and somehow disposed of the body. Then she announced to a curious hiker one day that her husband had left her as well.

"Local people were afraid of her. Some people thought she was a witch. She never went anywhere, and appeared to be self-sufficient regarding food. She used to farm when she was younger and I believe she still keeps a milk cow. When we did a check on your car and traced your home address, we learned you were in Wales on a walking holiday. We broke into your car, I'm afraid, and there we found evidence of the bookings you had made to stay, and ascertained you were indeed missing.

We decided we would watch the house for a while, but I can not really explain why we decided to come back tonight.

Call it fanciful if you like, but I had a curious dream. I was a child again, at a circus. There was a clown performing tricks in the ring in front of me. Suddenly this clown, with a funny hat and wild orange hair falling over his face, came right up to me, and despite his bright red nose and false smile, I saw eyes that were strangely hypnotic. The clown looked straight at me and said – "You must go back right now. They are in danger."

Well – explain that if you will. They say we Welsh can be a bit fey at times – but this dream was so strong I reacted at once, much to the annoyance of my colleagues. Can you possibly believe that?"

Mark looked at the very ordinary and pleasant face of the policeman in front of him and said, "Yes I can. I can quite believe it."

Angela could not wait to get out of the house.

Whilst Mark understood, he hesitated. There was something he had to do.

"You go on," he said to his wife. "I'll be with you in a minute."

Mark climbed the stairs and walked purposefully towards the box room where he opened the door and stood in the threshold.

He looked around at all the various boxes, the chairs and tables and the little chest of drawers. He imagined himself trying to sleep on the decrepit divan. Then, finally, he allowed his gaze to rest on the faded old Jack-in-the-Box.

"I don't know how you did it, and I don't understand it at all," he said. "But you did it – and I am so grateful. Thank you."

Then without a backward glance Mark left, shutting the door behind him.

———————————

THE HAT BOX

MEREDITH PARKER WAS of course *very* proud of the success her husband had made with his haulage company. It specialised in vehicles for long distances and were quite pioneering in their ability to provide refrigerated lorries.

Thanks to Francis – Mrs Parker insisted on calling him Francis even though he said he liked being called Frank – they were able to live in a good-sized house in a quiet residential neighbourhood in Woking.

It wasn't that she was ashamed of what he did. Meredith just wished she could make 'Haulage Company' somehow sound, well, just a little bit smarter. A little less 'common'. Try as she might, she could not think of a catchy alternative. 'Long Haul Refrigerated Vehicles' sounded slightly better, but Francis simply said:

"We are in the haulage business, so we do what it says on the tin."

Apart from that, Meredith was extremely pleased the way her life was going.

Francis was a good, hard-working man and he loved his wife. The fact that she was always wanting to 'better' them all didn't worry him. If it made her happy, he would do his best to remember to say 'sofa' and not 'settee'; the 'WC or loo' and not 'toilet'; 'drawing room' and not 'lounge' etc., etc. What's in a name? Frank couldn't understand why it would matter.

When the children came along Meredith, who had been Maude in her youth, thought long and hard about their names.

The flash of brilliance came when she was peering into the window of a second hand book shop and saw a copy of *The Forsyte Saga* by John Galsworthy for sale. Meredith had studied this book at school and always loved it.

Fleur was born first, followed by Jolyon two years later.

When, in 1967, the BBC presented this saga on television, Meredith was in her element. Her only slight disappointment was that her Fleur was not as pretty as Susan Hampshire, who was playing Fleur on television.

Frank/Francis was able to afford to send the children to a small private school. Meredith took endless photographs of the children in their various school outfits which were prominently displayed in her 'drawing room'. She was also inclined to bombard her friends and neighbours with countless stories of the 'famous' people she had met at Parent's Day, the School Play, Sports Day, and so forth.

The friends and neighbours were often left bemused having rarely heard of the 'famous' people she had boasted about.

However, Fleur and Jolyon did quite well. Fleur did not try for university but decided to enrol immediately into a secretarial college where she excelled herself, and landed a job working as a general secretary and part-time receptionist in London for a recruitment agency.

Jolyon was accepted at Southampton University where he made many friends with whom he travelled frequently. After graduation he too got a job in London, working for a firm of insurance brokers.

Of course, they were *thrilled* to recruit Jolyon after his excellent 2-1 degree, and they made it quite plain they expected him to climb the ladder, and eventually end up on the board!.

Meredith put huge pressure on Francis to raise enough money to buy a flat for their children to share in London.

Although it was not a particularly good area at the time, partly due to financial limitations, but also due to Francis's innate sense of a potentially good bargain, they were able to buy a small house in Clapham.

Fleur and Jolyon were delighted with this purchase and Meredith adored the fact that she could go to London – oops! she must remember to say *up* to London – on a whim and stay in the third bedroom.

It was just as well Meredith did not overhear two of her friends having a chinwag over a coffee one day.

"Honestly, who does she think she is?" said Carol to her best friend Milly. "If she gets any fuller of herself I swear she will pop!"

Milly did a perfect imitation of Meredith:

"Aim *so* sorry – Aim afraid Ai can't attend your bric-à-brac sale as Ai am orf to London for a day or two to do some shopping and meet up with some chums."

The two friends were convulsed with laughter.

Fleur made great friends with Julie, who also worked in her agency.

"Let's go to Ibiza," said Julie one day.

Wow! The thought had never occurred to Fleur. But then again – why not?

So they joined an Under-30s group and before leaving they spent all their spare time buying bikinis and glamorous outfits for the evenings.

They had fun. They overdid the sun, with many a red and peeling shoulder or back to prove it. They overdid the drink, resulting in extremely sore heads from too much Sangria or Tequila. They overdid the flirting, with too many close encounters with either swarthy Spaniards or lobster-coloured Brits. They did all this, but somehow survived, and above all they had great fun.

Back in London, feeling a bit flat, the two of them were sitting outside a pub on Clapham Common.

A large, black, extremely hairy dog suddenly bounded up to them with great enthusiasm, banging into their table and spilling their drinks.

"Gosh – I'm so terribly sorry. Jasper – down boy – *Sit.* Oh dear – what a mess – please let me replace your drinks. What were they? Both shandy? I'll get them at once – but could I ask you – I mean would you mind –' and here the dog's owner bent down to put a lead on his dog, 'looking after Jasper for a minute? He's normally very good. Just a bit young and excited."

Fleur and Julie were laughing at these antics. Fleur grabbed the lead and said that of course they did not mind.

The young man introduced himself as Philip Jones. He was in the Army but on leave at the moment, staying with his married sister. Jasper was his sister's dog.

After a couple more drinks, they all agreed they must get going. Encompassing them both, though in reality looking more at Fleur, Philip said:

"I say – could we meet up again? How about the same time tomorrow? I might bring a mate, if that's OK?"

It was very OK. The four young people were soon firm friends. Two of them, however, fell in love.

Philip introduced Fleur to his parents. Nice gentle people who lived in a small village in Buckinghamshire.

Fleur took him to meet her parents in Woking.

Meredith made a cake for tea which was placed on a gold doily. The best china tea cups were taken down from their display shelf and put into action.

Meredith's accent became even more extreme and was often hard to understand. Philip seemed not to notice. He chatted easily with both Fleur's parents, but basically had eyes for no one else but her.

Philip and Fleur had a small country wedding the following year and Philip was then immediately posted to Germany.

That Easter, Jolyon joined a party of university friends on a skiing trip to France. One of the girls in the party was Miranda. She was a sweet girl, not especially pretty with rather nondescript brown shoulder length hair that she kept in place with velvet hairbands in various colours. Her nose was a bit large for her face, and her mouth a bit small, but the whole effect was pleasant, due to her eyes, which were of a deep violet colour.

Miranda was a rather timid skier, and as Jolyon was still quite a beginner himself, they inevitably spent a lot of time together and then they, too, fell deeply in love with each other.

It was not until they had been going out together for several months that Jolyon discovered that Miranda's grandfather had been a Lord, and therefore her mother was The Honourable Mrs Pettigrew.

When Meredith heard this news she nearly dropped to the floor in excitement.

Out came the china and the cakes and the doilies again as Mrs Parker did her very best to impress such a distinguished young lady.

Oh how pleased she was she had named her children Fleur and Jolyon and not Flo and Jake as Frank had wanted.

Jolyon proposed and Miranda accepted. Then Miranda's parents invited them all to a dinner in London to celebrate the engagement.

"You need a new suit, Francis. You have grown out of your other one with your beer belly. We must go *up* to London and do some shopping."

Frank stifled a groan, and accepted his wife's wishes with good grace.

The London prices hit them hard but a very adequate 'off the peg' navy suit was bought, plus a new shirt, tie and shoes for Francis.

Meredith found for herself, after much anguished searching and sighs from her long-suffering husband, what she called a 'cocktail dress' with a co-ordinated bolero.

With her best 'hair do' and top to toe shining in new clothes, Mr and Mrs Parker somewhat timidly entered the noisy, obviously extremely popular London restaurant in the heart of Chelsea.

Meredith was a tad disappointed when she was introduced to the Honourable Mrs Pettigrew. She had built up an image in her mind's eye of someone tall, slim and very regal. She would have aristocratic features and wear dazzling jewellery.

The reality of a very pleasant, slightly plump, round-faced woman with blue eyes that sparkled with amusement, was not quite what she had expected.

Mr Pettigrew (no Hon. there) was a jolly chap. He had a good head of thick grey hair, and was somewhat red in the face. He was as loud as his wife was quiet, and it seemed that Miranda took after her mother.

Mr Pettigrew – "Now now – no standing on ceremony seeing as we are about to be outlaws! My name is Gerald and my good lady wife is Felicity" – was the perfect host.

He guided them round the menu, most of which seemed to be in French.

"The *Bisque d'Homard* is excellent here and the *Poulet à la Maison* is unlike any chicken you've ever had. No idea how they cook it, but it's damned good."

Meredith did her best to remember all her social manners, and only had to glare at Francis a couple of times when he spoke with his mouth full, or left his knife and fork horizontally across his plate, instead of, as she had noticed, neatly side by side.

Felicity tried to find something in common with Meredith, but failed. Upbringing – holidays – interests – friends – there was no meeting ground. Finally, they simply discussed plans for the forthcoming wedding.

Felicity's brother, the incumbent Lord Brewster, was lending his house for the occasion. The village church would be perfectly adequate.

"Do you have a large extended family you would wish to invite?" Felicity enquired, slightly nervously. "We are keeping our own friends and relatives to the minimum as our young couple have so many of their own friends they wish to include."

"Not too many," replied Meredith, secretly groaning at the potential embarrassment of her younger brother Bob, a bombastic loud-mouth, becoming totally inebriated, or even dear, deaf old Aunty Gwyn who was liable to come out with a most inappropriate statement at the most inappropriate time.

"That wasn't too bad, Mum, was it?" Jolyon said after the round of polite farewells and thanks.

"They seemed very nice, dear. Very nice indeed."

Meredith went through months of anguish trying to decide on her wedding outfit. The kitchen table was strewn with magazines: *BRIDES, WEDDING DAYS, BRIDAL NEWS,* etc., etc.

There were good sections on mothers of the bridal pair. Lots of hints and lists of do's and don'ts. In the end, she decided quite wisely to avoid London as she really did not know her way around well enough, and put her trust in a small boutique in Woking that specialised in 'occasion wear'.

At last the choice was made. An elegant shift dress, which cleverly hid the odd bulge here and there, teamed with a loose-fitting long coat. The colour was violet, which Meredith told Jolyon was to complement Miranda's gorgeous eyes.

"I suggest all your accessories should be in a dark cream, except of course for the hat. Now, it so happens, I think we have the very thing," and with that the clever young saleslady produced a wide-brimmed hat in the palest cream, trimmed with a bouquet of violets and lilies of the valley.

Meredith was ecstatic.

"It's perfect," she trilled, "and as the wedding is in May, the flowers are perfect too."

Francis was delighted to see his wife so happy, although for the life of him he could not possibly see why it had all cost so much.

For himself, he had to grin and bear it. Jolyon took him to Moss Bros and both men were suitably kitted out for a smart wedding in morning suits, waistcoats and matching ties.

The friends of Meredith could not wait for this wedding to be over. The more they heard, the more they mocked.

"Do you think Jolyon will be knighted as soon as he says his vows?" Cheryl facetiously asked.

"I have heard they will spend their wedding night on a *gold* bed!" Hoots of laughter all round.

The few friends who were invited to the occasion however were almost as excited as Meredith. However, Pam's husband Steve said he refused point-blank to get into one of those 'monkey suits' and he would wear his old brown suit or not go and that was that.

Lord Brewster's house was situated in the Lake District. The wedding was to take place on the Saturday, but family and close friends decided to go on Friday to Sunday, "to make a proper little holiday."

Meredith, with Miranda's help, found a small hotel that was able to accommodate all the Parker entourage and was only thirty minutes from the church.

Fleur had arrived two weeks before the event, as she had to find a suitable outfit which would not accentuate her exciting 'baby bump'. Meredith took her off to *her* shop and the clever young sales lady found the perfect 'coat dress' in cherry red, with a gorgeous red hat embellished with bunches of cherries to go with it.

The clothes were all placed in smart-looking garment bags, whilst the hats nestled among tissue paper inside their distinctive black hat boxes which were embellished with horse shoes, bells, bouquets and bottles of champagne in gold and silver on the outsides.

A debate as to whether or not they should drive to the Lake District was dismissed. "Too far." "We would need two cars." "Supposing we broke down – or worse, had an accident?" So the train it was.

Meredith was relieved. "Let the train take the strain," as they say. The actual journey wasn't too long, and they would hire a couple of rented cars to meet them at the station.

It arrived! The long-awaited week-end was upon them.

Fleur's husband joined the rest of the family in London, and the five of them had a jolly dinner at a local Italian *trattoria*. Spirits were indeed high.

Jolyon had organised for two mini-cabs to pick them up at 8.30 the following morning which would give them plenty of time to cross London to Euston Station in order to catch the 11.02 train to Oxenholme.

The luggage was piled into the small hall of the Clapham house. Five suitcases, various garment bags, hat boxes and Jolyon's separate case for his Honeymoon.

Jolyon was talking on the telephone to the taxi company. There was no sign of either car.

"What do you mean they are on their way? Fifteen minutes? You said that 15 minutes ago. We have an important train to catch."

Nerves were beginning to fray. To speed things up, Jolyon, Philip and Francis began to take all the cases, bags and boxes, etc., out onto the pavement in front of the house.

Meredith was standing guarding them while at the same time looking this way and that for any sign of a mini cab approaching. She was beside herself with anxiety. Jolyon had to get that train as even if all went well he would only just be able to get to the church in time for the 3pm rehearsal.

More shouting on the telephone.

"Where is it? Not *another 15 minutes*!"

Then the soldier took command.

"Look – the most important person to get on that train is Jolyon. I will drive him in my car to the station and we will take half this stuff. Somehow I will find somewhere to leave the car."

After piling bags into the boot of the small car, the two young men sped off.

Meredith went into the house to ring the taxi company once again: "Where *are* you?" And just as she was about to say they would never use them again the operator announced that a car was five minutes away.

The house was rapidly locked up and as soon as the cab arrived in they all scrambled with the rest of the luggage in the boot and on their laps.

"Why were you so late?" Meredith demanded to know.

"I no late," was the reply. "I only get call 10 minutes ago."

They must have been quite a sight running and pushing the large luggage trolley towards the platform.

Philip and Jolyon were on the lookout for them.

"Hurry – just get on the train. It's about to go. We will find our seats later."

They were on! Each one grabbed a bag and then they pushed and stumbled their way through several carriages until at last they found their reserved seats.

Meredith collapsed into her seat in a state of frayed nerves and utter exhaustion. The boys had done their best to stack all their paraphernalia as neatly as possible into the limited space available.

After about an hour Fleur made a visit to the loo. (She was used to calling it that now.) On her return she glanced at the luggage. She stared transfixed for a good minute, before she silently said to herself, "Oh no."

Looking at the cases Fleur saw the correct amount of garment bags, but only ONE hat box.

Praying quietly to herself that it would be *her* hat that was missing, she only needed to open the existing box a fraction in order to see the bright red cherries dancing in rhythm to the movements of the train.

Quietly Fleur went and sat beside her mother.

"Mum," she tentatively began. "I'm sure we can solve this matter, but, somehow, well I don't quite know how to say this, but somehow, your hat box is not on the train."

Meredith just stared at her daughter. All colour had drained from her face. She could barely take in the fact that her marvellous hat, so perfect for her outfit, was not there.

There were at least another couple of hours to go before they reached Oxenholme, and the rehearsal was due to start at 3pm.

Somehow she would have to find another hat, but from where? She knew nothing about the Lake District. If only they were still in London; that would have been so easy.

The family were all so sorry for Meredith. Despite her often tiresome and 'over the top' ways they knew she had tried so hard to make everything perfect.

Francis, ever-practical, said, "Well there's nowt to be done right now, so let's use these next few hours to rest, have a bite to eat, and then once we get to the hotel, we will ask their advice."

Meredith did her best to comply, but she sniffed into her hanky as she knew the likelihood of finding a suitable alternative at such short notice was extremely low.

At Oxenholme they saw the pound where cars were parked under a banner proclaiming 'Lake District Cars – Sales and Rentals'. Jolyon went over to enquire about their cars. He returned with a glum face.

"They only have one car ready for us as the other was a late return, and they have not yet had time to check it out and clean it."

What else could go wrong?

"Never mind that," said Meredith. "We need them both now. As it is you will be pushed to get to the church on time."

Jolyon, Philip and Fleur sped off in the prepared car, and Meredith and Francis followed them to the hotel.

The car was filthy. It stank of cigarettes, but it went, and as far as Meredith was concerned that was all that mattered.

The receptionist at the hotel looked somewhat startled when Meredith immediately bombarded her with questions about the whereabouts of suitable hat shops. She explained she needed to buy an alternative for the wedding the following day.

The receptionist was a kindly local woman and she replied, saying:

"There is only one place you have a chance of finding the sort of hat you want, and that is in Kendal. It is an exclusive shop with a good reputation. I know, as my niece used to work in the back room there, helping create new hats. The only problem is they do not open on Saturdays, and close at 5.30 on Fridays. If you leave now you have 45 minutes to get there, so as long as you don't go wrong, you should be fine. Just follow the main road and when you get to Kendal, drive straight to the centre, and park where you can, and ask for directions. The shop is called 'The Hat Box' and it is in Spencer Street."

Hardly stopping to thank her, Meredith rushed back to the car, and easily found her way to the main road. As she tried to get used to the feel of the car, she saw a sign which said, "Kendal – 25 miles." Her eye was then distracted by a flashing light on the dashboard. It was a symbol of a petrol can, and looking at the gauge she saw that the needle was entering the red area.

What to do? If she stopped to fill up she would be too late for the shop. If she continued, she might run out of petrol.

"Oh, why is this happening to me?" Meredith wailed out loud. She made the decision to continue, and arrived in Kendal slightly after 5.15. She parked the car at the first convenient space she saw in the centre of town and immediately asked a passer by the way to Spencer Street. The first reply was unhelpful and she was running this way and that when at last someone gave her proper directions.

Spencer Street was small. She ran down it past a hair salon, a gift shop and a newsagent before coming to 'The Hat Box'. The door was locked. Totally breathless, Meredith banged on the door, even though there was no one inside. She knocked again, and a smart-looking, middle-aged woman in a black suit appeared, opened the door and said, "I'm so sorry. I am afraid I am closing up the shop now and have just finished tallying the till."

Meredith burst into tears.

The woman, whose name was Mrs Hawksley, said, "I think you had better come in, dear. Sit down and tell me your problem."

When Mrs Hawksley heard about all the dramas, she said, "What you need is a nice cup of tea, and while you are calming yourself down I will see what I can find."

Sipping her tea gratefully and relaxing in a chair, Meredith described her outfit, and the lost hat, to Mrs Hawksley.

"I'm afraid I do not have a hat such as you have described in similar colours, but I *do* have something which might do. It was made to order for another client who needed it for a wedding a month ago. Somehow my silly little assistant muddled up the measurements and the crown did not fit properly. We therefore had to recreate the hat in double quick time."

The hat produced was totally different to her chosen one, and perhaps it was not quite 'her'. However, she liked it. The crown was a snug fit. Rather like a skull cap.

One side was longer than the other. It was a deep purple, and the crowning glory was a large purple feather, and a purple mini veil.

"I think Modom looks quite superb in that," purred Mrs Hawksley. "Let me show you the back."

Meredith could not believe her luck. So it wasn't cream, but it would co-ordinate very well.

"Thank you *so* much," she said. 'You have saved my day."

Mrs Hawksley very generously said Meredith could have it for half price as she would not have been able to have sold it locally.

Back in the car, the new panic started. It seemed as if every warning light available was flashing at her. Try as she might, she could not see any sign of a petrol station.

Just as the car was beginning to give the odd judder and hiccup, a petrol station hove into view. Meredith literally coasted to the first pump. Once out of the car she tried to turn the petrol cap. It would not move, this way or that, it was stuck fast.

"No!" she inwardly screamed. "I can't take any more."

A large haulage truck pulled into the station, and would you believe it, it was from Francis's company!

Meredith went over to the driver and told him who she was. He was so amused, then he asked her what was the trouble.

"I feel such a fool," she said. "I cannot unscrew the petrol cap."

The driver looked at her car and said, "I know these cars, and there is a trick. Something you have to press under the dashboard." He grovelled around and then said, "Try now," and the cap turned with ease.

"I'll fill her up for you," said the driver. "You look as if you've had a bad day."

"You could say that," replied Meredith, "and thank you very much."

———————————

A hot bath helped soothe jangled nerves. The rehearsal had gone well. The hotel was lovely, and they had booked a private room for their family meal.

Meredith sighed with relief, that after such a traumatic day nothing more could go wrong, and all was well.

Saturday dawned rather overcast. After breakfast, the rain started in earnest. Philip and one of the cousins took it upon themselves to go in search of umbrellas. They went no further than the Golf Shop where they bought the entire stock of golfing umbrellas.

Fleur looked lovely in her cherry red, and Philip was so proud of her bump. A really nice boy.

Francis had nicked himself shaving and had bits of tissue sticking to his face. Apart from that, he looked great.

Meredith's new hat was much admired, and the family congratulated her on finding such a brilliant replacement, and at such a brilliant bargain price!

The wedding cars at least turned up on time. Meredith, Francis, Philip and Fleur shared a car. They had to climb several steps up to the church, but a young man shielded them with one of the golfing umbrellas.

The little church was packed and Meredith felt all eyes were on her as Mother of the Groom. She and Francis were escorted to their seats.

Jolyon and his Best Man were already seated and he turned round and gave his Mum a surreptitious 'thumbs up'.

He looked so handsome and Meredith was filled with pride that he was marrying into such a prestigious family.

A flurry – the entrance of the Bride's Mother. Whispers that the little Bridesmaids and Pages were already in place. The Chief Usher escorted The Hon. Mrs Pettigrew to her seat.

"Doesn't she look terrific?" Meredith heard someone say.

She turned and looked up the aisle.

Felicity was wearing a beautiful silk outfit in a pattern of the palest green, accentuated by large deep purple flowers.

On her head, she wore a little purple skull cap, adorned by a wonderful purple feather, discreetly held in place by a mini purple veil.

The groan that escaped from Meredith's mouth could be heard all round the church.

———————————

Somehow they got through it. Somehow they managed to laugh it off.

Mrs Pettigrew of course realised that no fault lay with Meredith, and when she heard the full story she was full of sympathy. She explained to Jolyon's mother that she had been invited to an earlier wedding in the Lake District and had ordered the hat by telephone, and obviously the girl had made an error with the measurements.

Meredith was slightly mollified by this, but also a bit put out that Mrs P's outfit wasn't new for Jolyon's wedding.

The rest of the festivities passed in a blur for Meredith. She slept almost the entire way on the train back to London.

Feeling somewhat defeated and rather idiotic by the time they arrived at the Clapham house, Meredith walked into the hall, and stared at the black hat box, covered in wedding insignia, seemingly mocking her as it rested on the floor by the stairs.

The next day she would return to Woking. During the following week she would have to bear the ridicule from her friends and neighbours who undoubtedly would be chuckling with glee when they learnt that the Hon. Mrs Pettigrew and Meredith Parker wore identical hats at *the* wedding – all due to a forgotten hat box.

———————————

THE INDIAN BOX

1. ROSE

HAD SOMEONE TOLD Rose as she was nervously making her way up the long drive leading to Setherington Hall that the very steps she was taking would lead to her life changing for ever, she would have replied in her typically blunt manner, "Don't be daft."

No one did of course, so Rose had no inkling of what lay ahead. She was simply on her way to the grand home of Sir Desmond and Lady Veronica Broughton to apply for a job as a cleaner. Her aunt, who was friendly with the cook, had told Rose's mother there was a vacancy.

Rose was dressed on this late Spring day in 1961 in a grey pinafore dress over a long-sleeved pink shirt. Her thick dark hair was neatly tied in a ponytail. She wore no make up, nor did she need to. Her natural colouring was pure 'peaches and cream', with pink cheeks, deep blue eyes, and a pretty little mouth.

Rose did not want to be a cleaner, she had dreamed of better things. She had worked hard at school and the Head tried to persuade her parents to let her apply for university. If her father hadn't suffered a serious accident at work which resulted in him being laid off, she might have succeeded.

However, she was the eldest of four children and even the wages from a cleaning job would help the family at this time. "Maybe after a year I could leave," she thought to herself.

Knowing better than to mount the steps guarded by fearsome looking stone Chinese griffins to knock at the front door, Rose worked her way round to the back and as she did so she gazed in wonder at the impressive grounds. Despite having lived in the village all her life, there had never been an occasion to walk through the majestic, wrought iron gates.

She had been stopped by the keeper of the lodge house, who let her pass using the small side gate.

The drive was lined with elegant lime trees. The mass of daffodils everywhere were just past their peak. Huge lawns stretched on three sides of the house. One led all the way down to a serene looking lake.

"What can it be like," Rose wondered to herself, "to live in such a beautiful place?"

Box hedges clipped to perfection bordered the paths. Rose stopped in amazement at two huge yew hedges that had been clipped to represent an elephant and a camel. Neatly maintained flower beds, beginning to show signs of the myriad roses that were to follow, were still full of colour from tulips, wall flowers and a mass of primroses. Rose loved gardens, and only wished they had one at home.

The door to the kitchen area was through the stable yard. A young man was busy grooming a fine-looking chestnut horse. As Rose approached he stopped his work and looked at her appreciatively. A quiet whistle emanated from his lips before a cheery, "Hello there! Might you be after the cleaning job then?" Rose acknowledged this was so.

"Good luck," said the boy. "I hope you get it. Then it would be my lucky day too."

To her fury Rose realised she was blushing. The back door opened, and there stood a friendly looking woman of ample proportions who welcomed her inside with the words:

"Don't mind that cheeky lad. There's no harm in him. But your auntie did say you were a looker, and she was not wrong."

Rose was introduced to the housekeeper. Miss Mackay was tall, slim and looked to be at least 70 years old. She used a black cane to help her walk, due, she said, to a childhood injury.

Once this formidable lady had ascertained Rose came from a respectable background and was obviously intelligent, she decided to take her upstairs to be introduced to Lady Broughton.

The housekeeper led the way across a large hall with a double height ceiling which was topped by a glass dome.

A vast staircase with a marble handrail was dominated by large portraits of severe-looking people in ancient attire.

Miss Mackay knocked on a large panelled door, which she immediately opened and, indicating Rose should follow, entered the drawing room.

Rose for a moment was dumbstruck by the beauty of the room. Five full-length windows graced the walls. Two overlooked the front, whilst through the others Rose could see the elephant and camel sculptures with the lake beyond. A fire burning in the grate was surrounded by a massive marble mantelpiece. On either side were two comfortable-looking sofas, flanked by small tables burgeoning with photographs in silver frames, ornaments and books.

An elderly lady dressed in a deep blue skirt and light blue twinset sat on one sofa. Three furry King Charles Spaniels were curled up beside her.

"Oh thank you, Miss Mackay," Lady Broughton said. "I see you have brought the young lady who might join us as a cleaner. Please sit down my dear," indicating a pretty upright chair, "and we will be fine, Miss Mackay, thank you. I will ring when we are finished."

Miss Mackay looked quite put out at being asked to leave, but off she went with a slight huff in her step.

"Now," Lady Broughton continued, "what is your name?"

"I am called Rose, my Lady."

"Such a pretty name which suits you perfectly. If I had been lucky enough to have had a girl, she would have been Rose as well."

Rose looked at Lady Broughton and couldn't help smiling at her. She had such a kind face, even if it was surprisingly weather-beaten indicating a life spent outside in the sunshine. Despite the greying of her hair, she seemed very fit and cheerful, with lines of humour round her eyes and mouth.

"Have you worked as a cleaner before?" she asked Rose.

"Not really," was the honest answer. "Just at home. My mother is very particular and has taught me well. Actually, I had hoped I might have been able to attend a university, but as my father lost his job due to an injury, and with three younger siblings, I felt it my duty to help out if I could."

"I see. How disappointing for you. However, we do desperately need a good cleaner. Someone who will take care and pride in their work. Do you think you might be able to manage as this in such a large house?"

Rose looked around her and her eyes glistened with appreciation.

"It would be a pleasure," was her sincere answer. "Everything I look at is a treasure, and I would be ever so careful as I can tell how precious so many objects are."

"Well," said Lady Broughton, "that is an unusual but welcome reply. When could you start?"

"As soon as you like, my Lady."

"In that case you had better meet my husband. Sorry now, you girls, I will have to disturb you."

Pushing the dogs to one side, who immediately curled up together to finish their important snooze, Lady Broughton stood up and led the way to Sir Desmond Broughton's study.

"Desmond dear – I would like you to meet Rose, who might come and clean for us."

Rose bobbed a little curtsy, and said, 'Good morning, Sir Desmond."

Then, completely forgetting her words of training from her aunt on how to address the elderly couple, and to speak only when spoken to, she almost cried out as she said, "What a wonderful room. *So* many books. What an absolute treat. Have you read them all, Sir Desmond? It would take me years to read all these. How beautifully they are bound. Leather and gold. What treasures."

As she was speaking, Rose was wandering past the shelves of books which were lined floor to ceiling in Sir Desmond's study.

Sir Desmond and Lady Broughton were open-mouthed. No cleaner had ever before shown such admiration for the mass of books. Cleaners in the past had only grumbled at having to dust them all!

Suddenly Rose remembered where she was.

"I do beg your pardon," she said. "Me and my big mouth. It's just that I have never seen such a marvellous collection of books before, and I'm afraid– well – I'm afraid I was a bit carried away."

Far from being cross, Sir Desmond and Lady Broughton were highly amused.

"Seeing as how you obviously appreciate the books and *objets d'art* we have here, we have no hesitation in offering you the job. Miss Mackay will fill in the details, but I think it is Monday to Saturday, 8 am to 1 pm. Good bye my dear," and Lady Broughton went on, "and I hope you continue to find enjoyment in our house."

"Oh I will. Indeed I will. And thank you so very much."

Another little bob, and the door miraculously opened to reveal Miss Mackay who had obviously been listening, given the shocked expression on her face at having heard such cheeky behaviour.

So started a liaison – a friendship – that was to last a lifetime.

Rose was kitted out in a black dress with a white frilly apron. She succeeded in her refusal to wear a white cap, but agreed to keep her thick hair firmly tied back in a black bow.

Rose did her best with her cleaning, and her best to remember her place. Miss Mackay chivvied her endlessly: "You are too slow." "You don't have to gaze at every object you dust as if it was pure gold." "Remember to step aside when you see Sir Desmond or Lady Broughton. You should be invisible." And so on, and so on.

On the whole Rose remembered – except for one day.

She was in her favourite room – Sir Desmond's study. He was out, but on his desk was an open book the like of which Rose had never seen. It was a very large book, at least 12 inches by 20, she would guess. It was bound in leather of a deep maroon colour, and the pages were edged in gold. The text was small and old-fashioned in style. On several pages were reprints of etchings depicting scenes in various parts of India. The page that was opened concerned Kashmir.

One picture showed a vast lake with a backdrop of mountains and a fascinating large, ornately carved boat moored to a jetty. The caption read "Royal House Boat... Lake Dal, Kashmir."

Gently Rose turned to another page. Here a picture of majestic mountains was simply headed: "The Himalayas." The next page showed a village, with cantilevered wooden houses, again all so beautifully carved. This was Srinagar, the capital of Kashmir.

Rose did not hear Sir Desmond enter the room.

"Would you like to visit the continent of India one day?" he asked softly.

Rose was horrified. "I do apologise, Sir Desmond. I am so sorry. It was open you see, and I was just fascinated by it."

"Don't worry, my dear," Sir Desmond replied. "I am glad you like it. Sadly, I can't lend this exceptional book to you, but if you are interested in India, I have a modern guide book here which is very informative. You may borrow that if you like."

Rose was in fact particularly interested in the old book, but she was not about to refuse such a kind offer, and she looked forward to learning more about that historic country.

"You see," continued Sir Desmond, "as I am sure you know, I am attached to the Foreign Office. I am a diplomat, and I have just received my next and last posting, which is in fact to India. It will be my second tour in that wonderful country. I have always been fascinated with the history of India, Kashmir and Pakistan, and in particular their languages. I have made a special study of the ancient languages and dialects. One day I intend to compile a sort of dictionary, but until then, I must mug up on present day politics, as we are off in a couple of weeks."

"How exciting, Sir. How long will you be gone?"

"Definitely two if not three years, I should think," was the reply.

"Oh!" Rose was upset to hear this. "Will you be coming home in between?"

"I think we get one good period of leave, but frankly there is so much to see in that part of the world I expect we shall want to explore there while we have the chance. Anyway – do borrow the book. In fact, you can have it. I don't want it back."

Rose could not believe how sad she was to see her employers leave for such a long time. She knew she was now left not only to the mercy of Miss Mackay, but she had also heard via Bob, the cheeky groom, that no one enjoyed it when the son and heir came to stay when his parents were away.

Mr Frederick Broughton, his wife Amanda and their son Wilfred arrived soon after Sir Dudley and Lady Broughton had left.

The change in atmosphere was palpable. Amanda couldn't stand the spaniels, and banished them to the servants' quarters, where, truth be told, they were much happier being cuddled by Nora (the 'General Skivvy' she called herself) than being shouted at by Mrs B.

Wilfred was a slob of a boy. Sixteen years old, he had no interest in the house or its treasures. He only wanted to shoot. If he wasn't eating or sleeping, he was prowling about the grounds with his gun looking for something to shoot and kill. Rabbit, badger, fox, pigeon or duck – he didn't care what. He once shot a baby deer in the woods, and left it dying in agony. The keeper was incensed.

Wilfred seemed to take delight in taunting animals or people. He particularly 'had it in' for Rose, and took every opportunity to complain, or make unnecessary demands of her.

The whole house heaved a sigh of relief when, at last, Amanda pronounced that she was 'bored stiff' and the dear family returned to the excitements of London town. Only Wilfred was upset, as shooting in London was some-what curtailed.

During the three years Sir Desmond and Lady Broughton were away, two important things happened at Setherington Hall.

Old Mr Johns who had worked in the gardens since he was a boy helping his dad, had a sudden and unexpected heart attack, and died, as he would have wished, hoe in hand.

The second gardener, Charlie Wright, was promoted to Head Gardener and a new young boy, Peter Deacon, was hired to work under him.

Rose had never spoken to Charlie before, so when they met in the herb garden one day they were both surprised and very pleased to meet each other.

After a few chance meetings with Rose he plucked up courage one day to ask her to go for a walk with him one Sunday.

It was obvious that Charlie not only knew a great deal about plants and gardens but that he also had a great respect for nature in all its forms.

Rose and Charlie rapidly became almost before they realised it more than good friends. Each had knowledge the other did not and took delight in sharing it. Charlie said that although he felt very privileged to be working in the stunning grounds of Setherington Hall, eventually he wanted to be his own master. He had dreams of becoming a landscape gardener and his ambition was to win a gold medal for design at the Chelsea Flower Show. Rose admired the love and care he showed to his plants, but even more the love and the care he was showing to her.

The second item of importance was that Miss Mackay finally owned up to her 80-plus years of age and increasing frailty, and made the decision, even though the Broughtons were still away, to retire.

On her recommendation Rose was promoted to House-keeper, and a new girl from the village, Jean Willard, was hired to do the day-to-day cleaning.

It was such a happy day when the chatelaines of Sether-ington Hall returned home at last.

Large packing cases were delivered which contained some of the many gifts with which they had been presented during their travels.

Rose was overwhelmed when she too was given a present: a beautiful amethyst necklace. She couldn't wait to show Charlie! However, she was enjoying discovering some of the other fascinating objects they had brought home with them and one in particular surprised her.

At first Rose thought a small table was being unpacked, but then there was a huge object designed to sit neatly in the space at the top. About 40 inches high and 20 inches in diameter, this was a globe atlas of the world dating back to the early 19th century. The colours were gentle and, once in place, Rose so enjoyed turning the globe and working out the names of the countries that she knew.

Thinking she had seen all that was wonderful and intriguing, Rose could not believe it when she opened that last object, which had been sealed in a very secure case.

This was a box, about 14 inches by 10, that quite took her breath away. It was made of wood, sandalwood as she discovered later, and covered in delicate carvings set in individual panels of various birds and animals, all surrounded by flowers. She thought these carvings were gold, but Lady Broughton said they were made of brass. Lady B. opened the lid, and the interior was not only lined in soft green velvet, but contained many small compart-ments of various shapes and sizes, most of which had carved brass tops with mother of pearl knobs on them for potions and lotions. Behind a dusky mirror which was set in the lid, was a secret compartment for *billets doux*, and finally, with the press of a hidden button a little drawer sprung out from the side.

Rose was not surprised when Lady Broughton told her it had been given to them by a very important man, who would have been a Rajah in the old days, and it dated back to the early 1900s.

The spaniels Bella, Minnie and Dolly were thrilled to have their mistress home again, and as she sat cuddling them on the sofa in the drawing room Lady Broughton asked Rose to sit down a minute.

"Rose, dear," she said, "you have changed, and I don't just mean because you are now 22 years old. Is there something I should know about?"

This was definitely said with a knowing twinkle. The below-stairs gossip had already reached the hierarchy.

Rose blushed to the roots of her hair.

"It's Charlie, your new Head Gardener, my Lady. Well – you see – we have fallen in love and Charlie has proposed."

These last words had come out with a rush.

"But that's wonderful news!" beamed Lady Broughton. "I must meet him at once and make sure he is worthy of such a bride."

Charlie walked Lady Broughton round the gardens the following day. On her return, Lady B. pronounced: "I don't know which one of you is the luckier. You are both so well suited."

The wedding, when it took place, was a simple village affair. Rose's three sisters were all Maids of Honour, and Charlie's younger brother was his Best Man.

After the marriage service in the Parish Church, the festivities and wedding breakfast were in the village hall. It seemed everyone in the village had taken part, either by preparing a sumptuous feast or decorating the somewhat plain hall with a mass of wild flowers, and quite a few roses, to chipping in to make sure there was plenty of beer, cider and the very important sparkling wine for the guests.

The Bride and Groom enjoyed every minute of their special day, but the best moment was to come, when just before they were due to leave for two nights in Devon, they were handed an envelope from Sir Desmond and Lady Broughton. Inside was a card which read:–

"To You Both.

We hope you will agree to make the barn we have just finished converting into your new home. This will be yours for as long as you remain at Setherington Hall.

With our very best wishes from

Desmond and Veronica Broughton."

For the following two years, Rose and Charlie were happy, content and in love. The only slight anxiety was the fact that no little baby had appeared. Rose tried not to let this spoil her life. She knew she had so much for which to be grateful. She and Lady Broughton were becoming firm friends as well as employer and employee. Lady B. would occasionally confide in Rose about the concerns she had regarding her son and his family. Rose found it hard to reassure her.

"A baby will come at the right moment," Lady Broughton said, which Rose relayed to Charlie.

However, Charlie felt sure the fault lay with him. He recalled that the natives of the Amazon forests would use some of the trees that grew there as medicines for all sorts of conditions and ailments. Charlie was fascinated by the power of trees, and read up about these practices whenever he could. This way he discovered the belief that certain trees could cure infertility.

One day, Charlie wandered alone into the woods at Setherington. He looked at the British native trees and doubted whether the oak or ash, the chestnut or beech, could help in any way. However, with nothing to lose he stood still and spread his arms wide, saying, "If you can help me – please do." And then, for some reason, he felt compelled to take some leaves from every type of tree he saw, and when he went home he boiled all the leaves together in a pot. He waited until the liquid was cool, which he then drank, grimacing at the somewhat bitter taste.

Three months later it was confirmed. A baby was on the way.

How or why it had happened, Charlie had no idea. He had admitted to Rose what he had done, and she, as practical as ever, said, "A wonderful coincidence – but totally impossible."

However, deep within himself Charlie was sure the trees had indeed helped him, and that the future baby, whether a son or daughter would turn out to be very special.

2. ANNA

A baby girl was born on the 15th June 1966. Rose tentatively asked Lady Broughton if she would mind them giving their little daughter Lady Broughton's name. "I would be delighted and honoured" was the generous reply. So Anna Veronica was later baptised in the village church.

Rose had been harbouring fears about her ability to keep on with her job, whilst at the same time caring for an infant, let alone a toddler. Rose's mother had refused to help, saying she had enough to do as it was. Charlie's father had died the year before, and his mother had gone to live in Australia with Charlie's married sister.

Lady B. as usual came to the rescue.

"Just bring Anna with you and leave her somewhere in a pram and later a playpen while you work. When she grows too big for that, we will work it out."

To Rose's amazement, Sir Desmond said he loved babies and would be happy if the child stayed with him in his study, and he would be on hand to call Rose when she was needed.

"I would enjoy the company," he said, "as my work is quite lonely."

By this time Sir Desmond was well into the compilation of the history and meanings of the six classical languages from the Indian continent.

Sir Desmond was unusual as although he could converse quite easily in Hindi, he also had a good knowledge of Tamil and Sanskrit.

The old gentleman would sit at his magnificent mahogany writing table – "Not a desk, my dear," he would say, "never a desk. This is a writing table." The table was rectangular in shape, with most of the top covered in deep green leather kept in place by small brass studs. A silver salver was placed in the top centre, and this contained three inkwells of cut glass with silver tops. The inks within were black, blue and red. A blotter in the shape of a half moon with a handle was nearby, ready to rock into action when needed.

The rest of the table was covered with books and papers; a leather mug which was full of sharpened pencils, rulers and 'bungees' as Sir Desmond called rubbers. The last item was a small Dictaphone.

Sir Desmond only wrote in longhand when essential; otherwise, he dictated into his machine for his Indian secretary to transcribe at a later date.

At first baby Anna used to sleep peacefully in her pram. Then later she would chortle and gurgle and make little noises of happiness at discovering her toes – or watching something fascinating out of the window.

Anna never minded the playpen. She amused herself with her toys, and then pulled herself up on her feet and walked her boundaries with happy cries of achievements. Even at such a young age, she would sit contentedly turning pages of her picture books and talking to herself.

Sir Desmond would look at her fondly, but once he was engrossed in his work nothing could shatter his concentration. His deep voice quietly talking into the Dictaphone often lulled Anna off to sleep.

As the little girl grew older and was able to walk, she would either trot round the house with her mother, or 'help' her father in the garden. It was the perfect arrangement.

At the age of two Anna knew many words and by the time she was three years old she was talking like a child of five. She was a most inquisitive little girl, and always asking questions.

"How does water come out of the tap, Mummy?"

"Where does it go when it goes down the plughole?"

"How can birds stay in the air, Daddy?"

"Where do flowers go in Winter?"

"Oh my goodness!" Lady Broughton would laugh, "Does that child never stop asking questions?"

In Sir Desmond's study Anna somehow knew she should not disturb him while he was working. But as soon as he stopped – off she would go!

Two items in the study fascinated her: the Globe and the Indian Box.

She would stand in front of the Globe and slowly spin it, trying to understand how the round world worked.

"Where is this place?" she would ask. "Have you been there? Do they speak English or something else?"

Not only did Anna ask questions, she would also remember the answers. Soon her knowledge of the countries of the world was astounding for a child of that age.

The Indian Box, however, was her very favourite. She understood that she had to be *very*, *very* careful with it. She would open it up and discover all the little drawers, compartments and cubby-holes within. Sometimes she would hide a penny in it and challenge Sir Desmond to find it.

Without doubt she thought this beautiful box from India was the best treasure she had ever seen.

Sir Desmond had explained to Anna that the box had been given to him by a very important and grand gentleman who would have been a Prince in the old days. Sir Desmond had tried politely to refuse, indicating it was too precious to give away, but the Prince had insisted. From then on Anna always thought of it as the Prince's Box.

When Anna was four years old, a curious situation began to occur.

After Rose and Charlie had tucked their little girl up in bed, and read her one of her favourite Beatrix Potter stories, she would snuggle down under her covers, clasping her beloved 'Doggy' and go sweetly off to sleep. So far so good – but night after night Rose and Charlie were woken up by the sound of Anna talking. There was, of course, no one in the room with her, and her eyes were always tightly shut.

Charlie said, "At first I thought she was talking gibberish, but now I'm not so sure. I think it is a language."

Rose confided this strange phenomenon to Lady Broughton who in turn mentioned it to her husband.

"I tell you what," he said to Rose, "take my Dictaphone machine and see if you can record her one night."

Two days later Anna was in full spate. On and on she went, and Rose recorded it all.

The following day Sir Desmond, Lady Broughton and Rose listened to the recording.

When it was finished, after a moment's silence, Sir Desmond pronounced that at first Anna had been speaking Hindi. Then she had switched to Sanskrit with a little bit of Tamil thrown in!

"All," he added, "with perfect accents."

Sir Desmond was totally intrigued, but he said he had remembered a similar case once in the USA where a young child had absorbed a foreign language from hearing it from her mother's place of work which she could only speak when asleep.

"It must have happened this way to Anna, and her subconscious memorised the words I have been speaking."

"That's all very strange," said Rose, "but how are we going to stop her?"

"Leave it to me," Sir Desmond replied. "I have an idea which just might work."

The following day, Anna popped into the study as usual and was happy to see Sir Desmond was not, for once, working hard.

"Ah, my little friend," he said, "I have a question for you. Can you speak any of the funny languages I sometimes use?"

"No, silly," was the typical, rather cheeky response, "I only speak *my* words."

"Bring me the Prince's box then, dear, and come and sit by me."

Sir Desmond then proceeded to tell Anna that he had never properly explained that this box was in some ways quite magical.

The little girl's eyes lit up with wonder and total belief.

"Yes, you see it is a keeper of special secrets and thoughts. Sometimes I say something in an Indian language which I need to remember so I open a little drawer, and put the word inside it and close the drawer again."

"What happens to the word, Grandpa Demmund?" she asked. (Rose had apologised to Sir Desmond for Anna's familiarity, but the old man just laughed and said he was 'flattered'.)

"The word is kept safe until the time I might need it again. Would you like me to show you how I do it?"

"Yes please. Can I help?"

"I was hoping you would ask that," he responded. "You certainly can."

So, starting with Hindi and working his way through all six of the ancient languages, Sir Desmond solemnly spoke some words, and made a great show of putting them in one or other of the little drawers and shutting them firmly. When all six languages had been shut away, Sir Desmond said:

"Now – if you or I want to speak these words we must open the drawers. However, they can only be opened during the day. At night time the letters need to sleep. Come tomorrow and we will see if the words will wake up. Would you like that?"

"Yes – yes please, and then p'raps I might learn to say some too?"

That night Charlie and Rose had their first decent sleep in weeks.

The next day Anna raced to Sir Desmond's study as soon as she was allowed.

"Quick, Grandpa Demmund – open a drawer!"

The Hindi drawer was opened and Sir Desmond told her the word that came out was, "Thank you."

"*Dhanyvad*," Anna repeated it flawlessly. "More," she said, "let's find more words."

Anna repeated and memorised the words, which were of course somehow already lodged in her brain. Very soon she was able to create small sentences, much to the astonishment of the adults surrounding her.

Just before Anna's fifth birthday Charlie and Rose were summoned to the drawing room to have a meeting with Sir Desmond and Lady Broughton.

Rose was extremely nervous.

"I wonder what they want?" she fearfully asked her husband. "I hope they don't think we have been taking advantage with letting Anna virtually have the run of the house? Thank goodness she will start at the village school next term, although I worry that due to her reading ability, not to mention her strange Indian languages, she might not fit in."

Sir Desmond and Lady Broughton looked fondly on the couple who served them so well.

Not only was Rose a very efficient and reliable house-keeper, but Charlie had delighted them with his imaginative ideas for the gardens as well. So much so, in fact, that word had penetrated the county and several owners of large gardens were desperate to borrow him if they could. However, Charlie would never have considered working for anyone else, unless it was in his own time.

"Relax," said Lady B. having noticed how nervous they both seemed. "We have asked you here as we have a proposal to put before you. There is no doubt you have given birth to a remarkable child. We are not really surprised as both of you have good brains, and in different circumstances I am sure you would both have gone to a college or university. However, to use the modern vernacular, we are where we are. So this is about Anna. Sir Desmond and I, as I am sure you are aware, are extremely fond of your little girl. Therefore, we have decided to set up a trust to pay for her private education until she is 21. That is, if you both agree?"

Rose and Charlie were stunned into complete and utter silence. In fact, truth be told, they could barely take in what they had heard. Eventually Charlie spoke first.

"You mean," then he cleared his throat and started again. "You mean you would actually pay for our daughter – the child of a gardener and a housekeeper – to be educated *privately*?"

"We do. And it would be our pleasure. We both agree that it would be criminal not to give that amazingly retentive, enquiring little brain the very best opportunity to make the most of it."

Lady Broughton continued, "Anna is enrolled at St Cuthbert's as from next term. The Headmistress is first class and she is more than happy to welcome Anna to her school."

At last Rose spoke – barely above a whisper. "We will *never* be able to thank you enough. What you have both offered our little girl is beyond our wildest dreams." And with that, strong, capable, efficient, no-nonsense Rose burst into tears of gratitude.

St Cuthbert's was a huge success. At the age of five, the other children were totally uninterested about Anna's background. By the time she was eight, she spoke exactly like her contemporaries and had become a very popular girl in her year.

Anna would spend hours in the school library where she would often pore over large atlases and dream about the far-flung corners of the world.

She had to have extra tuition after school twice a week with Mr Sandeep (who was really the Chemistry teacher) to continue her tuition in Hindi and Sanskrit. Sir Desmond felt this unusual talent could be very beneficial to her in her eventual career.

The next couple of years life continued happily. Sir Desmond's book had been published to great acclaim from academics who studied India and her languages.

At the age of 10, Anna won a scholarship to the renowned Kingston House Academy. Charlie and Rose were bursting with pride, and Sir Desmond and Lady Broughton insisted on inviting them to a special tea, with Cook's best fruit cake, to celebrate.

It had been quite a while since Anna had seen Sir Desmond and she was sadly shocked at the sight he presented. He seemed a shadow of his former self. Very frail, and somehow much smaller.

Anna immediately ran over to him and held his hand. In the direct manner of children she asked him, "Grandpa Demmund – you don't look well. Are you all right?"

Rose tried to shush him, knowing the sad facts behind Sir Desmond's looks, but he waved her aside and replied to the little girl, "No sweetheart, I am not all right because you see I am very old. I expect the Good Lord will call me away quite soon, which is why I particularly wanted you and your parents to come today. It is not only to celebrate your scholarship, and I am *so* proud of you, but for another reason as well."

This rather long speech seemed to tire Sir Desmond and Lady Broughton went to his side and insisted he had a sip of tea and a little rest.

Gathering his strength he addressed Rose and Charlie:

"Thanks to you two, I have had a joy at the end of my life I never would have thought possible. To see the way Anna has embraced her school work and found such excitement in learning has given me huge pleasure." Then, turning to Anna, he said, "How are you getting on with French?" to which Anna promptly replied, "*Pas mal, Monsieur. C'est tout a fait un plaisir pour moi.*"

"Good, good. I'm glad to hear it. I hope you'll keep it up and add German, Spanish and Italian as well."

"Oh, I have started German and Spanish already. They are fun too."

"On the strength of that reply and your great interest in foreign lands, I think you would enjoy a successful career in the Foreign Office as a Diplomat. Therefore I will write an introduction to Sir Forbes Branson who is the current CEO in London to ask him to keep an eye out for you, and to make sure you have an interview when you are ready."

"A diplomat. That is what you are, isn't it? Well then I would like nothing better. Thank you, dear Grandpa Demmund, but please tell the Good Lord we don't want Him to take you away."

Gently the old man patted the little girl's head and then once more addressed her parents.

"Due to the laws in this country I have no options but to leave my estate and most of its contents to my son. I am somewhat fearful how he might treat it, but that is out of my hands. I just want you to know that Veronica, Lady Broughton, will move into a small house we jointly bought some years ago. This house is in a village about 15 miles from here."

Rose and Charlie looked at each other. Neither of them anticipated working for the son and heir with any great pleasure. They had, in fact, secretly discussed it and agreed they would hand in their notices.

Sir Desmond continued. "The house, though small in comparison to this one, is still a good size and Lady Broughton will need help in the house and also the garden which is about three to four acres. The back part of the house was originally the old kitchen and various sculleries, etc., whilst upstairs were a series of small rooms once used by domestic staff. The previous owners have converted all this and turned it into a delightful, self-contained annexe. Two good-sized bedrooms and bathroom upstairs, and a large open-plan kitchen and living room on the ground floor. If you agree, we would like you to live there and continue to look after my wife. Charlie, you should have plenty of time to pursue your dream of winning that gold medal at Chelsea!"

By this time Sir Desmond was seriously fatigued, and Rose whispered to Lady B., having told Sir Desmond how thrilled they were at such a prospect, that they should slip away now and let him rest.

"*No, wait!*" came a surprisingly strong voice. "I have something more to say. Lady Broughton will of course take her prized possessions and favourite ornaments and paintings to the new house with her. I have cleared this with my son. He and I have signed a legal agreement to this effect. Finally – and this has been agreed, too – when I die, I want Anna to have and to own not only the globe that has given her so much pleasure, but the Indian box as well."

Anna turned to Sir Desmond and put her arms around his frail body.

"*Dhanyvad. Dhanyvad*, darling Grandpa Demmund. I will look after the globe and the Prince's Box all my life and that way I will never forget you."

Exhausted by all this effort and emotion Sir Desmond was suddenly left speechless.

Charlie, Rose and Anna, as one, looked at their kind benefactor and tried to smile, though tears were in all their eyes. Charlie spoke for them all when he said:

"The days Rose and I started to work at Setherington Hall were the luckiest in our lives. We will never let you down, and will take care of Lady Broughton for the rest of her life."

3. ASHI

Akshayaguna had been named after Lord Shiva. He had been born into a grand and historic family in the province of Gujarat. His parents had agreed to call him Ashi as soon as he was born.

Ashi grew up to be a charming young man who was also very bright. His father had insisted his son would attend the same English Public School as he had, and everyone would have been totally shocked if Ashi had failed to win a place at Oxford University.

Ashi had entered university life with gusto and was one of the most popular undergraduates of his year. He was a talented athlete who had been awarded a Blue for rowing, despite the fact he only started this sport during his first year.

Not only did Ashi make many friends but he also broke quite a few hearts on the way. He tried to be careful not to become too involved with any girl, as he knew his future lay back home in India.

At the start of his last year he decided to join a couple of new clubs. One of them was entitled "The Knowledge and Appreciation of Antique Artefacts Society". Commonly known as KAAAS, it amused the members that people asked to join sometimes thinking it concerned cars!

Realising he was late for a meeting one evening, Ashi dashed into the room with apologies on his lips, which to his surprise were brushed aside by the Chairman saying – "Ashi – just the person we need. Tell us – what do you think of this?"

On the display table a young girl had just placed a stunning Indian box. For a moment Ashi just gazed at it, entranced by its beauty. Finally, after he had carefully opened the lid and admired the interior, he had half whispered: "Astonishing, and so very beautiful."

The young girl replied in equally hushed tones, "Yes, isn't it? It is indeed very special."

Startled, Ashi looked up at the girl in astonishment. Without thinking he had spoken in Hindi – and in this tongue the girl had faultlessly replied.

At the close of the meeting Ashi sought out the girl, whom, dear Reader, we all know was Anna, and insisted she join him for a drink to explain how she was able to speak in Hindi.

The drink progressed to dinner, which in turn became lunch the next day – and the day after that. Lunches became whole day events. Picnics. Rowing on the River Cherwell. Long walks leading to longer dinners.

Almost without knowing it was happening, Ashi and Anna fell deeply in love with each other and Ashi dismissed any disquieting thoughts that threatened to rise to the surface.

Ashi was fascinated by Anna's story – especially the bit about her speaking Indian languages in her sleep! He felt sure that his father would have met Sir Desmond sometimes during his years in India.

Anna could not hear enough about Ashi's life. A world away from her simple background, he had been brought up surrounded by luxury: endless servants to do his bidding at a flick of a finger; a stable of world class horses; and opulent palaces to live in in Gujarat and Shimla. She tried to imagine it all. To Anna his life sounded like a fairytale. But Ashi was very modest, and most undergraduates had no idea about his wealth, as he did not flaunt it.

For his part, Ashi was in awe at Anna's ability with languages. He found her not only a joy to look at with her honey-blonde hair, deep blue eyes and somewhat serious expression which would disappear in a flash when she smiled, he also admired her intellect and enquiring mind. She challenged him and really made him think. He loved her for that as well.

It was only a matter of time before they became serious lovers. Anna would often lie in bed after an afternoon of love such as she had not dreamed was possible, and watch Ashi's strong brown arm gently resting across her body. Cocooned by love, Anna would feel that life could never be more perfect. Ashi would look at her with such adoration in his eyes, and profess he would love her forever. Anna would put her finger on his lips and say, "Forever is too far away, darling. Let's be grateful for now." For deep in her stomach Anna knew that this happiness was unlikely to last.

Ashi wanted to meet Anna's parents. Anna had of course explained about their simple background, but Rose and Charlie had in fact risen in status in the eyes of the world.

Their dearest friend, Lady Broughton, had passed away the previous year. Rose was distraught and could honestly say she had truly loved her employer.

The house had been left to them. Rose and Charlie were once again overwhelmed by their good fortune. However, they decided the house was too big for just the two of them, and occasionally Anna, so they sold it, extremely well, and exchanged it for a delightful house with an unkempt garden of a couple of acres that Charlie was busily converting into a mini-Paradise.

Rose had turned her love of books to good use, and she had used the excess money from the sale to purchase a small shop where she ran an exclusive bookshop, specialising in rare and beautiful editions. Her reputation was spreading, and she was in her element.

Charlie by this time had a small team working for him, including the young lad from Setherington Hall. All his efforts at this time were concentrated on his entry for the Chelsea Flower Show.

Initially, Rose and Charlie were rather nervous about meeting Ashi but nerves were dispelled when Ashi was so natural with them and it soon became the most normal thing in the world to know that their daughter was in love with an Indian Prince.

The culmination of such a heavenly year was both Ashi and Anna being awarded Double Firsts.

Ashi's parents came for the graduation ceremony. They met Anna, and both were charming to her, although Anna distinctly felt a tension with Ashi that wasn't there before. His parents were always polite to her, but kept their distance.

At the final ball of their university life, Ashi held Anna very tightly as they danced.

Anna looked up at him and saw his dark brown eyes had tears in them.

"What is it my, love?" she whispered.

Pulling her away from the dance floor and out onto the terrace, Ashi turned to her and said, "Anna – you know that I love you. This year has been the happiest of my life. But I must be honest. You and I have no future together. My parents have arranged for me to marry the daughter of one of their Princely friends. I haven't even met her. She is very young still. Only 15 at the moment. The union, though, will be very beneficial for both our families, and it is important for people like me to marry someone from the same background. If there was any way I could change this situation, believe me, I would. My deepest regret is the hurt I know I will be causing you, my beautiful, clever Anna."

As her heart was breaking, Anna summoned up her strength of character and said, "Ashi, you have given me the most wonderful year. I have learnt so much from you, and I will never, ever forget you. I quite understand that it is important for you to make a suitable and beneficial marriage, and I only hope this young girl will treasure you, and realise how lucky she is to have you as her husband. Before we say goodbye, though, please could we spend one last day together?"

Their last day was perfect. Heavenly weather. They drove deep into the Cotswold country and found an adorable pub in a picturesque village. They talked and laughed as if they had the world before them. Anna had insisted they only lived for the moment and the future was not discussed.

In the evening they returned to Ashi's rooms and made love for one last time.

The next morning Anna was up and dressed long before Ashi. She sat down on the bed, and out of her bag she produced the Indian box. In perfect Hindi she said:

"This is a box of secrets. We will choose the biggest drawer and put our combined love in it. Then we shall shut the drawer – and I will treasure it all my life."

With tears in his eyes, Ashi complied. Anna gave Ashi the lightest of kisses as she said, "Goodbye, my darling love. Have a happy life."

Somehow Anna managed to leave Ashi's room just before her tears burst like a dam and cascaded down her face. She ran, stumbling down the path, tightly clasping the Indian box to her chest.

One month later, having been cocooned in the understanding and warmth of her parents' love, Anna came to terms with her loss.

Much as she had genuinely loved Ashi, she knew the life of an Indian Princess would not be for her.

Not only did she owe it to the memory of her dear 'Grandpa Demmund', Anna was truly excited at the thought of a career in the Diplomatic Service, and having the chance to travel and use her languages. As she walked to the letterbox to post her letter of application, she wondered if possibly in years to come, she might be posted to India and maybe even see her Indian Prince again?

"If that happens," she thought, "I must not forget to pack the Indian Box."

—————————

THE SILVER BOX

IT ALL STARTED with the solicitor's letter.

Paula had been idly leafing through the somewhat dull-looking morning mail when she came across a letter from "*Goodbody, Goodbody, Whiteman and Sons. Chichester.*"

"How curious," Paula thought as she opened the formal looking missive. "Dear Madam," she read,

> "We are the Executors for the Estate of the late Miss Marguerite Rousseau, and we are pleased to advise you that a small bequest has been left to your good self in her Will. There is one proviso, however, and that is that you should collect it in person from our offices here in Chichester, within seven days of your receipt of this letter.

We look forward to receiving a telephone call from you advising us as to when we should expect your visit, and please provide some proof of identity, plus a certain item given to you by our late client.

Yours very sincerely

E. P. Goodbody

Chairman"

"My goodness me!" said Paula out loud. Startled, her husband looked up from his newspaper to ask her what brought that on. "Dear Old Aunt Rita has left me something in her will. That's so sweet of her as I really didn't know her as well as I should, and I certainly never expected anything from her. The only odd thing is that I have to go to collect it in person, from Chichester within one week."

"How very kind of the old girl, but as you say, a tad mysterious," Nick commented, then added, "I could drive you there if you like on Monday or Tuesday? I am between assignments at the moment and quite fancy the chance of visiting Chichester Cathedral."

"That's really good of you, Nick," replied Paula. "I'd like that. Let's make it Monday and as today is Wednesday that should give them plenty of notice."

As it turned out, Monday was a beautifully hot June day and Nick was delighted to be able to show off his (almost) new convertible and drive with the hood down.

Paula glanced at him as they were racing down the motorway. She felt she was so lucky to have married Nick. Their wedding had been very nearly a year ago. So much had happened since then, what with finding their flat and doing it up, and getting to know each other's friends and workmates. Everybody loved the story of how they had met.

Nick had been Best Man at his brother Tim's wedding and Paula had been invited as a friend of the Bride – Juliet. She had even managed to catch the wedding bouquet by executing an immense lunge, which brought many an admiring glance as, due to her somewhat short skirt her beautiful long legs were shown off to their best advantage! Paula was becoming used to the teasing she received as the result of that little feat!

Nick was an investigative journalist for a well-known newspaper, and had every intention of remaining in the job. He loved it, even though there were times when he had to up sticks at short notice, and travel for a week or so, which tended to play havoc with plans.

So far Paula accepted this as part of Nick, the man she had married, and besides she had a demanding job as well. Paula worked for a large sporting organisation and helped plan various events and fixtures all over the United Kingdom. It was fine if she and Nick were away at the same time, but sometimes it happened that she had just returned from a three-day event, and the following day Nick would disappear for ten days.

At the moment this lifestyle did not worry them. They just enjoyed their love and friendship, and cruising the country lanes on a glorious day with the top down.

Goodbody, Goodbody, Whiteman and Sons were fairly tricky to find as the building they were occupying was tucked away in a small street in the old part of Chichester.

The perfect secretary, straight out of Central Casting, showed them in. Nick and Paula could scarcely contain their giggles as they looked at this mousy little woman, hair scraped back into a tight bun, long cardigan worn over a calf-length skirt, sensible shoes and of course little spectacles perched on the end of her nose.

"I didn't think such places like this still existed," whispered Paula. "It's so musty. Those books don't look as if they have been touched in years."

"Mr Goodbody will see you now," said Ms Central Casting. "Just you, Mrs Cavendish, if you don't mind. Mr Cavendish, may I get you a cup of tea – or coffee?"

Paula glanced at Nick and shrugged as she followed her leader to Mr Goodbody's office. Slightly flippantly, Paula wondered if she was seeing Mr Goodbody or Mr Goodbody?

"Sit down please, Mrs Cavendish," said the elderly gentleman in front of her. (Also perfect, thought Paula: dark suit, sombre tie, receding grey hair and rather thick spectacles.) "Before we begin, may I trouble you to show me your proof of identity?"

Paula produced her passport, and after studying it carefully, Mr Goodbody returned it to her with a smile.

"Miss Marguerite Rousseau had been a client of ours since 1963. Both my late father and I were privileged to count the gracious lady as a true friend. Forgive the impertinence, but I wonder how much you know about the life your dear Aunt had led?"

"Not very much, I am ashamed to say." Paula muttered. "I didn't see her nearly enough, especially when she was older, but whenever we met, we got on like a house on fire. She was a joy to be with."

"Indeed she was. If you permit me therefore, armed with some coffee, I will attempt to fill in a few details about her life. I am sure you are curious to know what your legacy is, but if you can bear to wait just a little bit longer, you will be in a position to understand more."

"Please forgive me Mr Goodbody, I don't mean to be rude, but I have a feeling I will be here for a while. Would you mind if I suggested to my husband that he might take this opportunity to visit Chichester Cathedral, as I know he has long wished to do so?"

So satisfied that Nick would be perfectly content exploring for the next hour, Paula settled herself in a large, leather, high-backed armchair, to listen to the solicitor.

"Marguerite, whom you know as your Aunt Rita, was the daughter of Emanuel and Sarah Rousseau. Sarah was English by birth, and she and Emanuel had met during the years he lived and worked in London. After their first child was born Emanuel decided to live in the south of France as by this time he was investing in merchant ships many of which were based in Marseilles, from where they ventured forth to Africa and the Middle East. The baby was a boy called Pierre, who of course became your father. Pierre later changed his name to Peter Russell due to circumstances... but I digress. Apologies, but I am inclined to ramble rather."

A sip of coffee later and Mr Goodbody was back on track.

"Your Aunt Rita was born in France in 1932 as Emanuel and Sarah, having visited and fallen in love with the region around Cannes, had bought a substantial villa situated up on a hill with stunning views over the Mediterranean Sea and in the distance the Alpes-Maritimes.

"The shipping business was proving very lucrative. The fleet expanded in size. Trade was brisk and stretched to countries all over the world. ER Shipping was one of the most successful companies of its day. Emanuel was an unusual boss in that he took great interest in every aspect of the company, and in particular the welfare, comfort and safety of the crews.

"Sarah had been a keen amateur artist, and to help her Emanuel invited other artists to stay so they could paint together and learn from each other. As time wore on, the Villa Rousseau became a hub of artists and, indeed, it is said, some very famous artists would occasionally stay for a week or two, such as Raoul Dufy and Henri Fantin-Latour, although I believe the favourite and most regular visitor was Marc Chagall. Monsieur Chagall was Jewish, as was Emanuel.

"Emanuel bought many of the paintings that had been created while staying at his villa. He also invested in fine furniture, porcelain, silver and jewellery. In those days it must have been a wonderful experience to stay in such a house surrounded by objects of beauty wherever one looked. I have seen photographs, and the house should have been preserved as a museum. However... but I am coming to that."

Paula was absolutely fascinated. She had had no idea that Aunt Rita and her father had come from such a background. Tragically, Paula's father had been killed in a riding accident when she was only two. She only had the vaguest and most fleeting of memories of nestling into a warm body, smelling slightly of horses, and strong arms comforting her after she had taken a tumble and grazed her knee.

"So you see young lady, your father and your aunt enjoyed an idyllic childhood in an exceptionally beautiful home until, that is, until World War 2 broke out. One can only imagine how worried Emanuel must have been when rumours of the anti-Semitic actions ordered by the charismatic but horrifying man called Adolf Hitler reached their ears.

"After the Fall of France in June 1940, the Jewish people were persecuted ever more harshly, especially in Northern France, the Netherlands and Germany. The south of France was under French rule and was governed from Vichy under Maréchal Pétain and so Emanuel assumed they would be safe. Surely the French people, who were now defeated, would not wish any harm to befall French Jews? However, Emanuel was soon to realise his trust in the French was misplaced.

The first priority for your grandfather was the safety of his family. He immediately made secret arrangements to send Sarah with Pierre and Marguerite to England on one of his ships. Sarah was torn between her desire to be with her children, while at the same time wanting to stay with Emanuel. Your grandfather insisted, and so the three of them were given a safe passage on a ship that eventually landed in Tilbury, and only had to hide once when the Germans boarded the ship in Le Havre.

"Back in the Villa Rousseau, Emanuel, having given each and every one of them a generous severance payment, dismissed all his servants except his butler, Jean. Together they began to pack up the smaller contents in the villa. They made many parcels of silver and china ornaments, as well as the rest of the jewellery that Sarah had not been able to smuggle out when she and the children had left.

"The paintings were more of a problem. Many of them were too large. Now," continued Mr Goodbody, "I was instructed by your aunt to enlighten you about these matters as she realised, the dear lady, that she did not have many months to live. I was sworn to secrecy, and not even my brother (the other Mr Goodbody) was allowed to know what she had divulged. The reason for the secrecy will become clear.

"Are you quite comfortable, my dear? I have nearly reached the end of the narrative, so if you will just bear with me a little while longer?"

"Of course, Mr Goodbody. Not only am I totally fascinated, I am also feeling extremely guilty that I never took the trouble to really get to know my aunt and to find out more about her past."

Adjusting his glasses, Mr Goodbody appeared for a while to be deep in thought, but then he continued with a little more pace.

"Once everything possible was wrapped up, the question was, where to hide them? I understand on the bureau in your grandfather's dressing room there was a painting in a standing frame which measured about 14 inches by 12. It turned out that this was a watercolour executed by Sarah. It was a landscape of an area surrounded by deep vegetation and hills in the distance, but featuring a dramatic gorge in the foreground. Over to the right of the picture there was a small ruin of what had once been a shepherd's hut. Behind the hut one could just make out some larger stones in a circular shape. Apparently Emanuel and Sarah had found this spot one day when they had been out riding. It obviously meant a great deal to them and Sarah had sketched the scene and painted it later.

"Your Aunt Rita found out these details relatively recently. I believe she has left you a letter confirming this. Emanuel told his faithful butler Jean that the circular stones were part of an ancient well.

"Emanuel and Sarah had kept their horses in stables on top of the local vast hill called the 'Col de Vence'. It was cooler for the animals and there were plenty of places to ride in the area. Jean was not a rider, but he had to accompany his employer to see if by any chance the well could be used as a hiding place. Poor Jean, I believe he was somewhat nervous as he sat upon Sarah's horse and allowed himself to be led by his master into the unknown.

"Emanuel found the spot, which was clever of him as there were no tracks to it. He used Sarah's painting as a guide. Together he and Jean examined the well. It was almost completely overgrown with vegetation, but the vast stone lid was only barely in place. Looking down the well, they saw the petrified carcass of a sheep about halfway down. There was no sign of water. The original mountain stream that fed it had obviously long since dried up. Emanuel decided this would make an excellent hiding place.

"Returning to the villa Emanuel and Jean began to collect items to hide. As much as possible, the objects were made waterproof and safe. Emanuel had also taken a rope hay bale from the stables and this in turn made an excellent 'basket' which could hold everything together. Poor Jean had to suffer another ride when the two of them, with bags and rucksacks and saddle bags hanging everywhere, returned to the shepherd's hut, and after stashing everything inside the hay bale, they lowered it into the well. It must have taken all their strength to heave and manoeuvre the stone lid into place, which they then covered with as much vegetation as they could find.

"According to Jean, Emanuel then gave the owner of the stables several hundred francs when they returned the horses, and asked him to treat them as his own. The following day Emanuel also gave a large sum of money to Jean, and thanked him for his loyal service. He had one more favour to ask of him. He told Jean that it was a real possibility he might not survive the war, and if this was the case, he wanted his heirs to benefit from his collection. Therefore he asked Jean if he would look after Sarah's watercolour until such time as a family member should require it. He also told Jean that he had written out instructions as how to find the hut in English, and had given the envelope addressed to Sarah, to the captain of a ship that was returning for good to England to entrust to the post after he had arrived. Those instructions were handed down to Marguerite.

"Jean did not want to leave his master, but Emanuel insisted, and told him to try and forget what they had done. He advised him to be careful with his money so as not to arouse suspicion from anyone. Jean was a relatively young man, but had been unable to fight due to being blind in one eye.

"Emanuel returned to his villa and made the decision to lock everything up as best he could, and to go to the port in Marseilles to board one of his ships, wherever it might be going. His company had already been requisitioned, but the crews still held him in high regard.

"Tragically, Emanuel stayed on one day too long. French soldiers under the Vichy command descended on the Villa Rousseau and arrested him. The villagers were aware of the arrival of the soldiers, and Jean hurriedly made his way to the Villa Rousseau and from his hiding place witnessed the way this gentle man was roughly manhandled and virtually thrown into the back of the police van.

"Then started the looting. Everything was taken out of the house. When they had finished, the soldiers then set the house on fire, and gathered round cheering as the flames engulfed the beautiful staircase, raced upstairs finally catching the roof which in turn collapsed. By this time hordes of villagers had turned up to watch. Then Jean heard someone say – 'The ignorant soldiers said there were many gaps on the walls and shelves. It seems that only large pieces were left. Where are the rest of the valuable possessions owned by that rich family? They must have hidden them – but where?"

"Someone saw Jean and recognised him. 'He worked there. He will know. Let's ask him." When Jean professed ignorance they did not believe him. They beat him to force him to tell. Somehow he escaped and managed to get back to his sister's house where he was staying. The beating left him not only severely shaken, but his arm was so badly broken it never recovered.

"That is as far as I am able to tell you at the moment. Your aunt's letter should fill in the rest. In the meantime, I have to ask you, do you have the item I asked you to bring?"

For a moment Paula did not know what Mr Goodbody was talking about. She had been so engrossed in his tale. Then, of course, she remembered.

When she and Nick were married she had sent an invitation to Aunt Rita. The old lady had politely refused but was obviously delighted to have been asked. With her reply she had enclosed a small present. When Paula opened the tiny package she discovered a little leather-bound box and inside, nestling on the velvet interior, was a delicate silver chain necklace which had one charm hanging off it. The charm was a tiny silver key with a little diamond on it. Aunt Rita had penned a note which read, "This, my dear Paula, is the first half of your wedding present. The second half will arrive in due course, but in the meantime

I urge you to keep this chain necklace and key extremely safe. You will need it some time in the future. With all my best wishes to you both, for your happiness and well being. Affectionately, your Aunt Rita." It was no hardship for Paula to wear this fine chain all day and every day. She showed it to Mr Goodbody.

Mr Goodbody lapsed into silence for a moment, and then remembering himself told Paula the time had come to give her her legacy.

Paula looked on in astonishment as the large portrait of a very stern-looking Mr Goodbody of an earlier age was swung to one side by way of some hinges. Behind the portrait an ancient safe was revealed, with a huge dial, which Mr Goodbody twiddled this way and that until this door also opened. The interior of the safe appeared to be completely stuffed with papers tied together with red ribbons. The old man rifled through a few before triumphantly extricating the bundle he required, and pulled out a violet-coloured envelope, which he handed to Paula.

Paula saw with astonishment that the envelope was addressed to her in Aunt Rita's distinctive, somewhat spidery handwriting. It also obviously had something inside as well as the letter.

"Before you read your letter there is something else to give you," and the solicitor handed Paula a package wrapped up in brown paper.

"Feel free to investigate," she was advised. Once the paper was discarded she held in her hands a delightful silver box. It was unusual in that it was heart-shaped, and was embossed all the way round and on the lid with charming country scenes. Paula immediately tried to open the lid, only to discover it was locked. Cleverly hidden in the design of the gathering of the harvest on one side was a lock. Paula was beginning to understand the significance of her little silver key.

Paula looked questionably at Mr Goodbody. The old man thought for a minute and then he said,

"You have had a good deal to absorb this morning. I suggest you defer reading your letter and discovering about the contents of the silver box for a little while. Maybe you and your husband could have some lunch and then find a quiet moment to read your aunt's letter."

Paula had to admit her head was reeling somewhat with the extraordinary story Mr Goodbody had told her. She agreed it would be a good idea to wait a bit for the letter.

As she bade Mr Goodbody goodbye, he looked her in the eye and said,

"What you will discover could in fact make you an extremely rich young woman. However, unfortunately rumours have abounded over the years, and there is no doubt you could also be in danger. Whatever you decide to do, I urge you to be very vigilant and take the utmost care about whom you choose to trust."

"I will, Mr Goodbody, and thank you so much for all the trouble and care you have taken. I will let you know what I decide."

Nick was waiting for her when she left the office, and together they left 'Goodbody, Goodbody and Whiteman & Sons' and walked out into the sunshine.

―――――――――

"So – how did that all go?" Nick was in a fairly jocular frame of mind. "Has the dear old girl left you the crown jewels, or was it all rather a disappointment?"

"Let's go and find somewhere quiet for lunch," his wife replied, "and I will tell you all about it."

They decided to leave the city, and headed towards the water where quite by chance they found a charming little pub with great views of boats of various sizes and shapes bobbing about on the water. During lunch, Paula filled Nick in with all the details. The pub had a garden, and in a sheltered spot they settled down with their mugs of coffee to learn what Aunt Rita had to say in her letter.

As she suspected, when Paula opened the envelope, a key, slightly larger than the one around her neck, fell out. Paula took the silver box out of her bag, and inserted the key, which allowed her to open the lid.

Inside they discovered a thick piece of paper, somewhat yellow with age, that had been folded several times in order to fit in the box. When Paula had carefully opened out the paper, it revealed a rudimentary map, drawn in ink, and underneath directions in writing remarkably similar to Aunt Rita's own hand.

Paula then began to read the letter written by her aunt.

3, Primrose Cottages
Bosham, Chichester

11 March 2000

My dear Paula,

By the time you will be reading this I shall no longer be alive. I am not concerned about dying, other than I regret not having had the opportunity to know you better. You have so much of your father in you, and I know he would have loved you dearly.

I have asked my dear friend Henry Goodman to fill in the details for you about your family. You will have gathered that your father and I certainly enjoyed a most idyllic childhood in the South of France. I have to admit we were very indulged, and had a large staff who instantly pandered to our every whim. We wanted for nothing.

Thankfully, we had a sensible English mother who had been strictly brought up herself, and I owe her the credit of raising two, I believe, quite likeable children!

We were surrounded by beauty both in and out of the house. We would watch with awe as famous painters came to stay and produced many well known works of art in the studio my father had built in the grounds. Our mother was a very accomplished painter herself and her watercolour of a landscape that meant so much to them both was treasured by my father.

As you know this perfect life tragically came to an end in 1942. I am grateful I did not know I would never see my beloved father again when he kissed us goodbye as we boarded the ship.

When we at last arrived in England we had to stay with relatives of my mother. They resented us taking up rooms and food, despite the fact that my mother made sure we always paid our way. As soon as possible we moved into our own home. What a shock that was! My brother Pierre and I had to share a room, and even though my mother had often spoken to us in English, we could not speak it well.

We attended the local school where we were known as the 'Little French Jewish Refugees'.

I learned later that my father had been very forward thinking, and even before war had been declared he had transferred a good deal of money to a bank in England in my mother's name. Eventually she was able to access these funds and we were from then on quite able to care for ourselves.

Pierre attended an English boarding school, but before he went, he insisted on Anglicising his name, and eventually legally changed from Pierre Rousseau to Peter Russell.

My poor mother had lived in anguished ignorance as to the fate of my father for years, but eventually she learnt for sure that Emanuel had died in Auschwitz Concentration Camp.

Peter married your mother, and was so happy, especially when you came along, so it was a terrible tragedy when he was killed.

I never married. I had fallen in love with a young man after the war, and we had plans to marry.

One day he told me that his parents would disinherit him if he married me as I was half-Jewish. I had hoped his love was strong enough to defy his parents but it was not to be, and I never fell in love again.

I was not lonely, as I had many good friends, and have lived a perfectly enjoyable and busy life. I tried in a small way to help young artists, and I am proud that several of my protégés have found fame, and some even fortune!

In 1979 I received a letter 'out of the blue', as you would say. It was written by my father's faithful servant, Jean. He asked me to meet him two days later in Victoria Station in London. He stressed I should tell no one, and should be very discreet.

When I arrived at the café he suggested, I looked around and thought he was not there. Then I realised an old man was sitting by himself at a corner table, and looking at me curiously. I caught his eye. "Jean?" I said. The old man rose from his seat, and as I went over to join him, he came up to me and clasped my hands in his, and I saw there were tears in his eyes.

I only just recognised him. I had been ten years old when we had left France, and then Jean was a young man in his early twenties. Now, despite being only just in his sixties, he looked about 80. He was obviously not well, and his left arm hung uselessly by his side.

Jean then related to me the actions he and my father had taken to try and save the treasures of the Villa Rousseau.

It broke my heart to hear how roughly my poor father had been treated when he had been arrested, and by French people as well. All my father had ever done was to try to promote the beauty of his country. He had of course volunteered to fight during the First World War, during which time he had been injured on his lower leg, which rendered him unable to fight again.

My father had given Jean the watercolour painted by my mother of the countryside where they had discovered the shepherd's hut. As Jean had never married, nor had a home of his own, he hung it on the wall of his sister's house, with strict instructions to guard it with her life, and if she should die, to make sure her family did the same.

Due to the fact that Jean had been so badly beaten up after Emanuel's arrest, he decided, as soon as he could, to leave the area and he ended up in Switzerland, working for a very rich and pleasant family until his retirement.

In the meantime his sister had died, and her son and his wife continued to live in the house. Jean returned to Provence, and visited his nephew. Immediately they wanted to know why the painting was so important. It looked pretty ordinary, they said, unless the rumours were true, and the painting contained a clue as to the whereabouts of the hidden treasures of Villa Rousseau.

Apparently, Jean did his best to feign ignorance. His nephew Didier Lamont, however, did not believe him. He was also a somewhat unsavoury character. Before he knew it, Jean was approached by a group of men who demanded to know what had indeed happened. Once again Jean was roughly treated. Then an older man applied pressure of a different kind, promising Jean a large cut of the spoils if only he would confess. In the meantime, the painting was taken off the wall, and these men studied it and tried to work out where it had been painted.

Poor Jean. It all became too much for him. Also, his health was beginning to deteriorate. He felt it important that I should know what was happening. He told me he thought the group of men who threatened him were hardened criminals connected in some way to the Mafia, being so close to Italy. He felt they were ruthless and would stop at nothing to get their hands on the treasures. He was too scared to remain in France and therefore decided to spend the rest of his days in the mountains above Montreux. Before returning to Switzerland, though, he wrote to me in order to meet me one last time.

Jean was so sad to learn of the death of my brother, and also that of my mother as he was so fond of them both. He knew about you, my dear, and realised it would be up to you to retrieve the items that would rightly belong to you if you so desired, when you had reached your maturity. He begged me to leave informing you of all this for many years, in order to give the gang of men a chance to give up the idea of finding anything and to disperse, and especially for you to be old and wise enough to understand all the ramifications. He was genuinely afraid of these people and of putting any family members in danger.

I felt so sorry for the dear man. He had been so very loyal to our family and it was cruel that he now lived in fear. I was relieved he was returning to Switzerland as he said he had made some good friends over the years, and he would keep in touch with me.

Finally just before he left, he handed me the packet, very discreetly which contained not only the silver box, but the address of Didier Lamont. The key he pressed into my hand as we said goodbye, and suddenly he was gone, before I had a chance to thank him and wish him well.

Jean was as good as his word, and he let me know he had safely arrived in Switzerland and found somewhere to live, but sadly he never gave me his address.

I am sure he did not live too long, as I fear he was not at all a well man.

So there we are my dear Paula. A strange tale, and I apologise for being so long-winded. My mother always said I would use three words when one would do! It seems I have never learned my lesson.

However, this is now up to you. Maybe you would prefer to leave the treasures of Villa Rousseau well hidden? Maybe they have already been discovered by someone else? I have a feeling, though, that you would like to find them. If that is the case, my dear, I can only urge you to be extremely careful. First and foremost, you will need to find the painting. Goodness knows where it could be now, but you should start with the Lamont family. Whilst the original men may have disappeared, there could always be descendants. It would be safer to trust no one until you are very sure.

If and when you find the treasure, it will be up to you what you do with it.

Your grandfather had always wanted to fund an art gallery with paintings from his friends, as well as sculptures and other items of artistic interest, but it was not to be.

Good luck my dear. Keep safe. I know I can trust you to do what ever is in the best interest of all concerned. I am sure you will make your Grandfather, wherever he might be, very proud.

With much affection,
from your
Aunt Rita.

When Paula had finished reading Aunt Rita's extraordinary letter, she and Nick just sat for several minutes in stunned silence.

At last Nick asked his wife: "What is your gut feeling? What would you like to do?"

"Go to France and find it, of course, and then decide what to do with it all if we find it."

"It will not be without danger," said Nick.

"I know," said Paula, "but I will have you to look after me, wont I darling?"

Nick looked at his wife, and knew why he loved her so much. She was gutsy and fun, and always prepared to have a go at whatever challenge presented itself.

Sitting in the late afternoon sun, with her dark hair tumbling about her pretty little face, he knew he could not possibly resist her – or indeed the challenge.

"Very well then, we will go. I just have to complete one more three-day assignment, and then I will take a week's holiday."

Paula squeezed Nick's hand, and looked up at him as she said, "Thank you darling. At last I would be doing something for my family."

As it turned out, Nick's three-day assignment turned into a full week. They agreed that Paula should go on ahead and carefully try to learn the lay of the land. A small Bed and Breakfast hotel half way up the hill to Vence was found and a car was booked for her to pick up at the airport.

"Now don't forget to drive on the *right* side of the road," warned Nick.

"I won't," said Paula. "I will remember always to keep my body nearest the centre of the road, and I will also use my mother's trick of putting a green sticker low down on the right side of the windscreen and a red one on the left."

While the plane was making its scenic and quite dramatic descent into Nice, Paula looked down at the sparkling blue sea dotted with small white craft, and the busy buildings along the coast gradually giving way to smaller villages and hamlets as they climbed up the mountain and onwards towards the Alps, which, on this clear day, were clearly visible in the far distance.

Paula's thoughts were a mixture of excitement and trepidation. What on earth would the next few days reveal? Would they be able to find the buried treasures without encountering any hostility? She knew Nick and she would need help with the actual recovery, but how would they know whom to trust?

First things first. The car, a small VW, was collected. Then Paula bravely tackled the drive towards Vence. The hardest task, it seemed, was actually leaving the perimeters of the airport! Once on the motorway she gained her confidence and was easily able to follow the route which led directly to the small hotel situated just off the main road.

This was when Paula regretted she hadn't worked harder at her French, especially with her background. Her language was fairly rudimentary, although she could understand quite well. It was her grammar that let her down. She did her best, but time and again, when she thought she had said something rather well, the person to whom she was speaking replied in flawless English. This was the case with Madame who ran the hotel. She had told the owner she was a photographer, and was compiling photographs of the area for a magazine. Her husband was coming later and they would have a few days' holiday together.

After she had settled into the sweet little room, Paula asked Madame how easy it would be to visit Tourrettes, which was the closest village to the home of the Lamont family.

"So easy, Madame. I tell you. It will be perfect for your photos. But it is best if you wait until tomorrow as it will be Wednesday, Market Day, and there is always so much to see. At this moment you must be tired, so I suggest you wander into Vence this afternoon as the old town is particularly beautiful and full of wonderful shops."

What a sweet and friendly woman, thought Paula, and *how I wish I could speak French as well as she speaks English.*

Madame had told her it was important to arrive very early in Tourrettes-sur-Loup as the Market Day is so popular. Paula skipped breakfast and as Madame had directed, parked her car and, following everyone else, took the ancient path into the village. Luckily, Paula had her camera over her shoulder, as on the way she stopped and gazed in awe at the sight of a stone house completely engulfed in the most vivid purple bougainvillea against the backdrop of a sky of the deepest blue. For a moment she totally forgot the reason she was there at all, as she took her photographs – along, it must be said, with a few other tourists.

Even at the early hour of 9 am the square was alive with busy market stalls, early shoppers out to get the best bargains, and the cries of the stallholders tempting passers-by to buy their honey, their olives, their 'designer' watches, their herbs or tempting pastries and bread. The colours and the sounds filled Paula's senses, and she just wanted to stand and 'drink' it all in. So – she did the next best thing, grabbing a table at a café overlooking the square and ordering herself a delicious Continental breakfast.

Paula had also taken a photo on her iPhone which she sent to Nick to check in with him, which she had promised to do regularly.

Gazing over the scene in front of her, Paula noticed a stall selling a variety of cheeses. A pretty young girl in an embroidered blouse and cheerful pinafore was serving customers with a smile. It was not just looking at this charming scenario that had caught Paula's attention. It was the fact that the sign behind the stall read: 'Les Fromages Traditionnels de la Ferme Famille Lamont'.

"My goodness," thought Paula, "could that possibly be the family of Didier Lamont?"

Paula wandered over to the cheese stall and saw a small packet of goat's cheese which she picked up and in her best French asked the girl how much it was. In perfect English the girl told her the price. As Paula hesitated, the girl looked at Paula and asked, "Is there something else Madame?"

Paula couldn't resist it.

"Is it possible that Didier Lamont is part of your family?"

The girl was obviously somewhat startled at this request, as she was expecting another query about cheese.

"Yes. He is my father. Why do you wish to know? He is not here today, alas."

"He used to know somebody connected with my family I believe. Jean Collobert."

"Would you tell me who you are, Madame?" the girl enquired politely, but with great curiosity.

"My name is Paula Cavendish. My grandfather was Emanuel Rousseau."

Paula was unprepared for the instant reaction of the young girl. She turned to the other woman helping her with the stall, and in rapid French, which Paula easily understood the gist of, told her she would be taking 20 minutes off for a *café*. Then, taking off her apron, she led Paula to another restaurant at the back of the market and marched straight inside to small table in the dark interior and ordered two espresso coffees without even asking.

"Madame," the French girl began, "I am wondering what would your business with my father be? He is an old man now, and not always in the best of temper. Oh – and my name is Marie-Annette."

Paula smiled at the girl, whom she guessed would be about 19 years of age. She knew she had to be very careful what she said.

"My dear aunt in England, who spent her early childhood here, died the other day. She wanted me to have a picture that my grandmother had painted when she was living here. Apparently it was of great sentimental value, and reminded my aunt of her parents. She had wanted to come herself to find it, but she was not a strong woman. Jean Collobert's sister was *your* aunt, I imagine? Jean told my aunt that his sister was looking after the painting until such time as a family member requested it."

Marie-Annette was quiet for several minutes. Finally she said, "There are many rumours, Madame, concerning this painting. No one knows if there is any truth in them. Do you know to what I am referring?"

"No I don't, I am afraid. When my aunt died and left me word about the painting, my husband (who is joining me the day after tomorrow) and I thought we would combine a holiday in the region, along with an assignment for photography for me from an English magazine, and at the same time see if we can locate the painting, just for family reasons. I also know that my grandparents had a beautiful villa somewhere near here which was destroyed during the war, but I would dearly love to see whereabouts it had been. I don't know if that would be possible?"

"The original Villa Rousseau was completely destroyed. Such a pity, as I have heard it was an exceptional building. Now there is a new villa on the same site, and they have kept the name. I can show you if you like. It is very modern and grand. The people who own it are foreigners and only come a few months a year. I believe they are there now, so we could only peep."

"I would really like that, thank you Marie-Annette. And please, call me Paula, as we are not very different in age and I have only been married for one year."

The French girl then continued, "Regarding the painting. I have not seen it for some time. It always used to be on the wall in the *salon*. A few years ago Papa lent it to some friends and I am not sure if they returned it. I shall try to find out. Now I must return to my stall. Can we meet again tomorrow? I could collect you at your *auberge* and show you the spot where your family used to live. For now – enjoy yourself exploring our beautiful little town – and do some shopping!"

Paula wandered up and down the steep cobbled streets, admiring the work of the artisans and allowing herself the treat of a totally delicious ice cream before giving into temptations on display in shops and on the stalls. It was a stunningly beautiful day and she wished Nick was with her.

For lunch she found yet another small restaurant and ordered the perfect *salade Niçoise* and as she ate it she went over the events of the morning in her head. Hopefully she had convinced Marie-Annette that she had no inkling about the buried treasures. Also, she very much hoped that the painting could be found. By the time she returned to the hotel she was tired out, and after a simple supper she went to bed early and amazingly had a dreamless sleep.

True to her word, Marie-Annette arrived on time to collect Paula and show her the modern version of the Villa Rousseau. They drove all the way through Tourrettes, and then followed a small road twisting and turning up a steep hill. Right at the top Marie-Annette stopped the car and when Paula was standing beside her she gazed at the stunning view in front of her. No wonder Emanuel had picked such a perfect spot to build his house.

A long, high, white wall abutted the road. At regular intervals niches had been carved into the wall and these had been planted with brilliant red geraniums. Close to the highest part of the wall was a pair of very ornate gates through which it was possible to see a sweeping gravel drive leading to the front of the house, but only tantalising glimpses of the property beyond. Cameras and security lights were very much in evidence. Every window of the house was protected by curved iron grilles.

The house looked attractive. Two-storey, with a deep green tiled roof.

Suddenly, the gates began to open, and a service vehicle belonging to a swimming pool company drove out, enabling Paula to see more of the garden, which looked immaculate and full of hibiscus, oleander and other colourful shrubs.

Although Paula knew the original Villa Rousseau would have looked nothing like this modern version, she was nevertheless pleased to know that the site was being well cared for and to a certain extent loved.

Briefly she closed her eyes to help her imagine Aunt Rita and her father growing up in such surroundings, and also what it must have been like when the villa had been the centre of the most amazing artistic abilities.

"My father would like to meet you," Marie-Annette said suddenly. "If you have time, I could take you home now for some coffee?"

Paula had not expected to meet Didier just yet. Once again she wished Nick was with her.

The Lamont farm was a 20-minute drive away. Paula took the time to compose herself and to make sure she stuck to her story.

Didier was a large man about 60 years of age. It was hard to tell, as he was totally white-haired, had virtually no teeth, and had a weather-beaten, lined face. He still looked however, a strong and fit man.

Didier spoke no English. Marie-Annette acted as an interpreter.

"Why have you come here?" – "Why now?" – "Why are you interested in that old painting?" – "How much do you know about Emanuel?"

Paula stuck to her story, and smiled and was as pleasant as possible. She did her best to appear totally ignorant regarding any rumours of buried treasures.

Paula did not like Didier. The way he never took his eyes off her when she was talking was unnerving. It was not a friendly look.

Finally, she plucked up courage to ask the old man if he knew of the whereabouts of the painting.

Didier shrugged his shoulders, and then said, "The painting was not up to much. More like a sketch. I gave it to a friend and I think he sold it to a local art gallery for a few Euros."

Paula knew Didier was watching for her reaction to this news, so she tried to appear suitably disappointed, but in no way particularly upset.

"Oh well," she said. "Thank you anyway. Now, I really must be going as I have my assignment to complete. Such a pleasure to meet you, Monsieur Lamont."

Marie-Annette drove her back to her hotel in silence. After she had left the car, Paula leant in again to say goodbye when Marie-Annette suddenly grabbed her hand and said, "Please take great care of yourself, Paula. I am not sure my father completely believed you. He is not the only person who wants to learn the truth of the rumours."

Paula tried to protest innocence again, but the French girl interrupted her.

"If you really need to find the painting I believe it might be in one of the lesser art galleries in Saint Paul de Vence." And so saying, Marie-Annette quickly drove away.

Paula had thought Vence was picturesque enough with its charming square and old fountain leading to tiny streets full of shops selling all types of delicious gourmet food, but her senses were once again assailed as she went under the archway, and trod on the decorated cobbled road into St. Paul the following morning. This was most definitely the home for artists and almost every shop seemed to be an art gallery.

Paula had to admit some of the paintings were not her style at all. They looked rather as if they had been churned out by a machine. Brilliant bright red poppies against startling blue skies flanked by the most virulent lavender fields were obviously popular buys. Whilst these strong colours could fit in well in Provence, somehow she could not imagine them at home on a dull English winter's day.

Not all the paintings were like that by any means. Suddenly a shop would be dedicated to one artist of exceptional talent and diversity. *Emanuel would have liked that one,* Paula thought as she admired a stunning painting of a village scene, with shafts of sunlight piercing the trees. So delicate and bordering on the impressionistic style. That would be a painting she would buy if she had the money.

The owner of the shop came out and smiled at her.

"You look for something in particular, Madame?" he asked.

"Oh – I was just admiring that picture. I think it is so charming and utterly captures the feel of these enchanting village squares. Sadly, I know that will be beyond my means, but I am really looking for something much smaller, and possibly in watercolour. Do you sell anything like that?"

The owner also happened to be the artist. He was most agreeable but did say he only painted in oils, acrylics or sometimes pastels. However, his friend who also had a shop, not only painted in watercolours, but also bought work from other artists. "Do you have a particular subject in mind?"

"Mmm." (Paula was trying to appear a touch undecided.) "Much as I love the village scenes, I also adore the rather wilder parts of the countryside. When my husband arrives tomorrow, one of the first things we will do is to drive up the Col de Vence and go for a long walk."

"I believe my friend has a few paintings that might appeal to you. This is his card. Tell him I sent you and he will give you a good price."

Paula's heart was beating quickly as she found her way to the other art gallery.

Might she find her grandmother's picture there? Would it be that easy?

On entering the little shop, her hopes subsided somewhat as there were masses of paintings all over the place. Not only on the walls, but in folders, on tables, and seemingly hundreds stacked up against the wall on the floor.

How could she possibly describe the painting she was looking for without attracting too much attention?

Once again she explained that she was looking for a more rustic scene, preferably either painted from or of the Col de Vence.

The young artist looked at her rather curiously when she had told him what she wanted.

"I wonder if you are, how do you say in English? When you know something strange?"

"Do you mean psychic?"

"*Exactement*! It is strange is it not, that a painting very much as you described came into the shop only last month. No one has bought it. I will show it to you."

Paula gazed at the beautifully painted watercolour showing thick vegetation, a ruin of a shepherd's hut with just visible the curved stones of an old well, in front of a dramatic gorge, and mountains in the distance. Goosebumps went over her body and she gave an involuntary shiver. To eliminate any doubt she might have had that she had indeed found the right painting, on the bottom of the right hand corner were the tiny initials of *SR*.

The young owner gave her a good price. Little did he know she would have paid double. He wrapped it up and Paula was able to fit it inside the canvas carrier bag she had with her. She left the shop, with smiles and thanks, and feeling extraordinarily light-headed, she quickly found a seat at a bar in the main square and ordered herself a glass of white wine. She didn't care if it was too early to drink alcohol, she needed something to calm her down.

Unnoticed by Paula as she sat gratefully sipping her restoring drink, her transaction had been observed by a man of about 40 years of age, who now sat on a wall, smoking a cigarette as he made a call on his mobile, whilst never taking his eyes off the English girl.

If she had noticed him Paula would have observed that this man was very dark. His skin was deeply tanned, and his rather long dark hair fell over his face. He was unshaven, and dressed in workman's overalls, which would have explained his dirty hands. No tourist was he.

The wine did its magic, and Paula returned to her hotel. Once safely alone in her room she undid the package and studied the painting which was still in its original frame.

She allowed herself to wonder why the area was so special to Emanuel and Sarah, and could only conclude they had enjoyed a wonderfully romantic time up there in the hills. Paula admired Sarah's attention to detail and the lightness of her touch. It brought tears to her eyes thinking about the happiness that prompted the execution of this painting, followed by such heartache and tragedy. She gently touched the frame, and felt a connection to both her grandparents.

There was no doubt in Paula's mind that once they had found the right place this painting would confirm it. However, the problem was finding the exact spot, and this is where the directions came in.

The silver box shone brightly in the light from the sun as Paula took it from her case and placed it on the table by the window. Once it was unlocked, she carefully removed the folded paper within. She studied the map and hoped it would eventually make sense.

Deep in her thoughts Paula was startled by her mobile ringing. Not Nick, as he was well on his way to join her by now, but 'Number Unknown'.

"Paula – it is I – Marie-Annette. I am calling to warn you. You were seen this morning and it is known that you have found the painting. I am afraid you might be in danger. You must keep the painting safe. I am so sorry. *Bonne Chance.*"

Marie-Annette did not give Paula time to respond.

The call definitely upset her. Thank goodness Nick would be with her in a few hours. In the meantime – think – think. A simple plan began to form in her mind and she set to work to execute it. Then she lay down on the bed, and despite feeling seriously peckish, she allowed herself to drift off to sleep until 3 pm when it was time to drive to the airport to meet her husband.

Dressed casually in her walking shorts and T-shirt, Paula left her hotel with her canvas bag slung over her shoulder to find her car. As surreptitiously as she could, she looked round about her while flinging her bag in the passenger footwell and driving off as quickly as she could.

The dark-haired man dressed in workman's overalls, who had been lounging against a tree on the other side of the road, suddenly crossed the road and mounted a small motorbike. Paula kept sight of him in her rearview mirror as she headed towards the airport.

Nick's plane was on time, and Paula rushed to meet him, immediately feeling safer and comforted in his arms. As a consequence of Nick's job as an investigative journalist, he had often found himself in tricky and sometimes violent situations, plus he kept himself ultra-fit.

"Darling," said Paula, "don't be surprised at what I say. Just act as if – which I hope you are! – thrilled to be here and as if all we want to do is to have a lovely holiday together."

"I have a surprise for you," she continued, and patting her canvas bag, said, "it's in here. But no – you must wait. I will show it to you later."

Nick looked at her curiously. "Is I what I think it might be?"

"You must wait and see. Now – let us find the car and head back to the hotel."

Once in the car Paula explained that she had indeed found the painting, but she had been seen and followed this morning. Just before she turned the car into the hotel's car park, she was forced to brake sharply as a motorbike lay on the ground in front of her. Before either of them could take in what was happening, two men appeared and wrenched open the car doors, and one, on seeing Paula's canvas bag grabbed it, shouting, "*C'est ici!*" While the second man righted the fallen bike, the package containing the picture was removed before the first man jumped on the back of the motorbike; both had disappeared before either Nick or Paula could take in exactly what had happened.

They sat in the car in a state of shock. Then Paula drove to her parking place, and motioned to Nick to bring his bags and follow her inside.

"Oh my poor darling," said Nick as he put his arms around his wife. "Aunt Rita was not wrong when she told us to be on our guard. I am so sorry. Now those wretched people have gained possession of that important painting."

"No they haven't." Paula had recovered from the shock and had a twinkle in her eye.

"The painting is safe and I have hidden it. I only had the empty frame with me this morning just in case something like this happened. My sweet friend Marie-Annette warned me to be extra-careful."

"You clever girl!" Her husband was full of admiration. "Where is it? Once they discover they do not have it, they will return with a vengeance, I fear."

"I managed to work the painting into the lining of the jacket I brought just in case we had a cool evening. The directions and map are in the inside zipped security pocket in these shorts I am wearing. Nick darling – I am absolutely famished. I have not eaten properly all day and there is so much to tell you. I suggest we behave like a couple of real tourists and I will take you to Vence where Marie-Annette said there was a superb small restaurant, and let's give ourselves a thoroughly good dinner and make plans."

Nick was only too happy to comply.

La Petite Armoire lived up to its reputation. Nick and Paula savoured every delicious mouthful and appreciated the way the Patron helped them choose the perfect wines. Paula was grateful they only had a short way to drive back to the hotel.

During dinner they had made their plans. They noticed that the directions began on a path on the other side of the road from the riding stables. They knew Sarah and Emanuel had originally discovered the site on horseback, and so they agreed this would be their best bet on finding it. Paula had ridden a good deal as a child, as her mother had been brought up with horses. Nick knew how to ride, although he was not so accomplished as his wife.

Madame in the hotel had rung the stables and explained their abilities, and so two horses were prepared for them. The wonderful Madame also gave them a picnic lunch to take with them, complete with a bottle of their own wine.

Paula continued to drive as she was pretty confident by now. They started the climb up the Col de Vence, and as they went ever higher, they passed several serious cyclists either struggling up or haring down at terrifying speeds, whizzing round corners and miraculously avoiding various cars and motorbikes also sharing the road. The views became ever more spectacular, and even the burnt-out areas, evidence of bush fires, did not detract from the overall beauty.

They were almost at the summit when they saw the sign for the stables on their left. Sure enough, two horses were saddled and ready for them. The stables were a family business and the present owners were third-generation. Paula wondered if they might remember Emanuel.

Tentatively, she asked the young woman who was holding the horses if there might be someone around who knew the Rousseau family?

Once again the name Rousseau caused a startling reaction. "A moment," she replied, and, handing the reins to a stable lad, she disappeared into a nearby house.

"Come," she called a few minutes later. She beckoned them to follow her.

A very old man was sitting in a chair in the *salon*. He looked at Paula for a long moment. In French he said, "Yes, it is true. I can see Rousseau in you. You are Pierre's daughter, no?"

The elderly gentleman explained that he had been a boy when Emanuel and Sarah used to keep their horses with them. He remembered his grandfather being very upset when they heard the news of Emanuel's arrest and the subsequent destruction of his villa. He had always held the Rousseau family in the highest regard, and were appreciative of all they did to promote Provence.

"Your grandparents loved this part of the country and knew it very well. I believe they explored the area overlooking the gorge. There are rumours, and there are unscrupulous people about. Take care, my children."

Paula shook hands with the old man, and looked him in the eye as she said, in her very best French, "Thank you so much. We will be careful."

The girl sent them off in the right direction with rather vague directions as to how to find the gorge. Nick was doing very well on his gentle mount and even managed to balance the bags containing the lunches on either side of the saddle. It was another beautiful day in Provence, and they both felt exhilarated and full of anticipation at what they might discover.

They had been riding for about 40 minutes when, seemingly with no warning, the dramatic gorge appeared in front of them.

"Goodness!" said Paula. "Somehow I didn't expect it to appear just like that."

Out came the painting, and they studied it carefully. Although they could recognize the mountains, the terrain in the foreground was quite different, and there was no sign of any hut anywhere. Nick then looked at the directions and concluded they still needed to travel further off to the right.

Trying to keep the gorge in sight, they continued. After another half an hour Nick suggested that they stopped for lunch, and give the horses a rest and then, fortified with food and wine, they would carry on with renewed vigour.

"I suppose it is possible the hut has completely disintegrated by now, which would make finding the well pretty near impossible."

"Possibly," said Nick, "but don't let's despair just yet."

They tethered the horses and found themselves a suitable spot to have their lunch whilst at the same time enjoying the scenery.

It was tempting just to lie on their backs in the sun, listening to the birds and the quiet chomping of their horses, and drift off into a gentle sleep. But they resisted, and while Nick cleared up the picnic, Paula took herself off into some bushes to do what comes naturally, especially after nearly half a bottle of wine! When she had finished Paula didn't turn back at once, but pushed her way through thick undergrowth in front of her as she thought she could see something that caught her interest.

Nick was just beginning to become concerned when his breathless and somewhat dishevelled-looking wife emerged from the bushes.

"Nick. I have found it! We are almost on top of it. It is so well hidden, as it is built on the downward slopes towards the gorge. Quickly. Come and see."

Nick had finished tying the bags back onto his horse, so he followed his excited wife at once.

Forcing themselves through the bushes (rather like a jungle trek, Nick thought), they duly emerged above a long slope leading down to the depths of the gorge. There, over to the right were the crumbled remains of a shepherd's hut. Surprisingly, most of the roof and walls were pretty much intact; it was the small outbuilding that was a virtual heap of stones.

"Where is the well?" whispered Paula. Then, at the same time they both noticed a rather odd-shaped bush and on closer inspection found that it concealed the remains of the well. Together they started to pull the vegetation away, and sure enough the stone lid of the well was revealed.

So intent were the young couple on their discovery that they did not hear the at first distant and then nearer sounds of engines. It was the startled whinnying of the horses that alerted them, too late, to the arrival of four extremely evil-looking men, one of whom was the father of Marie-Annette.

In rapid French, which even Nick only barely understood, Didier Lamont said: "So – you thought you could trick us, did you? That was not a clever idea, I fear. But you have taken us to the hiding place where we know we shall find the treasures hidden by your grandfather."

"Whatever is hidden does not belong to you, Monsieur Lamont, and if you take them you will be guilty of theft."

"And who will know? Sadly the word will be that the careless young couple both fell off their horses by the deep gorge, and their bodies will only be discovered when it is too late. The horses have been sent off, so there is no escape. Michel – Pascale – Georges – tie them up."

Whilst the old man was talking, the other three men stood guard over Nick and Paula. Nick was desperately trying to reach his phone, but there was no chance.

Paula asked him to ask Lamont why he was doing this, and why he obviously hated Emanuel so much. Nick also added that whatever might be found was already listed and a copy was in a bank in Switzerland. If he tried to sell anything he would be caught at once.

This information made the farmer hesitate – but only for a moment.

The three men produced some ropes and roughly tied Nick and Paula's hands behind their backs.

"Try and pull your wrists apart, Paula' Nick urged, 'to give some slack."

When they were satisfied that they could cause no trouble, the men manhandled the couple and pushed them roughly inside the shepherd's hut. They then set to work to try to remove the stone lid.

Paula couldn't imagine why there was such a heavy lid to the well, but Nick thought it was for use only during the winter snows, and that during the summer months the well was left with just a wooden lid to protect unwary animals.

Once their eyes accustomed themselves to the gloom of the interior of the hut, Nick noticed several sharp-looking stones. He immediately started to rub his rope bindings against one and his wife did the same.

There was a great deal of shouting and swearing as the four men, even with their combined strength, found the shifting of the lid well-nigh impossible. They would not give up, and nor would Nick as his rope binding was definitely responding to the sharp stone.

Then everything seemed to happen all at once.

The stone lid was finally removed and fell with an almighty thud on the ground.

All four men whooped with exultation and peered into the interior of the well with great excitement. They discovered the rope of the hay bale quite quickly and then, in their haste, pulled and jerked at it to bring up the bale. The rope snapped in two and the hay bale fell deeper into the well.

While they were all shouting and blaming each other, they were totally unaware of a group of men, armed with pitchforks and staves, advancing upon them.

Completely taken by surprise, Didier Lamont, Michel, Pascale and Georges were overcome by extremely fit young stable lads, who took pleasure in pinning their quarry to the ground with the pitchforks.

Nick managed to free his hands at the same time as the young woman from the stables found them, and she produced a fearsome-looking knife to free Paula.

Then another sound – and this time they all heard it: the sirens from police vans. Using walkie-talkies, the owner of the stables was able to direct the police motorbike riders to the right spot.

Cursing and swearing and uttering vile oaths on all descendants of the Rousseau family, the four men were frogmarched away by the gendarmes.

The owner of the stables, who was called Martin, explained firstly that he had been concerned when one of his lads witnessed, as he returned from a ride, the two motorcycles ridden by men whose reputation was well-known, heading in the same direction as Nick and Paula.

Martin decided to be on the safe side, and so he called the police, who were happy to have something to do as life was rather quiet at the moment.

It was, however, the return of his two horses with no riders that made Martin spring into action, and along with his strong team, and even his daughter, they jumped on their horses and galloped off to help. Although they only knew the general direction, the two horses ridden by Nick and Paula led the way unerringly. By the time they had all dismounted, the men were making such a noise they succeeded in taking them by surprise.

The police stood guard over the well until specialist equipment could be brought in to lift the hay bale. It was taken, intact, to the Mayor's office, where with great ceremony Paula was allowed to unpack the hidden items.

Emanuel and Jean had done such a good job, carefully preserving delicate items such as a Sèvres jug of untold beauty in one of the boxes.

Amongst the items discovered was the exact pair of the silver box in Paula's possession, decorated in an equally charming style, and in the shape of a heart. This one, though, had no key, but it was still locked.

The jewellery was stunning. Paula imagined her grandmother wearing it on grand occasions. She knew she would never live the sort of life that would require a beautiful little half-tiara, or indeed a choker of four strands of pearls held together with a clasp of the deepest sapphire surrounded by diamonds.

There was more silver, and some charming candle-sticks that they could definitely use. Also several rings Paula would be thrilled to own, as well as some delightful earrings.

But it was the pictures that almost outclassed everything else. They may have been quite small in size, but one and all were exquisite examples of the famous painters who had spent time at the Villa Rousseau.

Marc Chagall had been particularly prolific, and Paula made the immediate decision to donate all but one of the samples of his work to the museum dedicated to his memory in the old town of Vence. That one she kept.

The Mayor made sure the discovered items were kept under lock and key until the time Paula, with the help of Nick, had decided what to do with them all.

There was a charming little brooch, which had the possibility of being made into a pendant, of flowers decorated with precious stones, that Paula immediately gave to Marie-Annette. The poor young woman was devastated by the actions of her father. However, luckily the handsome young man who made fabulous items out of olive wood had fallen in love with her, and so she was happily able to leave the Lamont family home.

The more important pieces of jewellery Paula decided she would sell at auction in London. Anticipating a good result, she took Nick back to the art gallery where she had admired the painting of the village scene, and bought not one, but two as a pair!

Paula knew she would need expert advice regarding the other paintings by well-known artists. Most would be sold, and the money raised she decided would be divided between art galleries and museums in the area.

Paula made Nick chose one painting above all else for himself. He chose one by Raoul Dufy of the 'Baie des Anges' in Nice... At the same time Paula chose another work by this artist of horses, which she gave to Martin who owned the stables.

So much had happened, and so quickly, that it wasn't until they were home again that they had time to have the watercolour by Sarah re-framed.

Then Paula remembered the second silver box. Out of curiosity she produced the key she already had, and it worked. Paula lifted the lid and there inside, yet again, was a folded piece of paper. With slightly trembling fingers, almost as if she knew what she might find, Paula opened out the page.

Written in Emanuel's handwriting was a letter inscribed

To My Descendant

This is for you, my Descendant, whosoever you shall be. Man or woman?

I will not know.

I have been so blessed with my life, surrounded as I have been by beauty and love.

I have been lucky to have been successful in my chosen occupation, but mostly I have been lucky to have had the love of my wonderful wife, Sarah, and my two dear children Pierre and Marguerite.

Half of my heart was removed from me the day they sailed away to safety.

My life has been enriched by my friends, so many of whom were/are such talented artists. I wanted to create a museum of all their work, but it was not to be.

So you, my Descendant, by the very fact of your reading this note, now realise I did not survive the war. You have of course discovered what treasures I could save, and with the help of my faithful Jean we chose the best hiding place we could.

Enjoy what you have found, and please make good use of it all.

I trust you, and know that somehow you will find a way to help the young artists of your day, just as I tried to do in mine.

What lies ahead for me is unknown, but I am prepared for the worst.

Nothing can remove the memories I treasure of my life, love and happiness I have enjoyed.

My blessings will be upon you.

Emanuel Rousseau   *1942*

Villa Rousseau,

Tourrettes-sur-Loup

In 2010 plans were approved to create a haven for artists in the south of France.

This was to be built high up the mountain and set in a beautiful garden. Two purpose built studios were included, and the plan was to hold seminars there for students as well as for established artists.

The name of the building was to be:

THE EMANUEL ROUSSEAU COMMUNE FOR ARTISTS.

THE MAKE-UP BOX

PEREGRINE PETERS STOOD looking at his reflection in the long mirror in his bedroom for a good three minutes.

"Not bad," he said to himself. "Not at all bad, really."

He had done a good job of keeping himself in shape, and was particularly proud that he hadn't allowed himself to 'go to seed' after dear Arthur's death.

He turned sideways, and sucked in his stomach. Both sides – quite good. He was still handsome of features, and had worked hard to avoid a jowl.

The only problem – the only real give-away as to his living 72 years – was his hair. Or rather, the lack of it.

He had tried everything. Lotions and potions, and massages and heat treatments, but the hair obstinately refused to grow, and instead became even more sparse as day followed day.

Only Arthur and their cleaner Mrs Flower had been privy to his secret. The secret spent the night on its stand in Peregrine's bedroom. Carefully, after he had dealt with the few remaining strands of hair he had, Peregrine lifted the luxurious chestnut locks off the stand and firmly attached them to his own head.

"There. Peregrine Peters, you look every bit as young and handsome as you did forty years ago. What do you think, Arthur? Will I do?"

Arthur's voice would purr in his ear. "Perry my boy, you look divine. You wait until I get my hands on you!"

Perry turned to look at the mahogany bureau opposite his bed. A large silver frame held a studio portrait of Arthur as a young man, playing the part of Romeo. Blond hair and features like a Greek god. To this day Perry was so amazed that Arthur fell for him.

A similar-sized study of Peregrine in costume as Hamlet was on the other side, whilst a smaller photograph between the two depicted both young men during a performance of *Dial M for Murder*. This was where they had met in Adelaide, South Australia when they were in their late teens.

Their friendship and love had lasted for so many years, until Arthur's tragic death two years past.

"Now, now Perry," he heard Arthur's voice admonishing him. "No regrets. No looking back. You go and sort that lot out. Don't stand for any nonsense from those two overblown dames. You tell them. You are the pro. They are only amateurs, and they are more than lucky to have you as their director."

Perry smiled at Arthur's photo and blew him a kiss, and with his dead lover's words ringing in his ears, he virtually floated towards the door.

───────────────

Moira MacPherson was preparing herself with a fastidiousness equal only to Peregrine Peters himself. She was anticipating the moment, only a few hours hence, when she was sure she would be cast as Lady Bracknell in *The Importance of Being Earnest.*

She was, of course, perfect for the part. Not only due was she the right age – she only admitted to 62 of her 67 years – she knew the part backwards, having played it many times for the Lymington Players in the New Forest, the Chichester Dramatic Society and even twice for the Hong Kong Players during the time she and her husband lived in the territory before it was handed back to China.

Moira could be relied upon to always be on time, remember her lines and never miss a cue. She was as near a pro as she could be. She knew all the lingo, and called everybody 'Darling'. She knew about obeying the director, and controlling the urge to 'corpse' on stage – unforgivable, even if someone did their damnedest to make you laugh. She knew that 'flats' were part of the scenery, and not apartments, and that to 'strike the set' meant to take it down, and not hit it in frustration.

Moira had desperately wanted to act professionally. It was unfortunate that when she had been younger her face and figure had not presented themselves as ideal for the 'ingénue' parts. It was only as she grew older that she was able to 'let rip' in parts for the more mature and character-ful women. The part of Lady Bracknell in *The Importance of Being Earnest* she had virtually made her own. That is, after Dame Edith Evans, of course.

Aside from a tendency to overact – "Don't over-egg the part, Moira dear," many a director had beseeched – her successes had included Mrs Eynsford-Hill in *Pygmalion* and Madame Arcati in *Blithe Spirit.*

However, at this moment, confident as she was, there was a little anxiety that, possibly, that puffed-up old queen Perry Peters might just pick Diana Clarkson instead, if only to spite her.

The last time Moira had been in a Perry Peters produc-tion, he had not only directed it but also appeared in a small cameo role which was intended to show off all his talents. Quite unintentionally (although he never believed her), Moira totally upstaged him and virtually obscured him from the audience, due not only to her considerable size but also to the voluminous costume she was wearing. Perry had been distraught when he was barely visible in the photograph that appeared in the local newspaper a few days later. If indeed Peregrine did give the part to Diana, there would be no end to her crowing and lauding it over Moira.

Diana was a bitch. There was no other word for it. They had first met many years ago when they both audi-tioned for the part of Lady Macbeth for the charming little waterfront theatre in Devizes, Wiltshire. Diana had won the coveted role, and Moira, to her disappointment and chagrin, had only been offered a small part and the honour of being understudy to Diana. Moira had smoul-dered her way through the rehearsals watching Diana glorying in her superiority. Moira was word-perfect long before Diana, who rehearsed 'with the book' until the last possible moment.

Moira knew she was a much better actress. She had, after all, so very nearly been accepted for RADA.

"Don't forget, Moira dear," Diana would say in a patronising tone, "if for any reason you have to step into my shoes, it's the little nuances – meaningful looks – mannerisms with my hands that makes my performance so incredibly strong. If I were you, I should study me carefully. You never know, you might learn something."

Moira tried to be nonchalant but in reality knew how much Diana was enjoying her power and twisting a little knife deeper into the soul of someone she recognised as a serious rival.

Somehow, Moira managed to hide her feelings from the rest of the cast, but within herself she made a little vow, that if ever they ended up in the same production again, Moira would be ready for her, in no uncertain terms.

As she gathered the essential items she would need for the casting session, her eyes lit upon her treasured theatrical make-up box that her dear husband Dickie had given her. At the same time he had also given her a 'rabbit's tail' powder puff, which Moira considered her lucky mascot.

Of course she had been absurdly young, only 22 when she met and married Dickie. She had been performing in a ridiculous (even the cast agreed) farce for the sailors at the Chatham Naval Base. At the party after the last night this handsome young man, looking resplendent in his navy uniform, with a broad red stripe down the side of his trousers, came straight over to her and announced he had totally fallen in love with her and had seen the show four times!

Moira and Dickie had a whirlwind romance, and when he announced he was being sent to the Far East, Singapore and Hong Kong for a year, they instantly decided to marry and embrace the adventure of a new life together.

All was splendid at first, and very exciting. Moira was based in Hong Kong, but Dickie spent quite a large amount of time on his ship, travelling between Singapore, Korea and Taiwan amongst other places. To keep herself from becoming lonely, Moira joined the Hong Kong Players as well as successfully auditioning for the English-speaking radio station, where she was able to act the ingénue parts that had previously been denied to her.

Delicious Dickie was having a wonderful time in the Far East. Dear little girls dressed in tight-fitting cheong-sam dresses would sidle up to him with cheeky grins and inviting eyes, and even though he really didn't mean to succumb – Dickie did.

It was in Bali that he met his downfall – although he didn't consider May Flower a downfall at all. Dickie was totally smitten, and not only was poor Moira given the push, so was the Royal Navy. Dickie settled down to life running a bar on a beach in Bali and swapped his handsome red-striped trousers for a sarong.

Still, in her kind-hearted way, Moira understood. They had been young and foolish, and had enjoyed themselves immensely. Moira decided to stay on in Hong Kong as she had made some good friends and had found a job working as a receptionist at the Hong Kong Club.

The HK Players had decided to stage a Noël Coward musical called *Ace of Clubs*. Not having a bad voice, Moira won the part of Pinkie Leroy. On the first day of rehearsals the director announced there would be a new member of the cast called Diana Clarkson joining their team. Until she could prove her worth, she was to understudy Moira in the lead role.

Once she had overcome her surprise – and not a happy one at that – at seeing her old rival, Moira could not resist telling Diana to study her performance carefully, just in case she should be called upon to take over.

Moira could not believe Diana had arrived in Hong Kong. She quite thought she was safe from her on this island. Diana had decided to try her luck in the Far East, probably after hearing on the grapevine that Moira was doing rather well, and had simply arrived on her own.

For the ensuing months Moira and Diana muddled along together, although the green-eyed monster of jealousy was never far away. They took part in plays, in farces, in revues and pantomimes, and even though they would snipe at each other and try to score points, it wasn't until the comedy *Noises Off* was being staged that things went 'too far'.

Noises Off is a play about a play when everything goes wrong. Moira had the better part. On the final performance as she prepared for her last entrance Diana gave her the most almighty shove and Moira catapulted onto the stage before keeling over and landing flat on her stomach.

Luckily, as the play was all about the disasters that can befall a theatrical company, the audience thought it was part of the show and howled with laughter. Moira did some clever 'ad-libbing' and managed to carry it off, but she knew whose hand it was that had dealt the mighty blow.

Diana had professed total innocence and complete remorse. It hadn't been her fault. She had tripped on a weight holding down some scenery. She was *mortified*!

Moira knew better but could not prove it. She vowed one day to wreak her revenge.

The opportunity had come that Christmas when the HK Players decided to stage the pantomime of *Puss in Boots*. Diana was cast as the Principal Boy, with Moira playing the part of the Lord Mayor of London.

Diana never seemed to lose an opportunity to make snide remarks about Moira's figure. "Of course, this is why you could never be a Principal Boy," she informed her.

Hong Kong people love jokes, and it was no problem for Moira to find a shop that sold itching powder. Even during the winter months it could still be uncomfortably hot in the theatre, and members of the cast would dust themselves with talcum powder under their costumes to help them feel more comfortable.

With a sleight of hand worthy of a magician, Moira substituted Diana's usual tin with one doctored with itching powder on the first night. As the performance progressed, so did Diana's discomfort. Try as she might she could not stop scratching and wriggling about. The reviews that subsequently appeared in the newspapers the following week were not cut out and kept by Diana.

By the time the show was over, the tell-tale tin had been well disposed of and no one could possibly explain what had happened.

Diana had glowered at Moira. Moira had innocently showed her best caring and concerned expression.

Now, all these years later, Moira knew that if Perry Peters did cast her as Lady Bracknell, she would have to keep her wits about her, as no doubt Diana would do her best to scupper her performance.

Diana Clarkson was late. She rushed around her flat desperately gathering her tools of the trade. The forthcoming production of *The Importance of Being Earnest* produced and directed by Peregrine Peters was going to be the highlight of the forthcoming season, and Everybody, that is Everybody who is Anybody, would fight for tickets.

Luckily, a bus appeared at the right moment, and Diana sat in her seat trying to compose herself. It was inevitable that the part of Lady Bracknell would either go to her or that large, overweight pumpkin of a woman, Moira MacPherson.

Diana had made huge efforts to keep her figure, and she prided herself that she looked *years* younger than her true (almost a secret to herself as well) age. Some people might consider her a bit small and 'wiry', but Diana thought this was so much better than being rotund.

The bus took her to Chiswick and then with a running-type walk she would arrive at the rehearsal room above the pub in time. Perry was fastidious about time-keeping and this was rather a failing of Diana.

"Glad you could make it," Perry's voice resonated as Diana tried unsuccessfully to slide into the hall unnoticed. 'Now we can begin and have a read through the play after which my assistant producer and I will have a pow-wow and let you know what we have decided."

They didn't have too long to wait. The younger members were cast first, with the prettiest girls winning the parts of Cecily and Gwendolen, and two excellent young men as Algernon and Jack. Perry announced that he himself would play the part of The Rev. Canon Chasuble and then… (you could have heard a pin drop) the part of Miss Prism would be played by Diana and Moira would be Lady Bracknell.

Diana was sure she could actually see Moira puffing herself up to look even more like an excited pea-hen.

Moira was sure she saw Diana shrink visibly into the floor as she tried hopelessly to disguise her disappointment.

Perry wondered what he had done. If he had had his own way he would not have had either of those two warring women in his play, but he had to admit, they could both act rather well, and he knew he had made the correct choice under the circumstances.

Three weeks of rehearsals then followed. Three weeks with Perry Peters cajoling, shouting, begging and almost crying as he worked to bring together his disparate cast to meld in unison and to forget the distractions of the noisy world beyond their hall, and concentrate on living and breathing their characters.

Arthur was right. Perry was a very good director. He was firm, and stood no nonsense with histrionics and over-blown egos. He demanded the best from his actors, and he had the ability to prise a performance of note out of the most unlikely individual. His only problem, as he could see it, was trying to curtail the bitchiness that manifested itself every time Moira and Diana were in the same scene.

The play was going to be staged in a small London theatre. Although strictly an amateur production, it was eagerly anticipated by members of the general public.

Rehearsals were also attended by the wardrobe mistress, Miss Halfpenny. Trying not to disturb the proceedings, she floated about in an extraordinary mixture of loose-fitting, brightly coloured, totally mismatched clothes, clutching a notebook and pen with a large tape measure worn round her neck. Her flaming orange hair was kept short with tight curls, and from her ears dangled huge, intricately designed earrings. On her feet she wore brown sandals reminiscent of those she wore as a child on seaside holidays.

Miss Halfpenny and her friend, the minute Joyce Hickman who was in charge of props, were delighted to have discovered a company in Glasgow that had just finished the same play, and they were able to hire almost everything they required.

The serene and beautiful Ann Grainger was in charge of wigs and make-up. An actress herself in the past, she now was content to weave her magic backstage, and then to sit back and relax as she admired her handiwork during the performance.

Perry's right-hand assistant was a gentle, fair-haired boy who yearned to be on the stage. He had valiantly overcome a stammer, and was waiting to have contact lenses fitted so he would no longer need to wear glasses. He adored Perry and would do anything for him. Nothing was too much trouble. Every once in a while, Peregrine managed to find a small part for him.

He decided on this occasion he would reward the boy with the part of the butler during the teatime scene with the two girls and Philip could not believe his luck.

On the whole events were proceeding according to plan.

Moira would practise in front of her bathroom mirror the various ways she would say Lady Bracknell's celebrated line, "A *handbag*?" Should she emulate Dame Edith Evans and draw it out with a deep voice as in "*A HAaand Baaag?*" Or something quite different, more like

Judi Dench might do and keep it short and sweet: "*A handbag???*" Or perhaps with a note of disgust? Or fury? Moira could not quite decide, and Perry had left the decision to her.

The technical rehearsal was boring as ever, but went well, and even the dress rehearsal was not a total disaster, which it so often is. Photographs for the programme and Front of House had been taken, and rumour had it that tickets were selling like wildfire.

Diana was very funny as Miss Prism, and for a while Moira forgot there was any animosity between them as Diana suddenly seemed to be putting herself out to be friendly and sweet, especially in the hearing of other members of the cast.

Moira was not sure she trusted her, however, but it certainly made life more pleasant.

The play was due to last one week. There was to be a matinée on the Saturday and this was to be followed by the Gala Performance. The audience had been asked to dress up, and a party had been planned for the cast and select friends and relations in a restaurant near the theatre.

The First Night was fraught with nerves. Everyone seemed on edge. Moira, Diana and the two young girls all shared a dressing room. Moira arrived very early in order to secure the best position, and proceeded to set out her own space. First, she put down a pretty cloth to hide the somewhat scruffy surface. Next in pride of place was her make-up box. As she sorted the various creams and tinted foundations and blushers into their particular order, Moira had a sudden pang of missing Dickie, and she wondered where he was at that moment. She remembered when he had given her the make-up box and how delighted she had been. It was very professional and held everything so conveniently. After a good deal of use it had lost its pristine newness, but not only was it loved by her, it was indispensable for her performance as she knew it brought her luck.

Moira always used a mixture of '5' and '9' as her foundation. She tended towards high colour in her skin, especially if she was nervous. She liked the slight brown tone of this mixture. Her lucky powder-puff was poised above her powder tin, and her eyeliners, shadow and mascara were all neatly arranged.

The two young girls giggled endlessly and somewhat tiresomely together, but they were reliable, and charming in their parts.

Diana was somewhat miffed that she definitely had the worst position in the dressing room, but admitted it had been her fault for arriving last.

"Act 1 beginners, please." The announcement came over the Tannoy system. This was it. Moira waited for her call, and then went through her ritual of picking up her rabbit's fur and touching her forehead, her cheeks, her cleavage and her wrists. Then she closed her make-up box at the same time as she closed her eyes, and whispered to herself the words Dickie used to say: "Go for it, Moira old girl. Go out and wow them. You can do it." A little tap on the lid of the box, and away she went.

The play was well received. Of course this was largely due to it being such a delightful, and crazy, funny play, written with such incredible wit and humour by Oscar Wilde.

Still – if they had acted badly, or it had been ineffectively produced, it could have flopped.

Moira was so relieved that nothing untoward had occurred, and as they approached the Gala night, she was completely happy and relaxed during the meal with other members of the cast between the shows. Therefore she was totally unprepared for what happened next.

She and Diana entered their dressing room at the same time. Moira went to her chair, but as she sat down, she let out a cry of horror.

"My make-up box! Where is it? What has happened to it? It must be here. It can't have gone. Who would have taken it?" All the while these words were pouring out of her Moira was searching the dressing room for any conceivable corner or cupboard where her precious box might be.

The two young girls were solicitous and did their best to help with the search. Diana was incredulous. How could such a thing have happened?

The precious make-up box was nowhere to be found. Moira was sobbing, which she knew was the worst thing for her already high colour. Diana sweetly offered to lend her a tube of '5' and '9' mixed together. Moira plastered it on her face and tried to control her sniffles.

Moira did a good job of pulling herself together. The show must go on. She was as near as dammit a pro. Once on the stage, under the bright lights which obliterated the audience, Moira settled into her part and gave of her best.

During the interval she was rather shocked to see the colour of her face was looking distinctly orange.

"Oh dear," said Diana. 'You had better have some more '5' and '9' to tone you down."

After her next entrance Moira looked even more orange, and her face felt extremely hot. Other members of the cast looked at her curiously.

It was enough to put any great actress off her stride as gradually the truth dawned on her that the tube of make-up dear Diana had given her was somehow having the effect of changing her colour.

Mentally gritting her teeth, Moira vowed to ignore it, and as her great scene was approaching, when Miss Prism produced THE HANDBAG, she would still deliver the immortal words in a way that the great Dame Edith would approve.

For some reason Diana was not in her usual position, plus she seemed to be having a problem with part of her costume. Diana was standing extraordinarily close to the wings, and when Moira started to say '*A Haaand Baaag?*' Diana executed a weird twitch and there, swinging from a piece of scenery in the wings, Moira saw her make-up box dangling upside-down with the rabbit's fur attached on top.

The incredulous screech that emitted from Moira's lips as she cried out, "*A handbag?*" was unlike anything anyone had ever heard before.

Sitting in the audience, Perry could not understand why Moira had suddenly changed her delivery, but he had to admit it was incredibly effective. The audience loved it and burst into spontaneous applause. Still in a state of shock, Moira controlled herself and with the rest of the bemused cast, they finished the play on an extremely high note!

At last, alone in his apartment, Perry looked at Arthur's photograph as he heard his familiar voice asking how it had gone.

"Quite extraordinary," replied Perry. 'I am not sure what exactly happened, but all I can say it was a huge success, and despite my initial fears about casting Moira and Diana together, it all seemed to go surprisingly well, with Moira even changing her delivery at the last moment which turned out to be a total triumph."

"I knew you would pull it off brilliantly, you clever boy. I am so proud of you."

When Perry at last went to bed he settled down with a smile upon his face. His final thought, before sleep overtook him, was the recollection of hearing Moira crying out about her make-up box as he had passed by the door to her dressing room.

"What was that all about?" he wondered.

He never did find out.

THE THEATRE BOX

THE YEAR WAS 1893, and the streets surrounding the Royal Opera House in Covent Garden in London were alive with activity.

Even though the fruit and vegetable market had long since closed for the day, with traders and buyers already planning for the early opening the following morning, sounds of shouting and bartering joined the cacophony of noises made the by the horse drawn carriages and their occupants.

Flower sellers besieged the grandly dressed gentlefolk as they alighted from their hansom cabs, broughams or larger carriages, each one shouting louder than the other.

"Buy some sweet violets for Her Ladyship, My Lord-ship." – "Lucky white heather, Sir. We could all do wiv a bit o' luck now an' then." – "Luvverly roses – two a penny – Just in case your lady feels a bit faint."

Drivers urged their horses on, determined to find the best place for their beautifully dressed passengers to alight. Carefully avoiding puddles, though not so careful with people that strayed in their path, these men were skilful at manoeuvring both horses and carriages to reach their goal.

Although two people could easily fit in a hansom cab, when the ladies' fashion decreed the wearing of large crin-olines, this must have made for an uncomfortable journey for her escort.

Luckily, fashions were beginning to change and the mode of dress, still long and exaggerating the tiny waist as before, now had skirts that were distinctly reduced in size.

The gentlemen looked fine in their evening regalia, with their 'Opera' top hats, which were designed to concertina down during the performance.

The Opera House itself looked magnificent, with a blaze of lights which illuminated the handsome exterior of long windows, pillars and porticos. Abutting the theatre on its left side was the impressive and beautiful Floral Hall constructed of domed glass and wrought iron. Although founded as early as the 18th century, the theatre was destroyed not once but twice by devastating fires.

Various styles of entertainment took place within its walls before, in 1892, Queen Victoria gave her seal of approval, and the theatre became The Royal Opera House.

Therefore, only one year after this elevation of status – and with ticket prices beginning to match its newly regal nature – it was with great excitement that the high and mighty flocked to the Opera House not only to enjoy undoubtedly superb music and witness dramatic and visually beautiful performances, but also, most importantly, to be *seen*.

On this particular night in question there was the added cachet of being present at the latest production of the opera by Georges Bizet, *Carmen*.

The original première in 1875 had not been very successful. Audiences were perhaps not expecting such drama, excitement or ultimate brutality. However, by 1893, *Carmen* was fast becoming one of the most popular operas to hear.

What made it doubly exciting on this occasion was the fact that the title role was to be sung by none other than the highly acclaimed soprano known to the whole world simply by her nickname of 'La Stupenda'.

There were to be three performances altogether over two weeks, with the third and last being a Gala in the presence of his Royal Highness Prince Edward.

Although the audience on this first night was very favoured indeed, with not a spare seat to be had, it was for the final performance that people begged, fought, bribed and even wept to try and obtain tickets.

The hustle and the bustle created by the chatter and the laughter, combined with the clinking of glasses, the fluttering of fans, the rustling of playbills intermingled with the wafts of smoke from the gentlemen's cigars, only partially began to subside as gradually seats were filled in the auditorium.

Did I say not a seat to be had? True indeed, save for one exception.

The Royal Box was in fact used on this occasion by younger members of the Royal Family and their friends.

The box immediately on its left, however, Box number 66, was notable in that no one appeared to occupy it.

In all the other boxes the ladies produced their opera glasses, some with long handles for ease of use, to study the auditorium in order to espy people they knew, or even wickedly to mock their dress or, better still, discover that their beau was not their husband.

Occasionally opera glasses would meet each other, and thereupon the owners would either quickly look away, or wave a friendly hand in recognition.

The members of the orchestra, dressed in white tie and tails, were tuning up. The Conductor then appeared to be greeted by a large round of applause as gradually the chattering died down, and the house lights did the same.

Seconds before the audience was left in complete darkness a shadowy figure slipped into Box 66.

When the rich velvet curtains were parted there was a gasp from the audience at the intricate and realistic stage setting.

The moment came for La Stupenda to make her entrance, and this was greeted by a brief but loud round of applause. Looking stunning dressed in a black skirt, white embroidered top (that some ladies thought too revealing, but the gentlemen disagreed), La Stupenda flung her colourful shawl over her shoulders and shook her abundant black hair provocatively, as she fastened a red rose to her locks before beginning the 'Habanera' aria for which she was famed.

She sang superbly and with great character. As she swayed tantalisingly about the stage, her eyes strayed to the Royal Box. Whilst most of the auditorium was hidden in a pool of blackness, the soprano could easily see not only this Royal Box, but the one next door as well.

Sitting very still in Box 66, and dressed in black, was a woman. Occasionally a gloved hand appeared to flutter a fan before her face. Her face, however, could not be seen. A thick black veil obscured all but the glint of her eyes.

La Stupenda was a professional singer. Nothing could put her off her stride. Immediately she immersed herself in her part and sang faultlessly.

By the time the lights came up for the interval, the mysterious occupant of Box 66 was nowhere to be seen.

Once again, moments before complete darkness descended, she was back in her seat and quietly watched the rest of the performance.

Several members of the audience had noticed her, and speculation was rife as to who she was.

After the tragedy of poor Carmen's death, and the curtain had been parted for the audience to applaud and shout out their appreciation, the cast came forward to bow in humility. Then La Stupenda took a call on her own, and flowers cascaded down on her (some into the orchestra pit), which she gathered gratefully into her arms. Whilst doing so, smiling the while, the singer glanced up at Box 66. No one was there.

The hansom cab was waiting as agreed in the side street not far from the entrance for the artistes. The driver opened the door, and the cab had left the area before the first members of the audience began to take their leave.

"Did everything go well, Madam?" the driver enquired.

"Very well, thank you," was the reply. Then: 'Were you able to execute my instructions?"

"Exactly," was the reply. 'The rose will have been placed on the dressing table as you instructed."

"Most satisfactory. Thank you."

"The same arrangement next week, then?"

"Certainly. As we agreed."

"Will it be the same opera you will be seeing next week, Madam?"

"Yes," was the reply, 'it will."

The driver mentally scratched his head. *Very strange some people are,* he thought. Fancy going three times running to see the same show, and arrive late then leave early. Still, she was pleasant enough and the money was good, so he was happy to oblige. He did wonder, though, why she wore such a heavy veil. She looked quite young and had a good figure. Oh well – not for him to worry about.

The hansom cab drew up outside a terraced house in Belgravia. The door was opened immediately and a female servant came down the front steps to escort her mistress into the house.

La Stupenda was reeling from her success. Echoes of the rapturous applause abounded in her head, and smiling happily at all and sundry, still clutching several bouquets of adulation, she entered the calm of her dressing room.

Her dresser helped her out of her costumes and encompassed her in a beautiful satin robe.

"Florence, please give me ten minutes on my own. I am – a – I am in need of a leetle privacy to calm myself."

The dresser bobbed a tiny curtsy and, gathering the discarded costume in her arms, said, "*Si, Signora,*" as she left her mistress alone.

La Stupenda sat down at her dressing table and studied her reflection in the looking glass.

Reverting to her natural-born accent she said out loud,

"Well my girl. You are a *huge* success. Pity your Mam and Dad can't see it. As for Giuseppe, I bet he wishes he had stuck around a bit longer."

The soprano allowed herself a brief thought about the young man she had somewhat impetuously married when she was only eighteen, and as she chuckled to herself her eyes alighted upon a single red rose lying near her powder pot.

She picked it up to smell it, and then noticed it had a small card attached to the stem. The card had an inscription which simply read:

"*M. 1880*'

La Stupenda stared at the card a long while.

"No," she whispered to herself. "No – It cannot be."

"*Scusi, Signora.* It is time to prepare for dinner."

"*Che bello fiori,*" said the dresser, looking at the rose. "I put in water, *si*?"

"No," was the terse reply. "Throw it away."

La Stupenda did not allow herself to dwell on the mystery of the rose.

She was fêted as the Diva she was as she entered the famous restaurant at the Ritz on the arm of her escort, Lord Ambrose Belmont.

Four days later, the scene at the Royal Opera House Covent Garden was repeated in an identical fashion.

Once again, the empty box was occupied at the last moment by the mysterious, black-veiled woman.

On this occasion, however, La Stupenda found her eyes wandering on more than once occasion towards Box 66. The figure sat motionless apart from the intermittent flutter of her fan. The singer on the stage nonetheless could feel, even if she could not see, a pair of glittering eyes penetrating the veil in a relentless stare.

There was a slight gasp from the audience. La Stupenda, for the briefest of moments, gave the impression she did not know which way to turn. As the music rose to a crescendo, the singer composed herself and right on cue, began her famous aria.

The rose was there again, on her dressing table. The attached card was inscribed the same way.

La Stupenda summoned the stage doorman to her dressing room.

"Who gave you this rose?" she demanded.

"It was brought in by a hired hansom cab driver, Your Ladyship," was the response.

"Did he say anything?" she asked.

"Only to say he had received instructions that the rose be placed on your dressing table sometime during the last act."

It was hard work for the Diva that night, to smile and react gratefully and gracefully to the rounds of applause and congratulations she was receiving.

As soon as she could, and much earlier than normal, she escaped to the house she had been lent, and retired to bed.

Sleep, however, did not immediately come as a balm to her soul, or indeed as a solution to a slowly emerging feeling of fear.

1873. They had been ten years old. Two little girls coincidentally both from the same ancient English county of Wiltshire, albeit with differing backgrounds.

Beatrice was an exceedingly attractive child with long, chestnut-coloured hair. Her mother was a vaudeville dancer who had met her husband whilst he was performing as a singer in the same production.

When the baby came along, her mother juggled her career with bringing up her little girl as they moved between theatres and entertainment halls, and Beatrice was exposed to music, dancing and singing from infancy.

At the age of four Beatrice could hold a tune very well, and as she grew older, singing became her passion. Whenever possible, the little girl was given the chance to sing a short solo, much to the enchantment of the audiences.

Their favourite venue was the Salisbury Playhouse as it was so near their home. Beatrice was allowed to sing her little solo which she performed with great charm.

After one such performance a gentleman presented his card at the stage door and requested a meeting with the child's parents.

"I believe your daughter has great talent," he began. "I am sure her voice could be trained to be something quite special. However, she should cease at once from any more performances on stage as this could permanently damage her vocal chords. I am a teacher of the singing voice. I have studied with great masters not only in our country but in Italy, Germany and France as well. I would like your child to be my pupil. I can promise her a great future."

The parents of Beatrice were at once thrilled, proud and dismayed.

"You are too kind, Sir, but you see, Beatrice is becoming

quite a draw, and the money is useful, and in that respect, I fear we would not be able to afford your fees."

"You need have no qualms on that score," the gentleman replied. "No fees would be charged for such a talent."

The Maestro was persuasive. The parents were reluctant. Beatrice was overwhelmed. The Maestro won his argument.

Thereafter, Beatrice studied seriously with this eminent instructor, and learned how to control and save her voice; how to breathe from her diaphragm and how to pitch her voice at just the right place for trills or sighs. Beatrice also learnt how to be patient, and not to expect results at once. She avoided the temptation to sing too high, too low or too long. She learnt to treat her voice as a God-given musical instrument that she must nurture, treasure and preserve.

After only one year it was apparent the intuition of their kindly teacher and benefactor was correct. Beatrice's voice had the clarity, some said, of a boy soprano, with an innate gift of the ability to change the cadence of her voice seamlessly from romance to tragedy or from comedy to despair.

The few performances she was allowed to give during her training were greeted with wonder that such a voice could emerge from one so young.

Beatrice was not the only talented pupil to be thus treated by her tutor.

Maisie was almost exactly the same age as Beatrice, and came from a village deep in a large forested area which was not too far from Salisbury.

Maisie's father was a clergyman, and from a very young age the child had sung in the small village choir.

As she grew older and her voice became more mature, people began to hear about this sweet little girl who could sing, and some say even looked like an angel. The Rev. Simpson was delighted to have full congregations to listen to his sermons each Sunday, so he encouraged his daughter to learn even more difficult pieces to widen her fame.

Hearing about this child, the singing Maestro made a pilgrimage to this village church one day, and after hearing her, he once again made his offer of free tuition which was gratefully accepted.

Maisie had four siblings, and frankly, whilst recognising her talent, they were all becoming somewhat tired of her mannerisms and tendencies to show off.

For there was no doubt that Maisie was definitely aware of her ability and her looks. Her hair, almost jet black, with abundant thick tresses falling in soft waves around a pretty somewhat pale face, seemed to reflect in her dark eyes. The child had thoroughly enjoyed the adulation she received, and she did not take kindly to being almost shut away in the music school whilst she had to sing endless scales, and perform a multitude of what she considered boring exercises. However, she was not a silly girl, and she soon realised that indeed her voice was not only improving, but reaching heights she had never dreamed possible.

When the two girls reached the age of sixteen, the Maestro summoned both sets of parents for a meeting.

"I find I can no longer instruct your daughters as they are both turning into very fine singers in their own right. This is not to say that they cannot benefit from learning from masters of the art who are far greater than I. It has reached my ears that the world renowned 'Scuola di Musica' in Venice is opening its doors now to foreign students. Auditions to find suitable candidates are to be held in London and I propose that both your daughters should attend. Maybe neither, or maybe only one would succeed. Only think of the excitement and the honour if they were both accepted!"

The girls and their parents were excited and nervous at the same time. If only one girl was chosen, how awful it would be for the other.

It would not be true to say the girls were great friends. They had now known each other for many years and had often studied the same pieces.

Something made Beatrice a bit wary of Maisie. Strange things had happened to her at inopportune moments.

There was the occasion of an end-of-year performance in front of friends and families when they were 15 years old. Maisie had been furious that Beatrice had been given the better aria from *La Traviata* to sing. Waiting in the wings for her entrance Beatrice fluffed out the skirts of her ball gown, and slowly took her deep breaths in readiness for her entrance.

The musical cue came, so Beatrice stepped forward to make a determined and gay entrance only to find she was stuck fast. Somehow the back of her skirt was wedged tightly in the edge of the scenery, and when she tugged at it, the skirt ripped. Although she continued and tried to ignore it, she was conscious of trailing bits of costume and her own voice faltering. As she glanced back she was aware of Maisie disappearing into the gloom of the back-stage.

On yet another occasion, the prop of a letter from which her character was due to read/sing out her love had disappeared from her pocket. Beatrice was a careful girl, and knew she had placed it in her costume in plenty of time.

When it was eventually discovered in the box of other props, Beatrice was scolded for her carelessness.

Maisie came up to her after that and said, "You will never become a star if you can't even look after your props."

The Maestro rehearsed them both in the arias they had chosen for the audition.

After one such rehearsal, Maisie realised she had left her copy of the libretto with the pianist. She returned to the rehearsal room just in time to hear the Maestro saying: "In reply to your question, Mr Caldwell, there is no doubt that both girls are extremely talented. However, if I was forced to pick just one, it would have to be Beatrice. Her voice has the most sublime quality that no teacher can give her. It is part of her very soul."

Maisie's expression hardened. With all her being she wanted to be the one to attend this world-famous establishment in Venice.

The auditions were to be held in a very old, somewhat small London theatre.

The limited lighting on the stage was created by gas lamps, whilst candles, some of them in glass jars, were used backstage.

Beatrice and Maisie were given a small dressing room to share. It was very dark, and made the act of changing into their simplified costumes behind the modesty screen really quite challenging.

Beatrice was the first to be called to sing. The Maestro had agreed she could sing the aria from the first act of

La Traviata. This time she ensured her costume could not possibly snare on any scenery.

There was a moment of silence after she had finished and this was swiftly followed by a long and sustained round of applause. Beatrice knew she had sung her very best. She was proud to think that her parents were somewhere in the auditorium. Sitting a few rows in front of them was the Maestro, and he turned round to give a large smile and indicated that he was sure there would be no doubt about her acceptance.

Back in the dressing room, Beatrice was smiling happily. Maisie was preparing herself to sing a short while later.

"Can you help me fasten the buttons on the back of my costume?" she asked her fellow student.

Beatrice joined the other girl behind the screen and Maisie put her candle on a low stool to give a better light as it had already burned dangerously low... When she had completed the task, Beatrice returned to the dressing table and quietly relived her performance.

Maisie was called, and just before she left, she put the candle on the floor behind the screen, and trailed a piece of oil-soaked rag around its base.

Beatrice called out her good wishes for luck, and Maisie left the dressing room, quietly locking the door on the outside with the key which she then dropped on the floor and kicked into the shadows.

Maisie had chosen to sing the difficult aria for the Queen of the Night from Mozart's *The Magic Flute.* It was ambitious and challenging, but she did it very well.

Although she lacked the purity of voice that Beatrice innately had, Maisie was able to act convincingly and in this case somewhat menacingly. She too was greeted with loud applause, although the audience was surprisingly restless.

People began to murmur: "Smoke…" – "Burning…" – "FIRE!"

By the time everybody realised what was happening screams could be heard from backstage.

Immediately Maisie started rushing about and screaming. In so doing she hindered those who were trying to help.

"Is it Beatrice?" she cried, and pushing her way through, she raced to their dressing room. Men were valiantly trying to break down the door, and in the ensuing chaos Maisie quietly retrieved the key, which she then made as if to discover it lying by the door as it was at last opened.

Flames were destroying the wooden screen and the smoke was thick and acrid. On the floor in an inert heap of smouldering clothes, lay Beatrice. Her face and hands were blackened and she had fallen by the door through which she had desperately tried to escape.

Maisie stood still and looked at her fellow pupil. For a fleeting moment she regretted what she had done. She only meant to damage her voice a bit, and enough.

Galloping horses and the clanging of bells meant help was on its way.

The inert body of Beatrice, accompanied by her distraught parents, was taken away.

Despite the terrible shock which was felt by all, the results of the audition were announced.

Beatrice had indeed been offered a place, but as it was now unlikely she would be able to accept, even if she survived this horrendous ordeal, her place was offered to Maisie.

It was lucky for Maisie that her ensuing years would be spent in Italy.

The final performance, the Gala Night arrived. HRH Prince Edward was entertaining his guests in the private salon behind the Royal Box.

La Stupenda sat silently in her Number One star dressing room. Already, carefully placed by her powder pot, was a red rose with a card attached.

This time the message read:

"M. Never Forget. 1880'

Now La Stupenda knew. It had been rumoured that Beatrice had died. This was convenient and made it so much easier to forget.

Meanwhile, Maisie succeeded beyond her wildest dreams in the famous 'Scuola di Musica' in Venice.

At the start of her professional career she agreed to marry an impossibly good-looking Italian Count. She learnt Italian; like all musicians, she had a good ear and soon spoke it perfectly. She was also able to sing in French and German, although Italian was her favourite language.

Someone nicknamed her 'La Stupenda' and she liked it and encouraged this, so soon her English origins were entirely forgotten.

She and the Count grew bored of each other after a couple of years and went their separate ways. 'La Stupenda' found it much easier to cultivate several lovers and marry none of them.

This night, however, was different. This was the night she was performing in front of Royalty, and in the back of her mind was an eligible minor Royal Prince who would very neatly fit into her plans if all went well.

But the rose, the rose... Even though she picked it up and threw it in a temper across the room, the rose haunted her.

Was Beatrice still alive? Could that possibly be her in Box 66?

La Stupenda was thoroughly nervous. Her nerves showed with the way she snapped at her dresser.

Finally, she went up on stage before the audience was settled, to try to calm herself and get into her character. The audience was making its usual happy, chattering noises as people began filing into their seats.

Suddenly there was an audible gasp and sounds of horror, followed by an unnatural silence.

Quickly, the Diva pushed the stage manager out of the way as she managed to peep around the side of the heavy curtains. She could see the Royal Box, still empty, so unimpeded she could look at Box 66. There she saw a sight so ghastly and so horrifying, it made her feel quite sick.

The woman in black had already arrived and was standing up in full view of the audience as she slowly lifted her veil and revealed an image that could only be described as half a face.

Tiny piercing eyes unprotected by any signs of eyelashes or brows stared unblinkingly at the audience. The nose was only half visible, and the lips were not there at all, so teeth forced the mouth to appear in an horrific smile.

La Stupenda clung onto the edge of the curtain, and gasped in horror. What, oh what had she done?

"Dim the lights," she ordered the stage manager, and even though it was too early, and the Royal Party were not yet seated, he complied.

Gradually the sounds of talking quietened down. The conductor brought some order, and the Overture to *Carmen* began.

La Stupenda heard her cue, and taking a deep breath walked onto the stage, to be greeted by the usual round of applause. The orchestra began to play the accompaniment to the 'Habanera' aria.

La Stupenda – or was it Maisie? – opened her mouth to sing. Nothing came out. She looked up towards Box 66 and the ghastly face with its piercing black eyes stared back at her.

The conductor stopped the orchestra. He caught the eye of La Stupenda to indicate 'One more time'. Again the music played, and this time only a strangled note emanated from the famous singer, which suddenly turned into a high-pitched, strangled scream that seemed to have no end.

The curtains were hurriedly lowered. The noise from the audience reached a fevered crescendo. The Royal Party hurriedly disappeared into their salon.

When the house lights came up, all eyes turned to Box 66. No one was there.

The occupant was already sitting in her hansom cab, and as they left the Royal Opera House the driver politely asked

"Did everything go as planned tonight, Madam?"

"Oh yes, Driver," was the reply, "Everything went very much as planned. Thank you."

THE P.O. BOX

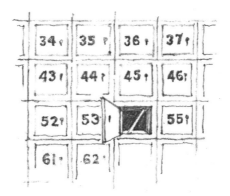

WHAT THE ENVELOPE contained was totally out of character for Mildred, who would be the first person to agree that she was an extremely private person who preferred to keep her views and sentiments to herself. But now inside this envelope, she was letting her guard down and almost – ALMOST – baring her soul.

She wasn't sure, in reality, whether stating what was your favourite colour or book actually amounted to 'baring one's soul', it was just that no one had ever asked her that before.

The envelope was addressed to 27 High Street, West-bury, Wilts. Despite it not being a million miles from where she lived, she thought she should follow the advice and her instincts so she had rented a letterbox in the post office in her local town of Shaftesbury rather than revealing her home address.

Mildred knew she was taking a risk. This was particularly rare for her as she certainly did not have the reputation as a risk taker. Quite the reverse, really. Mildred's whole life had been planned and orderly – so far.

She was an only child. Her father had been a country GP in the days when doctors would actually call upon their patients in their homes, and even become friendly with many of them.

Her mother Susan had been a school secretary. Mildred had then attended this school, and eventually proceeded to a 'red brick' university where she obtained a second class degree in English.

Always a serious girl, Mildred's friends were few, and even they were not particularly close.

When her university days were over, Mildred obtained a job in London with a firm of accountants. Here her calm and precise manner was very much appreciated. If someone were to ask her whether or not she enjoyed her job, she would reply, "Well, I have never really thought about it, but I suppose I do. I get on well with the partners, and I can cope with the work. So yes – I do like it."

The partners knew what a reliable treasure they had in Mildred, so they made sure she was paid well, and in time to come they entitled her to private health care should the need ever arise.

Mildred's parents had bought a flat for her in Stockwell, South London. This was quite pioneering of them, but Mildred loved the flat, in a Georgian house situated in a quiet square, from the moment she saw it. Mildred had the top two floors. The accommodation was light and airy, and the views of London from her bedroom window gave her pleasure all year round.

She tried once to have a flat mate, but it really didn't work out. Priscilla was a giddy girl who was always wanting to bring friends – mainly men – back to the flat. She never did her share of the housework, and constantly ran out of 'the basics' so she made vast inroads on Mildred's carefully stored supplies. Worst of all was how long she would talk on the telephone, with hoots of laughter and exclamations of disbelief, then totally 'forget' to pay her share of the phone bill when it came.

"No – I am much better off on my own," Mildred said to herself. At the time this is what she sincerely believed and it was a happy day when she shut the door behind a departing Priscilla.

A few years later the owners of the house put the freehold of the ground floor flat up for sale. With the approval of her parents, and thanks to glowing references from her bosses, Mildred was able to raise the money to buy it. The rent she subsequently received for the flat enabled her to pay the mortgage.

––––––––––––––––

Mildred did not care to travel on her own. It was not that she wasn't interested in other countries, it was simply that she did not fancy either being a 'singleton' in a jolly group, or simply meandering around an unknown city, guide book in hand, and then sitting alone in a small hotel trying to fathom the mysteries of *foreign food.*

Museums in London, however, were a great attraction for her. Wandering in and out of vast halls and fascinating exhibitions was no problem if you were alone. She would spend quite a bit of money in the gift shops buying beautifully illustrated and informative books that would entertain and educate her for many happy hours when she went home.

Whenever Mildred had a break she would head back to Dorset to stay with her parents. They lived in a charming cottage in the delightful village of Hinton St Mary. Both Doctor John and Susan had retired and they then surprised all their friends by splashing out and buying a second-hand Morris J4 camper van.

They were so excited by their purchase and couldn't wait to show Mildred the interior with its cleverly crafted cupboards, and a tiny kitchenette, together with a double bed and even a mini cool box. They didn't even mind about the somewhat garish bright green roof and paler green chassis. With no ambitions to go abroad, Mildred's parents just took off whenever the mood took them, for a week, a fortnight or just a couple of nights, to explore the United Kingdom.

Mildred thought she had never seen her parents so happy. They were quite rejuvenated, it seemed. They never appeared to mind if the weather was bad. "Part of the adventure," they told Mildred. Therefore, when they had, unwisely as it turned out, decided to visit Yorkshire one October, Mildred did not think it was up to her to suggest they might wait a bit and go perhaps in May.

Of course it was all in the news. Appalling floods affecting so many people. Mildred watched on television and saw people being rescued in boats from their houses, clinging on to a few precious belongings and their terrified pets.

As she watched the camera spanned the local river which had burst its banks. A car had been swept downstream by the strong current and was stuck fast again a crumbling bridge. But just beyond – really too hard to see properly – was another vehicle half submerged in swirling water.

As Mildred looked, she saw a bright green roof and she knew, instantly, that this was the camper van belonging to her parents.

Sick with fear, somehow Mildred managed to get through to the local police. She explained what she had seen.

"Don't worry, luv, it may not be your parents' van." She knew, though. She knew it was.

So when a couple of hours later she was called by a WPC with the tragic news that sadly the occupants of the van had both succumbed to the cold and the water, she simply said, "Thank you very much for telling me," before she hung up.

It was a nightmare Mildred preferred to forget. The identification – the repatriation to Dorset – the funeral arrangements – the solicitors and the well-meaning friends. Somehow Mildred survived it all as if cocooned in an ethereal bubble that wafted her from one event to another.

The thought that her parents died together and were enjoying their retirement so much was a deep comfort to her. She tried not to think how they must have suffered.

Mildred surprised herself at how quickly she made the decision. She put the Stockwell house on the market, and it was snapped up at almost double the cost of their initial investments. Before it was sold she had given in her notice to the firm of accountants, who gave her a generous fare-well bonus as they wondered ruefully how they could possibly cope without her.

Then finally, at the age of 48, she retired to her cottage in Hinton St Mary, Dorset.

———————————

Mildred did miss her parents. She realised they had found their only child a bit on the dull side, but they loved her nevertheless, and had made sure she was left comfortably off as by the time she had reached her mid-forties they surmised she was unlikely to find a companion of either sex with whom to settle down.

It took a while to adjust to not going into the office every day, and also not telephoning her parents every Friday at 7pm.

She made few changes to the house as she liked it as it was. Her only major alteration was that when she moved into her parents' bedroom (due to the en suite), she had the flowery wallpaper removed and replaced with a plain, slightly textured paper in the softest creamy-yellow colour which went perfectly with the existing curtains, patterned in fading green, yellow and dusky pink leaves.

The garden had always given her pleasure. It was under one acre, but it had certainly kept both her parents busy. Mildred's pleasure, alas, did not include knowledge, and she had no idea what to do or when. She was so grateful that dear old Sam the gardener had agreed to stay on. Mildred gave him a free hand and increased his wages. Sam was as happy as Larry.

Despite being on the edge of the village it was only a short walk to the little shop. Perfect for day to day needs. Shaftesbury with all its hustle and bustle was an easy drive. Her car was cared for by the local garage, and her parents' ashes were interred in the village church, which

Mildred, never known for her piety, made an effort to attend. The rest of the congregation were *terribly* friendly and always wanted Mildred to stay for coffee and biscuits after the service. As soon as she could, with a lame excuse hovering on her lips, she escaped back to her cottage and shut out the world with relief.

So therefore, after about six months of this 'perfect' existence, it came as a total surprise to Mildred to realise she was not, after all, 100 percent happy. She was missing something, and what that something was came to her as a bolt from the blue.

Mildred was an avid reader. She positively devoured books. She read classics and the latest 'must-read' biographies and novels. There was a good lending library in the town so she never ran out of something to read. Gradually it dawned on her that, whether they were successful or not, what the majority of the heroines in these books shared was love.

Love in all its forms. The excitement of being in love. The joy and contentment (like her parents) of lifelong love. The physical act of love and even the hurt and sadness of lost love. Above all the companionship and friendship that a lasting love could bring.

Mildred had never felt love of any sort in her life other than obviously for her parents. Once when she was a child of eight she had loved the hamster someone had given her, but when she found it dead in her empty bath in a pool of blood some time later, she was so traumatised she vowed never to own any sort of an animal again.

Despite her undoubted creature comforts Mildred came to the conclusion she was lonely. Not just lonely for a friend in the village, but lonely for love.

It was several weeks after this startling revelation to herself that her eyes lit upon an advertisement in the local newspaper that seemed to be written especially for her.

ARE YOU LOOKING FOR THAT SPECIAL SOMEONE TO SHARE YOUR LIFE?

Do you suffer from loneliness – or a lack of a friend or companion?

At LISA'S MARRIAGE BUREAU (Est. 1962) we offer a confidential and personalised service for discreet clients.

Contact us on Westbury 6428 at any time.

Mildred read and re-read the advertisement. She had heard about these marriage bureaux of course, but never ever thought she would consider approaching one. The fact that this was almost local tempted her and she argued that there was nothing to be lost by picking up the telephone and making an enquiry. So, feeling ridiculously nervous, Mildred did just that.

"Hello. You have reached the offices of Lisa's Marriage Bureau. Please hold on and your call will be answered as soon as possible."

Mildred hung on, and just as her nerve was about to fail she heard a friendly voice saying, "Hello – my name is Lisa and I am the owner of Lisa's Marriage Bureau. To whom am I speaking? Mildred Musgrave. Would you mind if I call you Mildred, even though we have not yet met? Tell me in your own words how I may be able to help you? Take your time as there is no hurry."

The warm, melodious voice babbled on and gradually Mildred relaxed enough to be able to tell this unknown person about her life. It all came out, about London, then the tragedy and now her life alone in Dorset, with no immediate family in her life. Lisa at the other end of the line made the most sympathetic and understanding noises and remarks.

Sending gleeful looks to the other two occupants of the cramped office above an Indian restaurant, Lisa scribbled on a piece of rough paper, "I think we may have the ideal person here," before she continued soothingly to Mildred, "I so understand and sympathise with the situation you find yourself in. You are not the only one, believe me, you are not alone in this. I detect that you will want to meet someone very kind, who maybe has also neglected his personal happiness in pursuit of a fulfilling career. Do you agree? To find the right person we would need to study our client list very carefully. In the meantime we will send you a questionnaire to your home address, but I suggest" – and Lisa was rather proud of this as she felt it made them sound very safe – "when corresponding with our clients it would be wiser to use a post office box number until you are sure you wish to see them again."

Mildred – head now firmly on her shoulders – indicated that she would inform them the following day of her P.O. Box number and she would prefer not to divulge her home address just yet, even for them.

Lisa pulled a face and looked at her colleagues who both mouthed, "Go along with it. It doesn't matter for now."

"That's fine, Mildred. You let us know when you have organised your box number and in the meantime we will start the hunt. I have a feeling we will be able to set you up with the perfect Mr Right very soon. All we need is a telephone number so we may contact you." And with that, Lisa turned to Josh and Pete and gave them the thumbs-up.

Before she could change her mind, Mildred drove into Shaftesbury and went straight away to the post office and paid for post office box number 54. She then telephoned the agency and again had to wait for a while, but luckily it was Lisa again who told her she would post the questionnaire that very afternoon.

Considering the organisation had been in existence for a number of years Mildred was a bit surprised at the slightly flimsy form she was sent. Somehow she was expecting it to be more formal, with a logo, etc. This one almost looked as if it had been typed on blank pages. Still, she filled it in, although she thought some of the questions were really irrelevant. She answered the questions on music, art, travel, cooking, etc., and mentioned she loved her garden. Mildred considered lying about her age, but in the end told the truth, and then explained she had worked all her life for one firm and was now retired and living in the country. She had to admit, she did not sound, even to herself, remotely interesting.

On reading the completed questionnaire Lisa turned to her two colleagues in the office and said, "Perfect. I think she sounds utterly perfect. However, from our conversation I detect a certain amount of timidity and so patience and a lot of assurance will be required to start with."

The younger of the two men stood up and went over to Lisa. He put both hands on her shoulders and looked straight into her eyes as he said, "Trust me, Lisa. You know I can do it. I agree. This time I feel a sugar plum has been dropped into our laps. But 'slowly, slowly, catchee monkey'. We must move bit by bit."

The telephone, which happened to be on the table right by her ear, burst into life with its shrill ring almost a week later. Mildred was momentarily startled. Very few people ever rang her unless it was something to do with the church.

"Hello Mildred, it's Lisa."

Lisa? Lisa who? Oh yes of course, the marriage bureau person.

"I was looking through our lists of candidates and was not entirely happy that we were on the right track, when lo and behold one of my colleagues interviewed a new gentleman this week and I think he sounds just the ticket. He is a bit younger than you – late thirties – but sounds very mature and quite serious. Not a 'fly-by-night' sort of character if you get my meaning.

"For his interests he put architecture, opera, reading, gardening and walking. I definitely think he would be worth a once-over. What do you think? Oh – and also from his photograph he seems very nice-looking as well."

Josh, who was standing beside Lisa at this moment, did a little mock bow.

Mildred was somewhat taken aback. Then she said, "I am sure a good-looking man in his thirties would have no interest in a boring old spinster like me."

It was a good thing there was no way Mildred could have seen the exchange of jokey expressions between Lisa and her colleague and lover Josh, completely endorsing the sentiments that Mildred had professed.

Knowing Mildred's P.O. Box was in Shaftesbury, Lisa asked if she was happy to go there for her first meeting. Mildred was relieved such a convenient place had been suggested.

"There is a nice pub at the top of the famous Gold Street. You could meet Josh there. Shall we say 12.30 next Thursday?"

Despite the slightly disquieting feeling that the rug was being pulled from under her feet, Mildred agreed.

So it was settled. Middle-aged spinster Mildred was about to meet a strange young man in his thirties with a view to becoming a possible long-term companion. Was this really happening?

Thursday dawned and promised to be a fair if slightly cool day in April.

"What on earth should I wear?" wondered Mildred. She had never bothered with clothes too much. At least not in the fashion sense. If she found a jumper or a pair of slacks, or even a jacket she liked, she would invariably order another one in a different colour. She eventually settled on maroon slacks with a fawn jumper and one of her slightly smarter London jackets to complete the outfit.

"Goodness! I look old and hideous," she thought as she gazed at her reflected face. She only had powder and lipstick, so that would have to do.

She saw him at once. As soon as she entered the pub. He was sitting by a window at a table for two and appeared to be reading a book about architecture.

Immediately he saw Mildred, the young man stood up and stretched out his hand.

"You must be Mildred. How do you do? I am Josh. Please sit down."

Lisa was right. Josh was indeed very good-looking. Thick, slightly wavy brown hair framed a face with regular features. Not too big a mouth and somewhat startling light blue eyes. He was wearing grey flannel trousers, a checked shirt and navy blue sleeveless jumper under a tweed jacket.

"Are you happy to drink white wine?" he asked.

"Yes thank you, although only a little as I have to drive home."

"Do you live far from here?" Josh asked.

Steady on, thought Mildred. *I am not telling him where I live just yet.*

"Not too far," she replied.

The wine was poured, then Josh began.

"I will tell you a bit about myself. My father was in the army and as children my sister Penny and I became used to living in different countries for a few years. We were in Cyprus, Germany and Ireland mostly. When Penny and I were nine and seven, the Army paid for us to attend a boarding school to give us some continuity. It was in 1956 that the headmaster summoned us to his study and had the difficult task of informing us our parents had been involved in a collision with a tank on the army base. Our father died instantly. Later our mother was repatriated to the UK where in time she made a full physical recovery but was never the same mentally. Eventually we had to make the sad decision to put her in a home where she still is. Penny lives nearby in Leeds and is wonderful at visiting her, but I regret I am not so good. The last time Penny saw her, our mother had no idea who Penny was."

Mildred listened intently and was so sorry to hear such a sad story.

"Anyway," Josh continued. "Life goes on. Our uncle and aunt stepped in to care for us and now I am happy to say we both have fulfilling jobs. Penny works for the NHS in the administrative department of a local hospital, and I was able to get a job with a private company that is slowly building up a fleet of well made and comfortable coaches – complete, would you believe, with a toilet on board!"

He was obviously so proud of this that Mildred made all the right noises and then asked, "Who will use these buses?"

"Ah – they are already in much demand by companies organising groups of people who wish to travel all over the UK and the Continent as well. I started as the most junior employee but have worked my way up to Assistant Manager in charge of Sales!"

"Well done," enthused Mildred. "My life is so dull in comparison."

"I don't believe it," replied Josh. 'Now, tell me everything. Do you live in a town or village? Is it friendly? If there is a good pub perhaps we could go there one day?"

Mildred surprised herself at how happy she was to talk to Josh. He too was wonderfully sympathetic when he heard about her parents. He reached out and touched her hand, and looked deep into her eyes as he said, "I do so understand, having been through something similar myself. We have this sadness in common."

Then, briskly changing, Josh looked at his watch and said, "Will you look at the time? Just as we were getting to know each other. However, if you agree, I would be happy to meet up again." On the nod from Mildred he continued: "How about the same time, same place in two weeks? Only this time I will make sure I don't have to rush so we can have lunch together. Next week I am off to Austria for a few days. Give me your address and I'll send you a postcard."

"That would be fun," said Mildred as she carefully wrote down: *Miss M. Musgrave, c/o PO Box 54, Shaftesbury, Dorset.*

"We're getting there," thought Josh and out loud he said, "I so enjoyed meeting you, Mildred, and I very much look forward to seeing you again in two weeks' time."

―――――――――――

"How did it go, darling?" asked Lisa.

"Like a dream," was the reply. 'She's as dull as ditch-water, poor thing, but perfectly pleasant and I would say totally naïve. She swallowed my story hook, line and sinker. There were even tears in her eyes."

"Josh, you are incorrigible!" laughed Lisa. "Come here and give me a kiss."

The first week passed very slowly and Mildred found herself thinking of Josh on several occasions.

Part of her felt distinctly giddy and girlish anticipating when they would meet again.

The sensible part of her gave voice to a stern warning:

"Mildred my dear, you are no looker. You are neither charmingly amusing or fascinatingly interesting. Why would a good-looking young man like Josh want to see you again? Be careful."

Mildred let a full week pass before she visited the post office in Shaftesbury. There was the bank of post boxes and she hopefully opened number 54. Disappointingly, it was quite empty.

"Oh well," she thought, 'probably just as well. I was much too old for him."

Two days before they were due to meet she could not resist going once more to see if the P.O. Box had some-thing inside. This time it did! She opened it up and removed a picture postcard of mountains in Austria. She turned it over to read the message.

"Dear Mildred – I have been thinking about you constantly since we met, especially on a long walk in this glorious countryside. Until next week. Love Josh."

Then Josh had added, squashed at the top of the card,

"Written in Aus. No stamp. Sorry. Posted here."

Mildred did think it was slightly strange that Josh had the time for a long walk when he was meant to be working, but she was so pleased to get the card she dismissed any such unwelcome thoughts.

The second meeting over lunch went very well. Josh told her all about his visit to Austria and how he was mapping out routes for future bus tours.

Towards the end of the meal he said, "I might not be able to see you for a while as I must visit my sister who lives near Leeds. I am very worried about her as she appears to be rather unwell."

"Oh dear. How concerning for you. And you seem to be very close to her."

"Yes, indeed, we are very close. She is a wonderful person and I would do anything for her. She is younger than I am and not married either."

Josh left and promised to write to her. "Check your P.O. Box," he had said, 'although soon I hope you will give me your proper address."

Two days later Mildred had an appointment with her dentist in Shaftesbury so she popped into the post office and saw that box number 54 had something in it. This time it was a letter which had obviously been written in a hurry.

"Dear Mildred – Please forgive the scrawl but wanted to dash this off before leaving to visit my sister Penny.

I don't quite know how to put this, but I really feel you and I have something going for us. I so enjoy your company and really want to see lots more of you. Who knows – you and I may even have a future together? I would also love to see your garden that seems to give you so much joy. Anyway, until then, take care of yourself.

With love Josh."

Mildred carefully folded the letter and replaced it in its envelope. This was the nearest she had ever come to receiving a love letter. Ridiculously her heart fluttered in her chest.

"Silly old fool," she said sternly, "he is just flattering you. Take no notice."

But she did.

She decided to have her hair done and told Sheree to give her a new, more up-to-date style. The hairdresser looked at her in amazement.

"Crikey!" was the response. "I will. But I also think it would be great to lighten up your colour as well."

"Why not?" said Mildred, and she let Sheree do what she wanted.

The result was certainly different. Sheree had cut away the boring, rather limp strands that hung somewhat lifelessly on either side of her face, and had given Mildred a layered look which was much softer and framed her face. The lighter colour was a big improvement and even Mildred had to admit the overall result made her look younger.

Mildred had been unable to reply to Josh as of course she didn't have his address either (pity, that), but the next time she checked her box there were two letters waiting.

The first one was again full of happiness at meeting and hopes for the future. The second contained some sad news. It appeared his sister had been diagnosed with a serious form of cancer, and the outlook was not at all hopeful. Josh wrote that he was about to have a meeting with her doctors. He told Mildred he would be back the following week and would she mind allowing the agency to give him her telephone number so he could ring her? Just call the office to say yes or no.

Mildred rang the next day and this time she spoke to a man. She gave him permission.

Lisa, Josh and Pete looked at each other as they all gave the 'thumbs up' sign and Lisa said, "YES!"

During their next meeting Josh told Mildred that unfortunately there appeared to be no cure in the UK to the type of cancer Penny had. Her only hope was to somehow get her to the USA. He had been told there was a team working on exactly the same cancer in Seattle, and so far the trials had proved more than encouraging.

Josh was bound and determined to somehow raise the money to send his beloved sister there. He had already found a buyer for his car, which would pay for a one-way ticket, but he needed so much more in order to fund her treatment.

Josh had told her he lived in Salisbury and had already put his flat up for sale. Even though this would only scratch the surface he was prepared to live in one room if it would help her.

Luckily their father had made a wise investment in a building society which neither he nor Penny had ever touched. Once they could get their hands on this it would help considerably.

"Anyway," said Josh, "enough of all this talk about money. What can I do to persuade you to show me your garden?"

Mildred's heart was full of pity for Josh in his dilemma. He looked so downcast. Surely now he had shown himself to be a decent and caring person, so what harm could there be in letting him come to her house?

"When could you come?" asked Mildred.

"Any time that suits you," was the reply.

And so a visit was arranged, and seemingly Josh did not have to worry about taking time off work.

There was no pretence in the appreciation Josh showed as he saw a delightful small house, with a perfect garden that had been carefully planned, full of mature trees and shrubs offering privacy, whilst at the same time allowing the eye to feast upon fabulous views of unspoilt country-side.

Mildred suggested they went into the house. *Deeply old-fashioned*, was Josh's first thought, but then he noticed a very handsome dining room table, and a majestic grand-father clock with a charmingly painted face. Several pieces of furniture looked 'good' and various ornaments and pieces of silver, together with quite a few obviously Victorian but saleable paintings on the walls, all added up in Josh's mind to an encouraging sum.

Josh followed Mildred into the kitchen where she placed the kettle on the hob. Before she knew what was happening he had taken her in his arms and then given the surprised middle-aged spinster a long and lingering kiss.

Mildred eventually broke away and tried to continue preparing the tea whilst her heart appeared to be leaping all over her body.

Walking her into the living room, Josh suggested they both sit down on the sofa.

"Darling. I can't tell you what a comfort you are to me. I know somehow I will raise the money needed. I am only just fearful I won't get it soon enough. Time, as they say, is of the essence."

Sitting side by side, with Josh's arm casually over her shoulder, Mildred told herself that this was companionship, and maybe even love. Surely she could trust him? The marriage bureau promised they vetted all candidates for their honesty. The seed had been cleverly planted, and slowly it grew into an idea forming in Mildred's head.

"Josh?"

"Yes, darling?"

"Perhaps I could help a bit. I could lend you some money to tide you over until you sell your flat?"

"No – no. I wouldn't dream of it. I couldn't possibly accept. It is out of the question. I only told you everything as you are such a sympathetic listener."

"Josh – I would be happy to help. How much do you need right now?"

Josh, still putting on a good act of demurring, whispered, 'It's a huge amount I am afraid. £10,000."

Mildred was taken aback.

"My goodness, that is a lot. I was imagining maybe £5,000 at the most. But anyway, let me talk to my bank and see what they suggest."

Mildred arranged to see the bank manager the following day. She hadn't seen Mr Plowman since her parents had died. When she entered his office she did not at first recognise him. She seemed to remember he was distinctly portly with at least a couple of chins, and a stomach fighting to emerge from his tightly buttoned waistcoat. Sitting before her now was a much slimmer and better-looking version of the same man, with only one chin.

"Ah Miss Musgrave, good morning. I see I have surprised you with my appearance. I have in fact lost over three stone, strictly on doctor's orders. I was in danger of becoming a diabetic. I have to confess I feel so much better as a result, and even enjoy my exercise these days," he laughed. "Now, to this matter. Do you mind explaining why you need to take out such a large sum? It does seem a little out of character, if you don't mind my saying. Are you sure it is for a good reason?"

"Yes it is. Very good. It is to help a poor young woman get some specialised treatment in America for her cancer. It is only a loan. Just until her brother's flat is sold."

"I see," pondered Mr Plowman. "Do you know this young woman, or indeed her brother well? What guarantee do you have that this loan will in fact be repaid?"

"I confess I have never met her, and nor do I know the young man well, but I am sure he is genuine. I have seen the particulars of his flat in Salisbury and it is valued at £15,000. It is in a good position and according to the estate agent it will be very easy to sell."

Mr Plowman looked at the woman before him. She too had changed her appearance quite considerably, and there was a definite sparkle in her eyes. Mr Plowman was no fool.

"I have to confess that it goes against my gut feeling to authorise this loan, but please take my advice and have the agreement between you and this man in writing. It is, after all, your money, so if you are really sure I will arrange it."

———————————

Josh was effusive in his gratitude.

"You are absolutely wonderful, darling. I can't thank you enough. Perhaps we should get married and then everything would be ours jointly?"

Mildred was not quite sure how he worked that one out, but the bells in her heart ringing out the joyful news that Josh had proposed to her drowned out the sounds of misgivings that lurked threateningly in the back of her head.

"You won't believe it," said Josh a few days later. "The So-and-So who was buying my car has disappeared. I have already booked Penny on a flight and the hospital is expecting her. I hate to ask darling, but could you manage another £10,00?"

Once again Mildred found herself sitting before Mr Plowman.

"How and where did you meet this young man?" he enquired.

Mildred was embarrassed, and it took her several minutes before she was able to admit to Mr Plowman that she had joined Lisa's Marriage Bureau which had been advertised in the local newspaper. She assured the bank manager that Josh had been carefully vetted before the introduction was made.

Mr Plowman jotted down this information, then he said, "Tell your friend that the money is on its way but due to it being held in a different sort of account it will take a few days."

Josh did not react to this news well. He was sitting in Mildred's kitchen drinking from a mug of coffee, which he then banged down on the table with such force that it broke and coffee spilled on her pretty tablecloth.

Mildred was shocked and unnerved by this behaviour.

"It's on its way, darling," she whispered.

"Well the thing is," said Josh, "I need it at once. Let's go to your bank now and withdraw as much as you can."

"I don't think that will be a very good idea at the moment," ventured Mildred.

"I don't care what you think. That is where we are going."

With shaking hands Mildred wrote out a cheque for her limit of £300, made out to CASH. They then drove to the bank and withdrew the money.

When they returned to the cottage, by which time Josh had firmly pocketed the cash, he announced that he would stay with her for the night, as after all, when they were married this is where they would live.

"But Josh," Mildred began, "I have not..."

Immediately Josh planted a kiss on Mildred's lips, successfully stopping what she was about to say.

"Now," he continued, 'show me how you can cook. Let's see how well you will feed me when we are married. In the meantime, I am sure if I look hard enough I will find a bottle of wine."

Mildred's mind was in a turmoil. What had happened to the charming Josh she had fallen for? Who was this domineering, rather unkind person trying to control her life?

Josh returned triumphantly holding a bottle of wine he had found in the drinks cupboard, and once poured out he handed Mildred her glass and clinked with his own whilst saying:

"To our marriage, darling."

"But Josh dear, I have not yet agreed to marry you."

"Nonsense darling, of course you have. Now let's get cracking with the meal. I am very hungry."

Stunned into complete stupefaction Mildred somehow managed to cobble together some sort of a meal while an awful fear began slowly creeping all over her body with its icy grasp. The terrifying realisation that she had been a complete and utter fool. That she, Mildred Musgrave, a stupid, plain, middle-aged spinster, had readily believed a good-looking young man in his thirties could possibly care for – yes, even love – someone like her. She had fallen for it, and now she didn't know what to do.

Josh ate his meal in silence, then abruptly left the kitchen, marching into the sitting room and banging into the hall table on the way which in turn knocked the telephone to the floor.

Mildred rushed out in panic. *Please don't let the phone be broken*, she thought. Part of her knew she might need this contact with the world outside. Luckily it had survived the fall.

Back in the kitchen, Mildred wondered what she should do. If she crept out by the back door Josh would catch her up in minutes. She could not call anyone (like who?) while Josh was there, as he would hear and stop her. She finished the washing up and went into her sitting room, and Josh was sprawled on the sofa with outstretched legs.

Suddenly he smiled his charming smile and said, "So sorry darling. I was a bit out of hand. Put it down to the anxiety over Penny. It's just that everything seems to be conspiring against me at the moment. Now don't worry. You go to bed and I will sleep in your spare room. I have a plan which we will discuss calmly in the morning. Off you go."

Dismissed in her own house! However, Mildred was glad to be able to escape to her bedroom. She wished she could lock the door, but there had never been any need.

Lying fully clothed on her bed Mildred could hear Josh talking on the telephone for hours. Eventually she drifted off into a fitful sleep.

Waking with a start, Mildred was instantly aware of a sickening feeling as she recalled the events of the day before. After a quick wash to refresh herself, Mildred started to quietly descend the stairs.

Halfway down she stopped abruptly, as to her incredulity she was aware she was hearing the sound of muted voices emanating from her kitchen. One belonged to Josh and the other was a woman's voice. There was something familiar about that voice but she couldn't quite place it.

When she entered the kitchen, Josh and the young woman looked up at her. As they clutched their mugs of coffee they also appeared to be studying sheets of paper which at a quick glance looked distinctly official.

"Ah darling," said Josh sweetly, "This is my lawyer, Miss Armstrong. I have asked her to draw up an agreement for us both to sign before our marriage. You needn't bother to read it all. Basically, it is saying that if I should die before you, you will inherit everything I own, and vice-versa."

Apart from the fact that, due to her training and work for the accountants, there was no way Mildred would sign anything she had not read, she said quite firmly:

"Josh. I have not yet agreed to marry you."

"Yes you did, darling," Josh laughed. 'Silly moo! Last night when we shared a bottle of wine, and we both agreed the sooner the better. Now don't say you don't remember. We didn't drink as much as all that! Well anyway, Miss Armstrong here has a colleague and he is one his way to be our second witness, and then we shall be ready to go. So exciting!"

Mildred looked at Miss Armstrong and said, "I am not going mad. We do not have an agreement, and I would like to make it clear to Josh I will not be getting married so there is no point in signing this form."

"Surely you will," purred Miss Armstrong. "You can't refuse Josh. He is such a lovely young man and would make a wonderful husband."

Then it was that Mildred remembered where she had heard that voice before.

She waited a moment whilst the two of them studied the papers again, and then she said sharply, "Lisa," and Miss Armstrong turned to look at her.

"I thought as much. So you two are in this together, and I have been taken for a complete mug. You are clever. You chose well when you picked on me. I should have realised how totally unlikely it was for a good-looking young man to fall in love with an old girl like me. Well, I can tell you this. You won't get another penny out of me."

At that moment the telephone rang. Luckily Mildred was still standing in the doorway of the kitchen so she was able to reach it quickly.

"Hello? Hello?"

A polite voice answered.

"Are you Miss Musgrave? Mr Plowman would like to speak to you."

"Put him on quickly," she said, but the girl at the end of the phone was too slow, and the receiver was snatched out of Mildred's hand by Lisa.

"Hello? Miss Musgrave?" asked Mr Plowman.

"Yes," replied Lisa sweetly.

"I just rang to warn you to be careful. Something is wrong. Just watch your step."

"Please don't worry, sir, on my account. Everything is perfectly all right. Thank you so very much for your kind interest."

Lisa put the telephone back on its cradle.

Mr Plowman hesitated only a second. "Sir?" That ultra sweet voice?

"Miss Jackson – call the police at once and tell them to meet me at Miss Musgrave's address. I fear she might be in danger."

Josh had pushed Mildred down onto a kitchen chair.

"These papers my dear are perfectly legal, whether we are married or not. The minute you sign them, witnessed by Lisa here, and –" to Lisa – "where the hell is Pete? – our other witness, Lisa and I shall be the proud owners of this house and all its contents, plus we shall have access to all your income as you will have, in sound mind, so gener-ously agreed to hand everything over to your intended husband."

"I don't know how you think you could get away with such a thing." Fear was making Mildred sound much stronger. "I will not sign anything you put in front of me."

Then Josh, without any warning, slapped Mildred hard across her face.

"You are a silly bitch, aren't you? To think you actually thought someone like me might actually find you attrac-tive, and then want to *marry* you. It's laughable. You are just a silly, sad, lonely old woman. However, you will soon make two people very happy indeed." And with this Josh smirked at Lisa and blew her a kiss.

Mildred looked at Lisa to see if there was any sympathy there. None at all. She too was mocking her.

"What about your marriage bureau?"

"That, my dear, was simply the bait to lure fish like you into our nets. I give you your due, though, I think you are definitely the biggest fish we have ever caught. As soon as we have sold your house, and what contents we don't wish to keep for ourselves, we shall be off to pastures new, to see what other fish we can snare. Where *is* Pete?"

Lisa went to look out of the front window. Not a sign of anyone.

"I suppose the story about Penny was a lie as well?"

"Yes – completely. Good one, though. I might use it again. In the past I have used my darling old mother, or my darling old dog. Both have been very successful."

"I hope you rot in Hell," Mildred spat out with a sudden venom that surprised even her.

At that moment there was knock on the door. Mildred tried to jump up to answer it, but Josh forced her roughly back into her seat.

Lisa opened the door to Pete.

"Sorry to be late. I lost my way."

"Idiot," said Lisa. 'We must hurry. She is being difficult."

A pen was thrust into Mildred's hand.

"I won't sign it," she said through gritted teeth.

"You damned well will," shouted Josh as he brutally gripped her hand and forced it onto the page.

Another knock on the door. They all froze.

"Are you expecting anyone?"

The adrenalin from fear enabled Mildred to think quickly.

"Yes. It's my neighbour who is coming to borrow my mower as his is broken."

"What's his name?"

"Bob."

Josh went to the door and opened it a crack. He could just make out the shape of a man.

"Bob," he said, "Mildred said can you come tomorrow to collect the mower as she is not feeling very well at the moment? I am her doctor and have just popped into see her."

As Josh started to close the front door a gruff voice said, "Doctor my eye," and then Josh was knocked backwards as the door was thrust open and in rushed two policemen, with Mr Plowman the bank manager following behind.

Mr Plowman immediately rushed to Mildred's side and was relieved to see she was not seriously hurt.

Josh put up a bit of a struggle but was quickly overcome, whilst Pete practically wept as he put his hands out to be handcuffed.

Lisa grumbled and kicked and even tried to spit at Mildred, but was firmly frogmarched out to the waiting police van.

There was an eventual court case, by which time many other victims had come forward. It seems the trio had jumped on the bandwagon of the newest craze for lonely people trying to find companions through marriage bureaux. They had unfortunately been rather successful. Sometimes Lisa had managed to snare a lonely old widower with promises of glorious romps in the marriage bed – a bed that had been sold off before any marriage took place.

Their skill was never staying too long in one area and only using local papers in which to advertise.

Mr Plowman had invited Mildred in to the bank after a week or so. He explained that he had investigate the bureau and discovered it to be bogus. When he rang to warn her he realised at once Lisa was not her, and that therefore she was probably in danger.

Amazingly, most of her money had been recovered as it had all happened so quickly they had not had time to squirrel it away. If Josh had been a little more patient and subtle he might have got away with much more. He was too greedy and wanted it all at once.

"Thank you, Mr Plowman. That sounds so inadequate, but I believe you saved my life. I do feel so incredibly stupid to have allowed myself to have been taken in by such a scoundrel."

"I am so relieved we were in time. Although only just as it turned out. If they had succeeded in persuading you to sign that form, even though you would have contested it on the grounds you were forced to sign it, the whole procedure would have taken quite a bit of time, giving them ample opportunity to spend what they could as soon as possible."

Mildred shuddered at the thought.

Slightly shyly Mr Plowman asked, "May I call you Mildred?"

"Yes, please do."

"Then in that case, will you call me Humphrey? And one day, if and when you feel up to it, would you allow me to buy you lunch? I can't promise anything dramatic, but I would very much enjoy seeing you again in more relaxed and non banking surroundings."

"Mr – er, Humphrey, that sounds a lovely idea, but wouldn't Mrs, Plowman object?"

"Well I suppose she might if there was a Mrs Plowman. However, I never managed to find her, so you see before you a somewhat dull old bachelor."

This was all said with such diffident charm that Mildred found herself warming to this kindly man.

"Humphrey, I would like to accept. That sounds a lovely. Maybe in a month or so? I feel I do need to recover from this ordeal. Perhaps you could ask some friends to join us?"

"Capital," said Humphrey. 'A great idea. I will do just that." Discreetly Humphrey made a little note in his diary for six weeks hence.

Mildred left the bank with a small smile quivering on her lips.

As she walked toward the car park she suddenly remembered to take a quick detour to the town Post Office, which she entered briskly, went up to a counter and closed P.O. Box number 54, and vowed never again in all her life to open another Post Office Box.

THE CAKE BOX

THE VILLAGE OF Minchinghampton was a buzz of anticipation.

Already, six weeks before the event, speculation was rife as to who the eventual winner would be this year.

The local shop became the hub of gossip. Mrs Tanner gathered every little bit of information that she could which she willingly passed on to ever-open ears:

"Her Ladyship was in yesterday and she hinted – with the broadest smile – that this year she had actually persuaded a VIP – a TV celebrity, no less – to come and be the judge. She wouldn't divulge the name. Said we would know in the fullness of time, but judging by how fluffed up she was I would say it is in the bag."

Sally and Shirley Thompson looked at each other with raised eyebrows.

"Well – well," they tutted in unison. "That's very interesting. That'll set the cat among the pigeons in no uncertain way."

"Wendy and Pat will be in a lather of excitement, I expect," muttered old Mrs Dunn as she wielded her shopping trolley through the door and began her slow plod back to her bungalow.

"Mornin', Ladies… How's it all goin' then? 'Ave you taken me up on the offer to start a book to name the winner of the icing competition? 20p a bet. Winner takes all. C'mon then – a bit o' a flutter is fun."

"Morning Jack. I think you might be right. I'll organise notices and you can pop one in the letter boxes on your rounds with the post."

Pat Johnson looked out of her kitchen window onto the High Street and noticed a group of ladies looking in her direction, and presumably, thought Pat, wondering what she would create this year.

Her arch rival Wendy Farmer was blissfully unaware of the mounting excitement as her little house was off the beaten track and her kitchen overlooked fields.

The competition between Pat and Wendy attracted a great deal of attention, as members of the public from neighbouring villages were keen to see what these two clever ladies could produce. Rumours had reached Wendy about a possible VIP judge this year, which meant the standard had to be higher than ever.

After a great deal of thought, acknowledging what a challenging decision it had been, Wendy was pleased with her idea. Now she had to plan how to execute it, as it was definitely going to be hard.

Lady Wentworth was speaking on the telephone whilst perched on a chair in the cosy sitting room of the Manor House.

"You really are *too* kind, and all of us at Minchinghampton are *so* grateful you have agreed to be our judge. I hope you won't mind if we now advertise the fact as I am sure you are aware your presence will make the most enormous difference to our numbers, and thereby we hope to raise a very generous amount for our cottage hospital."

A couple of weeks later the posters were printed and placed in every conceivable place in Minchinghampton and beyond. Lady Wentworth also inserted two good advertisements in the local newspapers.

MINCHINGHAMPTON FÊTE

SATURDAY 8th JULY 2017
10 am - 6 pm

BIGGER   BETTER   BOLDER

Jeremy Barker's Live Jazz Band
Even more stalls – new as well as the old favourites.
Children's games and competitions
Village Tug o' War
Teas and soft drinks and cakes served all day
Raffle with many Prizes.

PLUS OUR GUEST OF HONOUR OF
TELEVISION FAME
MARIGOLD MASTERS
*Who will judge our Home Produce **PLUS** our famous*

CAKE ICING CONTEST

Tickets available from village shops or at the door.
Adults £2   Children Free.

Although there were always several other entrants, nobody had yet managed to equal the skill and expertise of Pat Johnson and Wendy Farmer. They were indeed in a class by themselves.

Philip Johnson knew that from June onwards his wife would think of nothing else other than how she could produce an even more spectacular creation than her winning entry from the previous year.

Pat had then shaped her cake to resemble a boat in full sail. There was a figure climbing the rigging and another with a telescope to his eye in the crow's nest. The helmsman was at the wheel while the deck was being swabbed by a small boy. Ropes were carefully coiled and the Captain was smoking a pipe. The boat was on a blue/green sea with small waves giving the impression of movement. The cake was a sponge and the entire decoration was made from icing sugar and marzipan. It was indeed a masterpiece and a worthy winner.

The year before Pat's triumph it had been Wendy who had won with her Christmas Tree. Somehow Wendy had, after a few failed attempts, succeeded in producing a tree with branches that actually stayed in place. The clever combination of chocolate and hazelnuts was her secret here.

A silver star sparkled on the highest point, and the rest of the tree was adorned with colourful balls, tinsel and charming ornaments of birds, cherubs and cinnamon sticks. Under the spreading branches was a pile of mysterious and exciting-looking packages. This, too, was also a masterpiece.

Wendy had been into creating novelty cakes ever since her mother had taken her as a little girl to a wonderful French Patissérie in London called '*FLORETTE*'. From the amazing array of figures and animals made out of sugar and marzipan, to the variety of cakes for children and adults alike in extraordinary shapes like dragons, fairy castles or a tennis racket and balls, Wendy was fascinated and wanted to do the same.

Her mother had bought a cake for Wendy's 12th Birthday made into a pair of ballet shoes (as at that time Wendy thought she might be a cake making dancer as well!). The cake had arrived in a very smart white shiny box with the word '*Florette*' in fancy writing on the lid. The box was tied with a red, white and blue ribbon attached to a label made of icing with WENDY inscribed on it.

Ballet dancing was forgotten as all Wendy wanted to do was to make cakes. She was very popular with her family and close friends as they plied her with orders for their special occasions.

Wendy always placed her cakes inside her Florette box, but she would insist the box was returned to her.

Wendy married Bryan and together they had two children, now grown up. Although she still made fun cakes for birthdays and special occasions, Wendy never thought to turn her hobby into a business.

Bryan retired and they moved to Minchinghampton. It was here Wendy began to bake again in earnest and the rivalry began with Pat Johnson.

Pat, on the other hand, had taken her talent more seriously and had attended courses in the UK and France. Pat too was thinking and planning hard. She was searching in her mind for a novel and challenging idea, and rather wished she hadn't made the boat last year.

Pat wondered if Wendy was still planning to bring her creation in that somewhat battered old cake box. Honestly, last year she felt sure it was about to fall apart and whatever was inside would be ruined. But Wendy wouldn't be parted from it. She reckoned it was her lucky talisman. Well – it wasn't lucky enough last year!

Pat of course had a tin. Much safer and wiser. Still, if Wendy insisted on using that old box she was not the one to dissuade her.

Marigold Masters sent word that she was looking for originality, beauty, quirkiness and skill for the winning entry. No theme as such. "Just have fun, and see if you can surprise me," was the directive.

The fever pitch was mounting and Jack the Postie was happily collecting bets. Many other ladies and one gentleman also entered the cake icing contest, if only to say they had spoken to the famous Marigold Masters.

Both Pat and Wendy had banned their husbands from their kitchens so in desperation the two cake widowers took themselves off to the pub for a slap-up meal with some necessary liquid libation to accompany it. Somehow, they agreed, all other forms of cooking had been forsaken, as they both admitted hearing cries of frustration and anguish emanating from behind closed doors.

Seemingly just in time, the two ladies emerged covered in flour and icing sugar from their own kitchens. Each had a smile on her face, which is all their husbands wanted to see.

Saturday 8th July arrived at last, and praise be, the sun was shining.

Visitors came from far and wide. The Fête Committee had done a grand job and everyone agreed the stalls were indeed better than ever. In the large tent the jams and chutneys, cakes and biscuits were all laid out on trestle tables ready for the judgment.

Two entries, however, were still hidden from view. One in a rather smart tin, and the other in a distinctly battered looking box.

"Really Wendy, I am surprised you even dared bring your entry in that old thing. Let's hope that what's inside it is intact."

"I hope so too," Wendy nervously replied.

Pat glanced again at the box and noted that Wendy had tried to 'tart' it up with a newer looking ribbon and label, although even that was trailing untidily over the side. You could scarcely read the name of the shop as the writing was becoming quite illegible with age and even one corner of this precious box was missing. Pat couldn't resist the temptation to casually meander round the table to peer into the hole to see what lay inside.

NO! It couldn't be! Pat looked away quickly, then just to make sure she risked one more glance. There, staring back at her from the inside of the box, were two beady eyes, a little pink nose and yes – whiskers!

Pat very nearly shrieked. A *mouse* – inside the precious box. Wendy seemed totally unaware as she chatted to a friend.

The arrival of Marigold Masters provided a welcome distraction. A flamboyant character somewhat large of size, Marigold Masters did not disappoint. A mass of wild auburn hair was somehow stuffed in a rudimentary manner under a large purple hat adorned with orange flowers. Adjusting enormous spectacles of the brightest blue, Marigold proceeded to judge the entries with charm – and speed.

FINALLY...AT LAST... as the crowds pushed forward to see what emerged from the tin and box, a silence fell as collectively breaths were held.

Pat was chosen to reveal her entry first. Still somewhat shaken by what she had just seen, Pat nevertheless rose to the occasion and with care worthy of a craftsman handling the Imperial Crown, she lifted out her creation.

The cake was a church. A replica of their village church with its rather squat steeple. Stained-glass windows adorned the sides and the porch was decorated with seemingly hundreds of white roses.

A bride and groom stood posing for photographs in front of the photographer bent over his camera. Dear little flower girls should have been demurely standing on either side of the loving pair, but one child was sitting in a heap with her head in her hands as a scruffy dog was seen bounding down the path with a posy of flowers in its mouth.

Surrounding guests were laughing and pointing while a woman was hurrying from the church to pick up the distraught attendant.

Marigold Masters loved it. She thought all the details had been beautifully executed and the scene with the dog and the child utterly charming.

The crowd let out a breath. *Pat has done it again*, was the main thought. How could Wendy do better than that?

Now the judge moved closer to Wendy. "I see you too knew the wonderful 'Florette', now sadly long since gone. Is that why you hang on so lovingly to their old box?"

As Marigold was talking she edged round the box to the battered side, and Pat realised from her expression that she too had seen the mouse.

"I think perhaps you had better open this box rather quickly," the famous chef said, "I fear you might be in for a shock. I suggest you undo the ribbon right now and let us see what remains – ahem – I mean what in fact you also have created."

"I am afraid I can not open my box, Miss Masters," said Wendy.

"Why on earth not?" was the astonished response.

"Well, you see," said Wendy rather diffidently, 'the box *is* my cake."

Sally and Shirley Thompson were for once lost for words.

In fact no one spoke at all.

Pat Johnson's mouth had dropped open. She stared at the box and refused to believe it was in reality a cake.

Marigold looked at the cake box again, and wondered at the skill of making such a dilapidated box, particularly with a cheeky mouse peering out of the damaged corner in such a convincing way.

"Surely that is your box and you have just iced it?" Pat cried.

"I thought you might say that," said Wendy as she bent down to retrieve a carrier bag from under the table. Opening the bag she extracted her original box.

A ripple of applause went around the marquee as the onlookers appreciated how clever Wendy had been.

211

"Brilliant!" was the verdict and with that the famous TV personality began to laugh and laugh. Gradually the whole audience joined in, and even Pat had to concede how funny it was that they had all been taken in.

At last the laughter died down and Marigold Masters reached for the microphone. She then declared that in all her career she had never been so cleverly and artistically bamboozled.

The two final entries had fulfilled her criteria for skill, originality and quirkiness. No doubt about it, the ladies were in a class of their own, and as such, the first prize was to be awarded equally between them.

A week later and the village was still talking about the saga of 'The Cake Box that Wasn't'.

As no one had won outright, the Postie gave the money he had collected to the local Scout group.

Lady Wentworth was thrilled with the success of the whole event, plus the kudos of not only being featured in the local press, but appearing on the regional news on TV as well.

Seemingly everyone was happy, especially when Wendy and Pat decided to bury the spatula and go into business together.

NOVELTY CAKES FOR YOUR SPECIAL OCCASION
GUARANTEED TO PLEASE AND SURPRISE EVEN
THE MOST DISCERNING CRITIC.

THE RED BOX

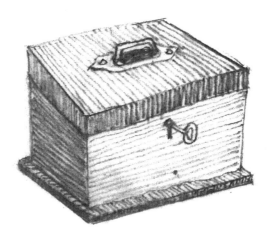

"YOU SOUND AS if you have your life all worked out," said Lizzie during their lunch break. "I wish I was as clear as you about my future. The only thing I know for sure is I want a gap year. I want to travel and explore the world, and I am *hoping* you will come with me."

Amy laughed. "You know I would love to. My major problem is money. I will have to fund myself as I can't expect anything from my parents."

"Mmm," murmured Lizzie. "I know I am extremely lucky and spoilt in that regard. Anyway, how are your savings going? Are you still working in the café on Saturdays?"

"Of course I am, and once exams are over Mrs Sharp said she'll give me more hours. I mean, I *so* want a gap year as well, but maybe just half a year, and I'll work the rest. I am bound and determined to get to uni. My mum is dead against it as she thinks I should work straight away and pay her rent."

"Gosh, how mean!" expostulated Lizzie.

"Well not really, as she does have the twins and then the Afterthought to cope with. She has no help and gets exhausted."

"You really are a kind girl, aren't you? Why don't you try and get work as a model? With your face and figure you should be a shoe-in. If I had your looks that's what I would do."

"I have thought about it, but really I think I would hate it. All that posing – all that make-up – endless waiting around – no, it's not the sort of life I want. You're right though, I do have my life worked out. A gap year which will be half-travelling and half-working, and then university, after which I want to train as a teacher. I have always wanted to teach."

So it seemed, that yes, indeed, Amy did have her life all worked out.

One important consideration was however, ignored.

This was *fate*.

Fate decided to disrupt her well-made plans.

Fate was in danger of taking control of the life of Miss Amy Swithun.

"Well you've certainly made a hit, young lady, with one particular customer. As you know, I don't hold with over-familiarity with customers, but I'm inclined to make an exception in this case as I must admit, he is extremely handsome, and also has very good manners."

"I have no idea who you are talking about, Mrs Sharp," said Amy as she finished carefully slicing a newly baked lemon drizzle cake into equal portions.

"Over there in the corner," Mrs Sharp whispered, "him with the dark hair."

Amy peeped round the door and looked at the man being referred to. She recognised him then. He had been in last week with his girlfriend. At least, she'd assumed she was his girlfriend, as she was all over him: constantly touching his hand and fluttering her eyelashes at him. Amy had served them coffee and whilst he had a home-made brownie, the friend had refused on account of her perfect figure. They had chatted with Amy for a bit, but that was all.

"Well go on then," said Mrs Sharp. "See what he wants."

"Ah, Amy," said the customer with a charming smile. "I want to know what you would recommend for me today with my coffee."

All the while Amy was making suggestions she realised the man was looking at her very carefully. At last he decided, and when she returned with the order he asked, looking straight into her eyes, "Do you have a boyfriend?"

Amy blushed. She was confused. She didn't expect personal questions from customers. She was, in fact, rather annoyed.

"No," she replied rather sharply, "I do not. Although I don't know why you would want to know."

With that she turned away and escaped back to the kitchen. "You can go and take the bill, Mrs Sharp. He gives me the creeps."

Two weeks later, Amy and Lizzie were casually strolling along the high street, arm in arm. Every so often they stopped in front of a shop window and giggled, pretending to chose the most outlandish outfits.

The windows of the travel agency though kept their interest so long that Lizzie said, "C'mon – let's go in."

Inside, they explained they were planning to travel in their gap year. The girl in the agency was so helpful. She also pointed out that Amy could combine travelling with working as an English teacher in various countries like Nepal or Africa.

Armed with brochures and full of excitement, they spilled out into the street and bumped straight into Mr Creepy Customer.

"Amy! What a coincidence. How are you? I'm sorry if I offended you the other day. I didn't mean to pry. Very rude of me. Let me make it up to you. Let me treat you and your friend to a glass of vino in the wine bar over there. Oh – and by the way – my name is Julian. Julian Morrison. I work for the local council for my sins, but I am free now, so how about it?"

Amy looked at Lizzie. Lizzie looked admiringly at Julian.

Rather against her better judgement, Amy accepted.

While Julian was buying a bottle of wine, Lizzie whispered, "Wow Amy. You didn't tell me he was so utterly *gorgeous*. 'Tall, dark and handsome' just doesn't do him justice!"

Lizzie was all over Julian. She chatted away and told him all about their plans. She made little flirtatious remarks, and knocked back her wine a bit too quickly.

Meanwhile Amy sat silently, as all the while Lizzie was doing her 'bit' she was aware that Julian was not so much looking at Lizzie, but at her. She barely touched her wine, and whilst she conceded that Julian indeed did have virtual 'film star' good looks, somehow she felt a little uneasy.

When Amy left the café the following Saturday, Julian emerged from the shadows and made her jump.

"I'm so sorry to have startled you, but you see I really wanted to see you again. May I walk you home, and if possible, might you introduce me to your parents, as I would love to take you out for a drink or a meal sometime, but I would only do so with their permission? You are 17, 18? Well, I am quite a bit older than you. Just two years off 30, so they might not approve."

But approve they did. Especially Amy's mother who was amazed her somewhat studious daughter had attracted such a handsome and obviously intelligent man.

Not that she meant Amy was in any way stupid. No not that. She knew Amy was a clever girl, she was just – well – not worldly. In many ways she was young for her age. Lizzie was far more worldly and grown up than Amy.

Julian put himself out to be helpful and charming. He carried the tea tray back into the kitchen, somehow avoiding the toddler who was careering about pushing his dog on wheels. He charmed the nine-year-old twins, and flattered their mother, while being deferential to Amy's father. How could they not allow this delightful man to take their daughter out to dinner the following week?

During their first dinner date Julian discovered that Amy had never had a serious boyfriend. That was one big tick. Her life had centred around school – work and activities. He was impressed to hear she had ended up as the Deputy Head Girl.

When he heard Amy wanted to go to university and had been offered a place at Exeter, he was less than enthusiastic. This puzzled Amy as Julian had said he had thoroughly enjoyed his university days.

After that, once a week Julian took Amy out, and in between times he telephoned constantly, and left her masses of messages.

Mrs Swithun then invited him to Sunday lunch, but it was a bit chaotic with the younger children. Julian had endeared himself even more to Mrs Swithun by arriving with a bunch of flowers for her. He also noted how helpful Amy was with the younger children.

Amy's father noticed that Julian rarely took his eyes off his eldest daughter, but he had to concede that his manners were impeccable.

Julian explained his parents lived in the North of England and sadly he rarely saw them. He was working in the housing section of the County Council where he had free range in the running of the section, and had good prospects for being promoted in the near future.

Throughout the summer holidays Amy worked not only double the hours at the café but also in the local library. She loved this job as when the library was not busy she was able to read the travel books that so interested her. She also mugged up on environmental issues as she planned to read Environmental Science at Exeter.

When their results came through both she and Lizzie had achieved their grades, and celebrated big-time with all their friends. Everything seemed to be going to plan.

The week after her results had been declared, an enormous bouquet of flowers was delivered to her house with a note attached which read:

"Amy – You are a very clever girl. Come to dinner with me next week and we will celebrate in style. Love Julian."

Amy didn't really know what to think about Julian. She was of course incredibly flattered that such a devastatingly good-looking older man appeared to be so obviously infatuated with her. However, she wondered why he did not date girls nearer his own age? She really did not know what to feel.

He was always utterly charming, and never tried anything untoward. He quite often held her hand, and he would kiss her lightly on the mouth when greeting her or parting from her, but nothing more.

Lizzie, very envious of Amy and wishing it was she who had won his attention, nevertheless kept pumping Amy with questions.

"So do you know any more about his background?" – "Has he introduced you to any of his friends?" – "Do you know any more about his family?" – "Has he tried to get you into bed?" – "What is his agenda?"

Lizzie's last question was the most prescient, if only Amy had known it at the time.

Julian told her he was taking her to a very special restaurant for dinner. It had a Michelin star, no less. He told her to dress up and to look as glamorous as possible.

Amy's father had given her some money as a reward for her good exam results. She and Lizzie went shopping in earnest and bought a simple black dress which showed off

Amy's figure to full advantage. There was enough money left to buy her first ever pair of high-heeled shoes. These were in red. Lizzie offered to lend Amy her red clutch bag to complete the ensemble.

Together they tried different hairstyles, but eventually opted for a loose chignon which rested softly on the nape of Amy's neck, which they thought was more sophisticated than just leaving her long blonde hair loose.

When Amy went down the stairs to wait for Julian, her father emitted a low whistle then said, 'What a beautiful daughter I have." Then he added, "Have fun tonight, my darling, but don't drink too much or you never know what might happen."

Mrs Swithun looked at her daughter admiringly and thought how lucky she was to be going out with such a 'dish'. She then turned round to shout at the twins to hurry up and get out of the bath.

The restaurant was indeed amazing. Dark – discreet and glinting with sparkles from silver ware and crystal glasses reflected in the candle light.

Charming small floral arrangements were on every table which were covered in crisp white tablecloths. Amy had never been in such an establishment.

The black-coated Maître d' smoothly showed them their table. Julian immediately ordered two glasses of Champagne whilst they looked at the menu. Amy was disconcerted as this was all in French.

Julian took charge. He ordered a chilled Vichyssoise soup, followed by grilled Dover sole and tiny tarte tatin for dessert.

"I thought it best not to have too rich a meal," he said, "and this way we can stick to the white grape."

Wow – this is incredibly grown up, Amy thought to herself.

"Did you notice how everyone looked at us as we walked in?" asked Julian.

"No," replied Amy. "Why should they?"

"Their looks were of admiration. You are looking absolutely stunning, without doubt the most beautiful woman here, and together I think we make the most perfect couple."

Amy could scarcely believe he was referring to her. She knew she was blessed with prettiness, and was lucky with her figure – but beauty? Nah!

During the meal Amy tried to find out more about Julian's family. He explained he had been brought up in a small village in Northumberland and both his parents had good jobs, but she couldn't quite understand why he had left home at the age of 18 and as far as she could tell, had barely seen his parents since. He felt a bit bad as he was an only child. However, he told her leaving home was like starting a new life. Fresh and clean. Amy thought that was a slightly weird comment. He enjoyed his job and was obviously comfortably off.

Amy felt her head swimming a bit. The food was delicious but she was not accustomed to eating quite so much. She excused herself to Julian and made her way to the ladies.

A young woman was applying her lipstick as Amy walked in.

"Wow! You are the lucky one. Tell me your secret. How was it you captured the best-looking guy for miles around? I have often seen him," went on the girl, putting her lipstick back in her bag, "but he has never given me a second glance. Looking at you, though," at this the young woman stood back and looked Amy up and down, "pretty though you are, I would say he has a predilection for very young girls. I bet you are a virgin." And with that she swept out of the ladies room.

"At last," said Julian on her return. "I was about to send out a search party."

"Sorry," said Amy, who was somewhat distracted by what the strange girl had just said to her.

The dessert plates were taken away, and then Julian ordered a 'flaming Sambuca' each.

"What on earth is that?" asked Amy.

"Oh how I love the fact that you know so little. I will have so much fun teaching you about all sorts of delights that await you. Our drinks are cocktails made with Sambuca and a coffee bean floats on top which is alight! You have to let the flame die down before you drink it, though, or you will scald your lips. Take tiny sips and savour the experience."

Amy was definitely wafting along. The drink was certainly an extraordinary experience for her.

She tried to focus on the handsome man opposite her who was gazing deeply into her eyes. He took both her hands in his.

"My little darling," he began, "it must by now be obvious that I am totally smitten with you. In my book you are quite perfect. You are bright, intelligent, eager to learn and explore, and have not been spoilt by grubby, pimply youths pawing at you. You are like a wonderful new book with clean pages just waiting to be filled. The fact you also happen to have the looks of a goddess is the icing on the cake. Put yourself in my hands, my darling, and I will continue the creation that God started in you, to turn you into the most perfect human being."

Amy was utterly stunned. What on earth was he talking about?

"Julian – I am not sure I understand what you are saying," she said.

"Put it down to the unusual amount of drink you have had which has succeeded in making you obtuse. I am saying, my dear girl, that you will make the most perfect wife. *My* wife. I am asking you to marry me, and…"

Here Julian reached into his right-hand pocket and produced a small leather box which he put in Amy's hands. "Open it," he instructed.

Amy felt her heart thumping against her chest. She wanted to get up and run. She never expected this. She did not want this. She certainly did not want to get married. She wanted to go on a gap year with Lizzie before going to uni.

She sat in front of Julian in stunned silence, and held the box in trembling fingers.

"Open it," repeated Julian in a surprisingly sharp voice.

She did. Inside was a ring with a small diamond solitaire. She said nothing.

Julian took it out of its box and put it on the fourth finger of her left hand. He then held her hand up so other diners could see. Immediately there was a ripple of applause, the sound of clinking glasses and people calling out their congratulations.

Julian was beaming. Amy was speechless. Champagne was produced 'On the House'.

They left the restaurant to more good wishes, as Julian laughingly explained that his 'Little Darling' was so overcome she was lost for words.

Amy sat in the car trembling. Julian put his arm around her. "I can see I have taken you by surprise," he casually observed. "I will take you home and we will talk tomorrow."

Like a zombie Amy let Julian walk her to her door, where he kissed her lightly on the cheek and said, "Good night, my perfect little bride-to-be. Sleep tight."

The house was in darkness as Amy crept up to her room. Flinging off her fine clothes, she took the ring off her finger and replaced it in the box. Then without bothering to wash she climbed into her bed and wrapped herself in her duvet, and burst into uncontrollable sobs.

"Wake up Amy," her mother's loud voice penetrated her sleepy brain. "Wake up! It's gone ten o'clock and look at you. Your lovely new dress in a heap on the floor, and your make-up smudged all over your face. You obviously didn't wash last night. Quickly now, get yourself clean and tidy then come downstairs. Julian is here, talking to your father."

What? No! What is Julian doing here? He has no right to talk to my Dad. I have not accepted his proposal, and I won't. I don't want to get married yet. I'm too young. I want to live a bit first, and see the world.

All the time these thoughts were whirring around in her head, Amy was cleaning her face, having a shower, and then dressing simply in jeans and a T-shirt. After giving her long fair hair a quick brush, she grabbed the box with the ring in it which she stuffed in a pocket and went down the stairs.

Julian and Amy's father were sitting opposite each other when Amy entered the living room. Both men stood up at once.

"My darling," said Julian, "I have been speaking to your father in the fervent hope that he will bless our marriage plans."

"But Julian –" Amy started to reply, but could get no further as Julian was immediately by her side and put a finger on her lips.

"Your father said the decision to marry must be yours. So here I am, darling –" and astoundingly Julian went down on bended knee – and then he looked at her hand and whispered, "Where's the ring?"

Slowly Amy pulled it out of her pocket. Julian removed the ring and once again placed it on her finger as he said, "Beautiful Amy, will you do me the honour of becoming my wife?"

Mr and Mrs Swithun looked at Amy anxiously. Amy's mother was willing her to say 'yes'. It would be brilliant to think of Amy being married to such an utterly charming and handsome man. A man who would look after her properly, and get her to forget her silly ideas of university and teaching. No money there. It would also help her housekeeping to have one less mouth to feed. Plus it would be one in the eye for Marie who had never stopped crowing ever since her Joyce had married a naval officer.

Mr Swithun looked at his daughter carefully. He saw confusion in her eyes. There was no doubt about it, though, Julian seemed to all extent and purposes to be a good catch. But it was all rather quick. She had after all only just left school. She needed to live a bit as a grown up first before settling down to married life.

Amy felt three pairs of eyes looking at her. She was in such a turmoil. She did of course, like Julian. What was there not to like? Deep down, however, she knew she was not ready for marriage. And marriage usually meant motherhood as well. NO WAY! She was nowhere near wanting her own kids. One day for sure, but right now the Afterthought fulfilled any maternal instinct she might have.

The silence seemed charged with electricity. She had to turn the switch on to flood the room with light – or switch in the other direction and plunge everyone into darkness.

"Julian," she tried – then faltered – then tried again. "Julian, thank you for your proposal. I feel extremely flattered. However, I feel I am too young and inexperienced to consider marrying you or anyone right now. I desperately want to go to university, and before that I want to travel and see some of the world. Eventually I want to train as and become a school teacher. I really do not want to lose these opportunities to enhance my experiences and education."

"Well said," said Amy's father, and then to Julian, "I think my daughter has given you a very fair answer."

Mrs Swithun looked aghast. "Well, you won't have another opportunity like this again, my girl, and I for one think you are a fool to turn Julian down."

Julian – by this time standing once more – seemed unperturbed.

"Darling. You are so right to be cautious. I admire you even more for that. As regards travelling – we will do that together. We will visit lots of countries, and who knows I may have cause to go to the USA soon which would be with you of course. As for being too young. You are mature beyond your years, darling, and don't worry, I will guide your reading matter so you can continue to broaden your knowledge while at the same time learning to be my wonderful, perfect wife."

Mrs Swithun beamed. Mr Swithun looked anxious.

Amy, indeed showing her maturity beyond her years said, "Please will you let me have some time before I give you a definite answer?"

"Of course, my darling. Think it over, and discuss it with your parents. I will return this time next week to hear what you have to say. In the meantime – keep the ring, even if you don't want to wear it."

Then with effusive polite goodbyes to Amy's parents, Julian left the house.

Amy slumped onto the sofa and her father came and sat beside her and put his arm around her.

"There's no doubt Julian is a great charmer – and I'm sure he would give you a good life. But don't feel pushed into this marriage if it is not what you want."

"Well I for one think she'd be an idiot to turn down such an opportunity. Imagine ending up with somebody like Cheryl has with that useless Jason! Not only does she have two kids now but has to work part-time as well, as Jason spends all his time and money playing the machines at the Troubadour. Is that the sort of life you want? Not many what you'd call *eligible* men around here."

And with that, not giving Amy a chance to explain that her chosen path of teaching might introduce her to someone of a different calibre to Jason, Mrs Swithun left the room, slamming the door behind her.

Fate. Do you remember Fate? Fate decided to rear its ugly head.

The following day Lizzie had come round and she and Amy were in deep discussion in her bedroom. Lizzie had gazed admiringly at the ring, and even put it on her own finger to see what it looked like.

"Wow-ee wow wow!" was Lizzie's eloquent reaction. "Gosh – I have to admit I'd be awfully tempted. But really – like you – I think I'd want to *do* a bit more before settling down as a wife for the rest of my life. He obviously loves you, though...' and as her voice trailed off Amy heard her mother calling for her in what sounded like a state of panic.

Amy and Lizzie tumbled down the stairs to find Mrs Swithun almost incoherent as she pointed into the living room whilst saying, "Your Dad – your Dad..."

Mr Swithun was lying on the floor and was obviously unconscious.

Amy hurried over to him and immediately started to try and hold him while calling his name. Lizzie sat Mrs Swithun down on a chair and then sensibly dialled 999 for an ambulance.

As they heard the sounds of the approaching ambulance Mr Swithun slowly opened his eyes and stared at Amy.

He tried to speak, but only the sound of a grunt came out of his mouth.

The paramedics breezed in and swiftly ascertained what had happened.

"Your husband has had a stroke," they told Mrs Swithun, 'and we need to get him to hospital right away."

Amy, her mother and Lizzie sat in a state of shock. Then Lizzie busied herself by making a pot of tea.

The telephone rang, and it was Julian. Somewhat incoherently, Amy explained what had happened.

"I'll be right round," said Julian – and he was – barely 20 minutes later.

Julian immediately took charge. Taking Lizzie with him, he collected the younger children from school. Then he helped Amy prepare a meal for them all.

Lizzie offered to stay with the children whilst Julian drove Amy and her mother to the hospital.

"I'm afraid Mr Swithun has suffered a severe stroke," the doctor told them. "The next few days will be crucial. All being well I think he should make a partial recovery, however I expect the right side of his body might be paralysed. He may regain some use in time, but never completely. His speech should return to something like normal, but not for some time. Be prepared for him to talk nonsense – like asking for a bus when he means a drink, and then getting cross if you don't understand him. That's all part of the recovery process, and great patience is required. You must accept he will no longer be able to work."

Amy cried, and Julian held her tight and promised to look after her and her family.

After a couple of weeks Mr Swithun was allowed home. They made up a bed for him in the lounge so he could watch TV and be part of the family.

Amy was desperately sad to see her father reduced to such a state. She felt he was trying to say something to her, but for the life of her she could never understand him.

The following month Julian appeared with a huge bouquet of white roses for Amy.

"Darling – I need your answer now. Please will you marry me?"

Amy realised he had been so helpful since Mr Swithun's stroke, and she was beginning to rely on him. She had also come to the conclusion that she had to abandon all thoughts of travel and university, as her mother needed her nearby to help.

She looked at Julian for a long time and only saw a handsome young man in front of her, offering her his hand in marriage. She firmly put any disquieting thoughts to the back of her mind. (She was aware that Julian had never actually told her he loved her since the night he had proposed.)

Taking a deep breath she returned Julian's gaze and said, "Yes, Julian. I will marry you, and thank you for being so patient."

"Wonderful," said Julian, and planted a kiss on her lips before giving her a big hug.

Amy thought to herself – *I ought to be feeling thrilled. I ought to be full of excitement and anticipation. I think I ought to be feeling I wanted to go to bed with him.* But Amy felt none of these things.

They told her mother at once, who showed all the excitement Amy lacked. Then they broke the news to Mr Swithun, and once again Amy felt he was trying to tell her something, but all that came out was: "Please – don't tickle the dog. It's not real gold, you see."

"Yes Dad," said Amy, and gently kissed his forehead.

Due to the circumstances Julian said they should forgo a church wedding and large reception and instead get married in a registry office and have a family meal somewhere nice afterwards.

"Well I suppose he's right," thought Amy as she banished all thoughts of a white wedding dress and Lizzie and her siblings being attendants.

Julian's next surprise was to announce he had bought them a house.

Thanks to his position on the housing committee, he had learnt of a small close of eight new houses that had recently been completed and were ready for occupation.

Julian took Amy to see the one he had bought. It was a corner property with similar houses on either side. It was perfectly acceptable and despite herself Amy felt quite excited at the thought of owning her own house, and immediately began to plan how she would decorate it.

There was a through lounge on the left of the front door, and on the right a small office, a cloakroom and then the kitchen.

Upstairs the master bedroom had an en-suite shower room and there were two more smaller bedrooms and a bathroom. Amy imagined having the children to stay sometimes. The kitchen appeared to be well fitted out with cupboards.

Outside the garden which had fences on either side, stretched down about a hundred feet towards open country. There were two trees, one of which was an apple; otherwise, as Julian put it, the garden was a blank canvas.

"Do you like the house, darling?" Julian asked.

"Yes. It's very nice. We'll have fun decorating it, won't we?"

Then Julian dropped a bombshell.

"It *is* decorated," he said.

"But it's all white. Everywhere. Surely we can have a bit of colour – or some nice wallpaper somewhere? Like in the bedrooms? It's a bit sterile like this."

Amy looked again and realised the white paint was all fresh. Although most of the floors were wood veneer, the kitchen and bathrooms had white vinyl tiles.

"Darling, you are far too young and immature to make decisions like that. Leave it all to me. Trust me. A white house is perfect. I am spending my savings on furnishing it and everything will be delivered next week. You'll love it. You'll see."

———————————

Before Amy could give Julian's prophetic words a chance, they had to get married.

Looking at herself in the long mirror, Amy thought she looked liked a frightened waif.

She wore a simple dress in an oatmeal colour with beige shoes and bag.

Her fair hair was tied back with a bow, also in beige. In her hair Lizzie had fixed a tiny pink rosebud and a sprig of white heather, for luck.

As she stood before her father, he reached out and held her hands. He managed to say – "Boot-ful girl. Take care," as tears welled in his eyes.

Before she knew it she was Mrs Julian Morris.

"We'll take a proper honeymoon later," Julian promised, "somewhere wild and exotic. But for now I have booked a room for the night in the Valiant Hart hotel."

For once Lizzie wasn't brimming over with enthusiasm.

"What is it with this guy?" she asked. "First no proper wedding, then secondly no proper honeymoon, and thirdly he buys and furnishes your house with no input from you at all. Also, you haven't done it yet, have you?"

"No," Julian said he had always wanted to marry a virgin. He wants everything to be fresh and new – including me."

During the family dinner in the Valiant Hart restaurant, Amy tried to smother her nerves by drinking a bit too much red wine.

As she lay on the bed in the Bridal suite, she tried to control the swirling of her head and the nausea in her stomach.

Julian emerged from the bathroom stark naked.

Amy averted her eyes.

With no preamble, he pulled back the covers, removed her nightdress and clambered on top of her.

Of course Amy knew what was happening, but what she hadn't expected was that not only did he hurt her – quite a lot, as he was none too gentle – but there wasn't a word of endearment before, during or afterwards. In fact, as soon as Julian was satisfied, he rolled off her and told her to go and have a wash. By the time she was back in the bedroom he was asleep.

Their house was number 5 Maryport Close. Number 4 appeared to be occupied by a working couple with no children. Number 6 was still awaiting its new occupants.

Julian had brought her to the house after their hotel breakfast. Her suitcases were in the hall, and in the kitchen was a mass of boxes containing kitchen china, glass, pots and pans, etc., all waiting to be unpacked.

"So now, I am off to the office. You have plenty to do to keep you busy. Let's see how you get on sorting everything out and putting it all away. I have arranged for an order from the supermarket to be delivered, so you can chose what you want to cook for our first meal."

With that he kissed her lightly on the cheek, and left her alone.

Amy sat on the stairs and surveyed her new home.

Furniture for the reception room had been delivered. All white.

She went into the kitchen and opened all the empty cupboards and wondered where on earth she would put everything.

Amy took out her mobile and rang her mother. As she spoke she began to cry. This wasn't how she had ever imagined the first day of her married life.

"Pull yourself together, Amy," said her mother rather sharply. 'You are a married woman now. Do as he says and put everything away so when he gets home the house will be neat and organised."

Amy decided to call Lizzie, who immediately said she would come round and help.

When she opened the door to her friend she found Lizzie standing there with a bunch of yellow roses and blue cornflowers. In her other hand she produced with a flourish a bottle of red wine.

With Lizzie's help they sorted out the kitchenware. The food order came and they made cheese sandwiches as they tackled the red wine. The flowers gave a welcome touch of colour on the white painted table.

"Oh Amy," said Lizzie, none too helpfully, "I do hope you haven't made a mistake. He's a bit weird with this mania for white, and everything, even his wife, being new and fresh. How was last night by the way?"

"Not much fun," said Amy. "Jolly painful actually."

"Well, I hope he was kind and loving to you afterwards. I remember my first time with my old boyfriend Tom, and it was only made bearable by him being so kind and understanding."

Amy couldn't bring herself to admit that Julian had simply fallen asleep.

"How are your plans getting on?" Amy changed the subject.

Lizzie was full of it. First she and three others were going inter-railing all over Europe for six weeks. After after a spell back at home, the *big* adventure. First they were off to Nepal where they were going to work as volunteers building a new school before joining a group to go trekking in the Himalayas.

Amy was filled with envy, and wondered how she had, against all her instincts, ended up as a married woman at the age of 18.

Time was passing quickly and helped by the wine, both Amy and Lizzie were thoroughly enjoying themselves, chatting and laughing as in times of old. Neither of them heard Julian coming in.

"What on earth is going on here?" he asked in the voice of a head master. "Nice though it is to see you, Lizzie, I must ask you to leave now, and please do not come round again unless I invite you."

"Julian," expostulated Amy, "Lizzie is my oldest and best friend. I intend to see her whenever I want."

"My dear girl," said Julian, "you will be far too busy. Now, what is this? Red wine? You have no business to be spending the day drinking wine when you have the house to organise. No – I must ask you to leave now Lizzie," then looking at the cheerful flowers on the table, "I will be the one to give my wife flowers, so you may take these with you." So saying, he removed the flowers from the jug they were in and unceremoniously pushed Lizzie out of the door.

Amy burst into tears, and put her head in her hands whilst sitting at the table.

"Now, now darling," Julian was using his softer voice, "we are married now and life is you and me. You have gone up in the world. You are now a wife. *My* wife. So dry your tears and show me what you have planned for dinner."

Not only had Amy totally forgotten about dinner, she incurred Julian's anger a second time when he saw the plates and glasses she and Lizzie had used still unwashed in the kitchen sink.

"When I come home," he explained, "I don't expect to see so much as a teaspoon not in its right place. Now come here. Don't worry there is a lot to learn about being a wife and I forget how young you are. Just think about what you have learned today and I will help, as it is only your first day, with the meal."

That night there was a repetition of the night before. Julian made some strange noises, but for Amy, she just lay there, biting her lip to stop herself from crying out, and trying to control the tears that were escaping from her eyes. This was her first night in her new home.

The following day Amy stayed in the house checking everything was in its place. There was a cupboard for the Hoover and household products which was convenient. A man came to plumb in the dishwasher and washing machine and kindly showed her how to work them.

"Are you all right, Mrs Morris?" he asked. "If you don't mind my saying, you look a bit nervous. I guess you are about the same age as my daughter – 18, is that right? Quite young to be married, aren't you?"

Amy tried to be non-committal and to act like a responsible married woman.

"I am perfectly fine, thank you," she said, "and please leave the bill, and my husband will pay it."

The plumber gave Amy a strange look, scratched his head, said nothing more and left.

When Julian came back to the house that night he had something in a carrier bag which he plonked on the kitchen table.

"There – you said you wanted some colour. Open it up and see."

Out of the bag Amy removed a box. It was about half the size of a shoe box, but the same depth. It was a wooden box and its colour was bright pillar-box red, with black borders.

"What is it for?" asked Amy.

"This, my little darling, is your learning box. Every time you make a mistake – forget something or do something wrong – I shall write it down from this note pad here, and put it in the box. At the end of the week I will examine the contents of the box. If there are more than ten misdemeanours I'm afraid that will mean a punishment. However, if you have succeeded in learning your lessons well, the relevant pieces of paper will be removed and you in turn will be rewarded. So now – I will write down:

Dirty dishes in the sink
No dinner prepared
Entertaining without my permission
Leaving your coat over the bannisters."

Amy was aghast.

"I don't understand why you are doing this, Julian. I had to go and see my dad today, so I confess I forgot to hang up my coat in the cupboard. But it's not a *crime*."

"It is, in my book," said Julian. "I chose you, as I intend to make you into my perfect wife. Soon I will need your help in entertaining some very important people. It is imperative you make a good impression. To this end I have bought you some books I want you to read in order that you can talk intelligently."

So saying, Julian placed three books on the kitchen table. One was about politics in Britain during the last 100 years. One contained potted biographies of famous people up to the present day. The third contained a brief description of every country in the world, including their demography, politics, population and language.

Amy was a clever girl and in actual fact she thought the books looked interesting, but Julian spoilt her glimmer of enjoyment by saying he would randomly test her on all three books at the end of every week.

Lizzie rang to say goodbye, as she was off on her travels.

"I'll email you whenever I can," she said. Bubbling over with excitement as she was, she still became aware that her friend was sounding very downbeat. "Are you OK, Amy?" she asked.

Amy told her about the red box and the books.

"Oh my goodness," said Lizzie "I can't believe it. He seemed such a super guy, and yet, if I'm honest, I did begin to feel there was something a bit strange about him. Oh I do wish I wasn't leaving tomorrow. Please take care. Talk to your mum, why don't you?"

Imagining Lizzie and her friends excitedly boarding Eurostar at the start of their adventures, Amy visited her parents. First she tried to talk to her mother.

"You silly girl. He is just trying to educate you. He said he'd do that, didn't he? I reckon you are very lucky to be married to such a thoughtful young man. Now stop complaining and do as he asks."

Amy looked at her father. He returned her gaze and tried to speak. "He's not...he isn't... Happy – happy – go, go, go."

Amy could see he was becoming distressed, so she gave him a quick kiss and left.

Hurrying back to her house, Amy wondered what to prepare for supper. She had never been much of a cook. She helped her mum of course, but she found thinking of a new meal every night somewhat daunting. She reckoned she could manage 'spag Bol" and thought all the ingredients were there.

As she was softening the onions she heard a knock on the door, and upon opening it she was confronted with a woman of about 30, with a lovely smile, wearing a medley of delightfully colourful clothes, who said, "Hello – my name is Mena. I and my husband, plus our two kids, have just moved in next door. I wanted to introduce myself and to say *when* we are settled, we would be delighted to entertain you and your husband for drinks one evening."

"That's so sweet of you," Amy replied, "but as we are here first – just! – we should be inviting you."

"Are you cooking onions?" asked Mena.

"Heavens. I forgot. Oh, please don't let them be burnt – Julian will be furious."

They both dashed into the kitchen and luckily the onions were saved.

Mena was looking round the kitchen, which was spotless. Amy washed up every knife or spoon as she used them.

"My, my – you are a tidy cook. You should see my kitchen. Mess all over the place!"

"I have to be very tidy. My husband insists on everything being clean and in its place."

"Really?" said Mena. "I saw him leaving this morning and he sure is a handsome chap."

"Yes he is," Amy quietly replied.

"Well Amy, I'll leave you to get on. I must get back to do some of my own sorting and tidying while Suki and Nelson are at school."

"How old are your children?" Amy asked.

"Suki is eight and Nelson – named after Mandela, of course – is nearly seven. My husband is called Obi and he is a solicitor. I am a midwife, but have taken some holiday to move in. Very nice to meet you, Amy," and she was gone.

Over supper Amy told Julian about meeting Mena.

"Yes. It's really unfortunate they've moved next door. People like that just lower the whole tone of Maryport Close."

"What on earth do you mean – people like that? Mena is a midwife and Obi is a solicitor. They are educated people and Mena was delightful."

"I mean, my dear ignorant wife, that people like them – coloured people from Africa, or somewhere – do not fit in with our society. I do not want you to have anything to do with them, and we will certainly not be going round to their house or inviting them to ours. Now – let's see how you are getting on with those books. And are my shirts ironed? No – why not? Oh dear – another misdemeanour to be placed in the red box."

That night Amy silently cried herself to sleep. She could hardly believe what was happening to her. She had failed her test on the books, even though she had read and enjoyed the biographies on Livingstone and Mussolini, as Julian's questions referred to pieces she had not yet read.

Her punishment was to stay in the house, and not visit her parents, even though she was wanted to help with the younger children.

The following day was sunny if windy so she decided to take the washing out into the garden to hang up on the line. As she struggled with a sheet, the wind took hold and it escaped from Amy's hands and flew over the fence into Mena's garden. There was nothing else to do. She had to go round to the next door house to ask for its return.

What a contrast Mena and Obi's house was to theirs, even though the layout was similar.

The house burst with colour. Fabulously patterned rugs covered the wooden floors, and joyful curtains in reds, yellows and greens hung in the living room. A few pictures were on the walls, with more stacked and ready to be found a place. The feel of Africa pulsated through the house. Several carvings of animals were already displayed on shelves, and one wall was hung with a tapestry made of hundreds of small pieces of material which somehow conjured up the sun, blue sky and mountains.

Amy stood stock still and just looked.

"It's wonderful – your house. It's so *alive*. It really feels like a home, and you have only just moved in."

"I'm glad you like it," said Mena. "If you like colour maybe you could introduce a little of it into your house? Not quite as bright and bold as us Africans, but a little gentle colour here and there might make quite a difference?"

"You are right, Mena, but the problem is that Julian doesn't like colour. He insists that everything in the house that can be white, is white. White and pure and perfect he calls it."

"That's very unusual," said Mena. "Did you know this about him before you married him?"

"No I didn't. In fact I didn't know him very well at all."

Amy looked at Mena and was conscious of the other woman looking at her with deep concern in her eyes. There was warmth there, and Amy suddenly felt here was someone she could talk to.

"The thing is," she faltered slightly, "I tried to refuse as I had only just left school, and was planning on travelling with my friend before going on to university. I had been offered a place at Exeter. Sadly my father had a sudden stroke and the burden on my mother with three younger children was too much. She told me it would help her out by having me, as it were, 'off her hands'. Plus Julian was so helpful at the time, and we were all upset, so I sort of fell into it."

"I thought you were very young," said Mena.

Suddenly, looking at her watch, Amy panicked.

"Mena, please can I retrieve my sheet which blew into your garden? I will have to wash it again, and that will be another sin to be posted inside the red box."

As Mena was helping Amy disentangle the sheet from a bush in her garden she said, "I had noticed that red box. At least there is no way one can fail to notice it, and I was wondering what possessed him to have that one object in colour?"

"It's my punishment box. If I have ten misdemeanours a week, I am punished."

"My dear girl. You certainly are in an unusual and not very pleasant situation. Now listen – we are just next door. Feel free to call on me whenever you want, even it it's only for a quick chat."

"Thank you Mena. I will. Now I must hurry back."

Despite re-washing the sheet and having a meal ready in a spick and span kitchen, when Julian arrived home he was in a furious temper.

"I told you I do *not* want you mixing with those black people next door, and the first thing you do is to disobey my orders. Just your bad luck I saw you as I was taking potential clients round the last remaining house in the Close. That will count as four misdemeanours, and your punishment is to stay inside the house for the next four days, and to hand over your mobile phone."

This time Amy cried out loud.

"Why did you marry me? Why did you want to so much and insist I was the one for you? If all you wanted was someone to do your bidding you could have paid someone. You only pretended to love me. I know now that you never really did. I am doing my best to please you, and you are never satisfied. I don't want to stay married to you. I want to go home."

Julian's face contorted with rage. He felt like striking out at this silly, unappreciative child.

For goodness sake, he had set her up in a beautiful house and was doing his best to improve her mind and all he got was disobedience and abuse.

However, Julian also knew he must calm her down. Perhaps he was pushing her too quickly. She was very young, after all. His plans seemed to be going so well, and she must not be allowed to spoil them. He would let her go eventually – but not yet. After he had won. Still he can't let her get away with this flagrant disobedience, so he marched over to the red box and added the notes confirming her sins. To Amy he said:

"Go upstairs and calm yourself down. There is no way you can go back to your parents as you well know. This

is your home now and here you will stay until... that is...
anyway, you stay here."

To Amy's surprise when she had calmed herself and
tidied up she found Julian had laid the table and was
cooking some steaks, whilst on the table was an open
bottle of wine.

"Darling girl – I'm so sorry. I was a bit harsh. Put it
down to tiredness. Work has been very pressured lately.
Anyway, sit down and have a glass of wine. I have a
surprise for you."

Amy was still not used to drinking very much, so she
sipped the wine tentatively and wondered what Julian's
surprise could be.

It turned out it really *was* a surprise. A nice one at that.

"I am taking you to Paris next week for a couple of
nights."

"Paris? – Oh, that is exciting! I have never been and
Lizzie has sent me some postcards saying it is wonderful."

"Of course it is wonderful, dear girl. One of the most
beautiful cities in the world."

They travelled on the Eurostar and stayed in a tiny
hotel on the Île de la Cité. Amy was entranced and turned
into an excited child.

"Can we go up the Eiffel Tower? Can we go on a boat
on the Seine? Can we go to Montmartre?"

Julian of course had his plans.

First stop was the Louvre. Amy was a tad disappointed
at the 'Mona Lisa'. So small, although she was sure the
woman's eyes did follow her.

After a brief lunch they visited the huge art gallery
called the Musée d'Orsay which used to be a railway
station. It was of course magnificent and there was a good
deal Amy loved, but she was feeling quite tired and longed

to be outside, in the streets of Paris. She wanted to soak up the atmosphere.

Their hotel was close to the Notre-Dame cathedral which was such a sad spectacle after the dreadful fire in 2019, but at least some of it remained.

Amy hoped they might finish the day in a glamorous and romantic restaurant. Instead Julian opted for a somewhat characterless modern bistro with no atmosphere at all.

Over dinner Julian quizzed her on what famous paintings and statues they had seen.

The following day he took her to the Rodin museum. Again lovely – but oh how Amy yearned to walk by the Seine on the Left Bank, looking at all the intriguing book stalls.

Julian allowed her a quick trip to the Sacré Cœur, but no meandering in the Place Pigalle, despite the fact that the young artists were clamouring to draw such a pretty young girl.

It was exhausting and tantalising not be able to 'savour' Paris more, but it was better than not having gone at all.

Once again Amy's mother was full of praise for Julian's magnanimity.

———————————

It was rapidly business as usual, though, and try as she might Amy incurred Julian's disapproval, resulting in more notes filling up the red box.

Once a week she was permitted to go to the supermarket, and there she bumped into Mena one day.

"Amy! Where have you been? I've been trying to catch you, and also to call your mobile but I could never get through."

Amy explained, first about Paris, and then her punishments which were usually to stay indoors and to read the books Julian had chosen, after her work was finished. As he had confiscated her mobile she couldn't ring as not only did he check the calls she had made, but he also rang throughout the day to make sure she hadn't gone out. She was allowed to call her parents once a day.

"Let's have a quick cup of coffee in the café," Mena suggested. "I confess I am worried about you Amy. I hope he doesn't hurt you? How is he in bed?"

Blushing to her roots Amy confessed that after the first somewhat unsatisfactory attempts Julian had shown no interest in sex.

"He doesn't hurt me physically," she said, "but I can't really make him out. He has this mania about turning me into the perfect wife, and anything I do wrong he treats like a crime. Paris was wonderful in a way, but we didn't exactly have *fun*. He quizzed me the whole time and if I couldn't remember who painted what he was furious."

"Listen," said Mena, "I will get you a mobile and pay for three months. I will put my number in it, and you install your parents' number as well. Keep it somewhere safe as you might need it. Will he allow you to visit us?"

Amy looked embarrassed, "I'm so sorry – but he has forbidden it."

"I thought as much. It's because we're black, isn't it? Well, it doesn't stop you and I bumping into each other by mistake, does it? We can be secret friends if you would like?"

"I would like that very much," said Amy. 'My mother will not hear a word against Julian. I think my father was worried and that might have brought on his stroke. I would love you to be a friend with me, Mena. It will be such a comfort. I have missed talking to Lizzie so much."

For the next couple of months Amy managed to keep Julian reasonably happy. She was becoming a more confident cook, and her ironing had improved.

Julian continued to provide her with mind-improving books which she actually enjoyed. She hated to think her brain might stagnate.

Mena managed to 'bump into her' reasonably regularly and Amy gratefully received her new phone and hid it in a sock in the back of her drawer.

Julian came home early one day, and told Amy he had something important to tell her.

He poured her a glass of wine and they both sat down at the kitchen table.

Julian then explained that there was an American magazine called *Mr & Mrs*. It was hugely popular in the States and there was even a TV show of the same name.

Every two years a competition was held, world wide, to find the perfect couple. The *perfect* 'Mr and Mrs'. The prize was absolutely huge. This year the lucky winners would have the full use of a fabulous mansion in California plus a car for two years. During this time there would be dinners with celebrities and film stars. They would have a holiday in the Caribbean and another in Aspen, Colorado. As if this wasn't enough, the lucky couple would be offered the chance to audition for the movies and to make their life in the United States.

Julian, with his devastating looks, had always imagined himself in films. Although he had never actually visited the States, he was sure he would end up there one day. The prize could be his for the taking, bar one problem. There was no 'Mrs' in his life.

The competition rules stated that the couple should not have had any other relationships. They must be properly married and living the life of a perfect husband and wife.

Behind all the glamour and temptations of the prizes was the fact that the *Mr & Mrs* organisation was in fact a deeply religious cult.

It had been founded by a husband and wife who had been childhood sweethearts. Their aim was to bring back the purity of marriage not only to the USA but in fact to the whole world.

They despised people who were 'partners' instead of being married. They also despised and despaired of 'same-sex marriages'. Our Lord would never have condoned these sinful arrangements, they wrote in their magazines and broadcast on their TV shows.

Heterosexual marriages were the only *true* marriages, according to the Scriptures.

Despite the huge lesbian and gay communities who abhorred every word written in the *Mr & Mrs* magazines, there was amongst the Bible Belt in the US and similar areas in other parts of the world a huge following that agreed with the sentiments expressed. These people gladly donated to the 'Mr & Mrs' Charitable Fund which helped promote their thesis world wide.

"So you see, my perfect little wife, I reckon you and I, in our perfect home with our perfect looks, have a very good chance of winning this competition. We do, though, have to be assessed by an American couple who are over here now. They have to chose three couples out of about ten to fly to the States for the final judgement."

"Golly," said Amy, "I don't think I have a hope in hell of ever being considered 'Perfect Wife" material. Also, I really do not want to live in America."

"Well you see, as you are my wife, you must do as I want. The judges are coming to dinner here quite soon. Between now and then we will practise your cooking, and your table manners. I will teach you how to be the perfect hostess. We will start right away, and I hope there won't be too many misdemeanours to put in the red box. To win this prize would be the fulfilment of all my dreams. I know my destiny lies in the US of A."

The next day, after Julian had left for work, Amy retrieved her mobile and rang Mena who was astounded at what Amy had told her, and said she would Google '*Mr & Mrs*' to try and find out more about the organisation.

"What do you want to do, Amy?" Mena asked. "Do you want to stay in this marriage?"

"I would dearly love to escape, Mena, but I have nowhere to go, and I cannot support myself yet."

"What time does Julian get home as a rule?"

"Normally by six, except on Wednesdays when quite often he stays out to dinner, or even later."

"What does he do then?"

"No idea. He just says it is the night for a work gathering."

"How is your father doing?" Mena's next question quite surprised her.

"Actually, amazingly well. He has recovered his powers of speech, although the right side of his body still doesn't work very well."

"Can you confide in him?" Mena enquired.

"I suppose I could, but I would hate to stress him out."

"Well," said Mena, "a plan is hatching in my head. I need to chat with Obi, and then let's meet up in the supermarket in a couple of days. In the meantime, visit your parents and try gently to put your dad in the picture."

They met up two days later and while they were sitting in the coffee shop of the supermarket Amy listened to Mena. She was so engrossed that unluckily she was unaware the Julian had also entered the store to buy more ingredients for the practice dinner. Pushing his trolley full of his purchases Julian looked up and saw, to his fury, his wife and that black woman sitting and talking, just as if they were the world's best friends.

Julian stormed over to the café and roughly grabbed Amy by the arm as he said, "*You* are coming home with me now." To Mena he said, "I would prefer you not to meet up with my wife. She needs to concentrate on more serious matters than just having a mindless gossip."

Frogmarched out of the store, Amy felt many pairs of eyes looking at her curiously.

"Leave me alone Julian," she said, as she tried to wrestle free from his grip, "people will think I've been caught shoplifting."

Julian said nothing until they were back in the house.

"Sit down," he commanded, "and listen. It is a burning ambition of mine to live in America and what better way to start than living in a large house in California, courtesy of the *Mr & Mrs* organisation. I chose you very carefully to be my wife, as you were unspoilt and very pretty. We could have a wonderful life there. We just have to convince the judges that we are indeed a perfect couple, and that we would be prepared to embrace their doctrines and rules of life. If we win, and I feel in my bones we can, and if after the two years you wish to return to the UK, I will consider it. Now – let's get going with the dinner, and make sure you know how to serve the drinks properly. As for that woman you were talking to – what's her name?"

"Her name is Mena, short for Philomena."

"Whatever... By now you know my feelings about them and you have decided deliberately to disobey me. So, four notes into the red box, and I fear this week that will definitely be more than ten."

Like a zombie Amy went through the ritual of preparing the meal, which she had got taped by this time.

Julian quizzed her about the latest books and also more questions about Paris. Amy did well.

He then told her she was to smile more, and do her best to overwhelm the judges with her British charm and manners.

By the end of the week her misdemeanours had mounted to eleven. Her punishment was to re-wash all Julian's shirts and iron them, plus to clean all his shoes, before weeding the garden. She was forbidden to leave the house. Julian said he would do the shopping.

"It's tomorrow!" Julian burst into the kitchen, his face flushed with excitement. "Mr and Mrs O'Leary are coming tomorrow, Friday as ever is. I have taken the day off work so I will buy everything we need. You clean the house and make sure there is not a speck of dust or a dead fly anywhere."

As soon as he had left the house Amy found her hidden mobile and rang Mena.

"What a coincidence," said Mena, "I was literally on the point of ringing you as I noticed Julian leaving. I have some rather startling news for you."

"Well so have I," said Amy, "but you go first."

"Firstly, I have been investigating the *Mr & Mrs* organisation. Primarily it is a religious cult. You are too young to remember, but years ago there was a similar cult called the Moonies. They too were full of 'good works' but they enticed young people to join them, and then brainwashed them in such a way that many of these young persons never returned to their families. If you did indeed win this competition and went to the States to live, you would be required to be ambassadors for their cult, and to entice as many people as possible to join up and once they had, they would find it extremely hard ever to leave again. The same would happen to you as very cleverly they would ensnare you with lots of legal gobbledegook which could tie you up for life. As far as I could see, no winners had actually broken into the Hollywood film world."

"Heavens!" said Amy. "What I can't understand is if you have found that out quite easily, why hasn't Julian?"

"I think he feels he is clever enough, and handsome enough, to avoid the pitfalls. Anyway, this next bit of news is *far* more significant, and you need to be sitting down before I tell you."

Amy perched on the end of her bed and wondered what on earth could be more startling than the news she had just heard.

"It seems, my dear girl, your husband has married you under false pretences."

"What do you mean? Other than the fact that I know all his protestations of love were lies."

"Not just that," said Mena. "Listen. Last night Obi had dinner with a client in town. As they left the restaurant and were walking towards the car park, they passed the pub called the Bullingdon Arms, which was on the other side of the road. At that moment the pub door opened and a couple came out, laughing and probably a bit tipsy. They walked in the same direction as Obi and his client for a bit, when suddenly they stopped, and there in the street, they kissed and embraced each other."

"Goodness," said Amy, "that is quite bold, but it is not illegal, is it?"

"No, it is not illegal, unless one of them is pretending he is the perfect husband to a perfect wife."

For a moment Amy said nothing, then she asked in a whisper, "Are you telling me he saw Julian? I was beginning to wonder if there was a secret girlfriend he was seeing on Wednesdays."

"I am, my dear, except – it wasn't his girlfriend he was kissing, but his *boyfriend*! Apparently that pub is *the* meeting place for Lesbians and Gays to find partners."

Poor little Amy. Her head was reeling with all the information she had just heard. To Mena she said, "Though I am totally shocked about Julian, in some ways I am not surprised. It explains quite a lot about his behaviour. But what on earth am I meant to do now? My news for you was that the American couple are coming to judge us tomorrow. Also if by any freakish chance we did win, I could never go to the States with him now. Actually the more I think about what he has done to me, the angrier I am becoming."

"That's the spirit. For what he has done to you he deserves to be punished, big time, and we will make sure he is. Obi says you have an excellent chance of having your marriage annulled. He has married you under false pretences. You need to be prepared to return to your parents, and it is not too late to take up your place at uni. In the meantime, I could get you a job in our practice as a receptionist as our usual lady has suddenly announced she was leaving and we need someone intelligent in charge. So – now that is sorted – here is my plan…"

Amy listened intently, then fearing Julian would return soon, ended the conversation and replaced her mobile in the sock.

"Mr and Mrs O'Leary, how very nice to meet you."

Julian, in the words of the song from *My Fair Lady*, was 'oozing charm from every pore'.

"This is my wife, Amy."

"Please come in," said Amy smilingly. "May I take your coats? Do come through to our living room. May I get you something to drink – a cocktail, or some wine perhaps?"

"Oh my – how delightful," said the American lady as she sat down on a white upholstered armchair, and gazed around her at the white walls hung with a few country scenes painted in pastels. She noted with approval that the Holy Bible had a prominent position amongst the interesting collection of books on the shelves.

(Julian had thought it was rather a masterstroke to find a Bible which he inserted on the shelves along with the library books.)

"A glass of white wine, please dear," Mrs O'Leary said. 'Your home is so – pristine. It must be hard work to keep it so."

"Oh I don't mind," smiled Amy. "Keeping the house clean or the garden tidy is all part of God's criteria for a wife, I always think. When I married Julian –" and with this Amy glanced over to where Julian was standing and talking to Mr O'Leary, and she gave him a beaming smile – "I quickly put behind me all thoughts of backpacking round the world, or going to university. Being the best housekeeper and wife that I can be is all that I ask in life, until –" and this time she looked coyly at Julian, who in turn was staring at her with a look of total surprise – "until we should be lucky enough to hear the pitter-patter of tiny feet in our home."

Then with a quick 'Excuse me', as if covering her embarrassment, Amy dashed into the kitchen to fetch the wine.

Dinner had been set up at the garden end of the sitting room. The table looked very pretty, with tall glass candlesticks holding white candles, and an arrangement of white roses.

Everything went without a hitch. The food was excellent. Amy was demure, but was not shy of voicing her opinion if she was asked. She spoke enthusiastically of the wonderful art they had seen in Paris, and the interesting biographies she had read.

For his part Julian praised Amy for so quickly adapting to married life, straight from school. He couldn't wish for a better wife.

It was clear the two of them had made an excellent impression on the judges.

"I guess I shouldn't say this," said Mrs O'Leary, "but I am sure my husband will agree with me when I say I would think you two stand a very good chance of winning this competition."

Julian was thrilled to hear this.

"That is most encouraging," he said. "Both my wife and I would dearly love the chance to live in your beautiful country and to help promote the *Mr and Mrs* message all over the world."

Smiles all round and graceful thanks between them, but as Amy was handing the coat to the American lady in the hall, she inadvertently lost her balance and knocked the red box onto the floor.

"So silly of me," said Amy, "I do apologise," and she made quite a show of picking up the box and carefully returning it to its place.

Then Mr O'Leary asked, "I have one question for you. I am curious to know, in this predominantly white house, why you have this red box in your hall?"

"I told you to put that away," hissed Julian, but Amy serenely replied:

"Oh, that. Well you see, this red box is my punishment box. You see, as I am still very young I have a huge amount to learn. Every time I make a mistake, which I confess does happen a great deal, Julian writes it down and puts the note in the box. He will then give me a suitable punishment – that of course I deserve."

Amy looked at the shocked expressions on the faces of the O'Learys before she went on.

"However, I must confess," and in a stage-whisper she continued, "Julian doesn't know this yet. I put in one of my own today. I actually found a misdemeanour that my husband committed, rare though that is, I can tell you, so just for a bit of fun, I wrote it down and put it in the box. Would you like to see it?"

Amy took the box and put it in the astonished hands of Mr O'Leary.

Julian, desperately trying to treat all this as a joke, tried to snatch the box back, but the American said, "Well Julian, let's see what terrible misdeed your little lady has accused you of."

Still smiling, Mr O'Leary opened the box and took out the only piece of paper inside. He read it in silence. His wife prompted him – "Go on, dear, what does it say?"

Mr O'Leary looked at Julian for a full, tense minute and then he read:

"Julian

Your misdemeanour this week – and presumably for all the weeks we have been married – is that you were seen this Wednesday evening outside the Bullingdon Arms kissing your lover, your boy friend.

Your punishment is that I am suing you for marrying me under false pretences and I am leaving you now.

Amy."

And with that Amy opened the front door and walked out into the arms of Mena and the protection of Obi.

Speechless, the couple from the USA managed to get themselves into their waiting car.

Julian was left alone in his white 'house of cards' that had all come tumbling down in one disastrous moment.

His planning and plotting and painstaking preparations had so nearly brought him the perfect prize he so deserved.

Now he had nothing, and Amy, with those dreadful people next door, would be laughing at him.

He looked at the red box and picked it up. Oh, how he regretted ever having had the idea of creating a punishment box.

In a fit of despair he threw it into the living room where it collided with a table and broke in two.

Then Julian sat down on the stairs, put his head in his hands and wept.

———————————

THE LOCKDOWN BOX

"DON'T WORRY, MUM, we will be in touch all the time and now you have your 'smart phone', I can FaceTime you so you will be able to see us and chat to the children."

"That sounds amazing," I said to my daughter. "I am sure it will be almost as good as actually seeing you all in the flesh."

I made up my mind to put a brave face on this new and somewhat unnerving situation we were all finding ourselves in.

How long would it last? Who knows? It is totally unprecedented and somehow I get the impression we are all floundering about in a rough sea, shouting at each other to swim this way or that to avoid the sharks or the rocks, but whichever way one goes, another hazard looms before us.

I counted myself one of the lucky ones. I was quite used to living alone, ever since Gerald had finally succumbed to dementia just on three years before this virus raised its ugly head.

There is a little shop in our village, and several very kind neighbours. I was not worried about myself, and was sure I could cope. Besides I had my darling Tiger Lily for company. I was in a much better situation than many people, and for that I was extremely grateful.

The worst aspect was the thought of not being able to see Lara and the girls. The children are at such a sweet age now – six and eight – and I have established quite a bond with them.

It gives me huge pleasure to have them to stay. We have such fun together. They love to hear stories of my past, and about their mother when she was a little girl.

I have a drawer in the chest in my sitting room and periodically I put in a new game or toy that I have found in a charity shop which they take pleasure in discovering.

Dressing up in old clothes gives them hours of amusement, and sometimes I tell them stories regarding the time I wore that extraordinary hat I once thought was so wonderful, or the dreadful pair of shoes which were excruciatingly uncomfortable but *so* trendy!

Anyway, it is what it is, and at the moment all I can do is make the best of it. Use the time usefully to give the house a really good clean, and sort out some of those cupboards that I have successfully been ignoring for years.

I have to admit to a feeling of satisfactory smugness when I look at my gleaming kitchen, and open any cupboard I like to see the china neatly stacked, bottles and tins, and even all the tiny spice jars in alphabetical order, labels to the front so I can actually see them. That is how I like my kitchen to look. Why can't I keep it like this? I do enjoy cooking, and entertaining. After Gerald had died I found more time on my hands and so took up playing Bridge again. We took turns in each other's houses, but I always enjoyed it when it was my turn, as I would produce what they all called – and I did like it when they did! – "Another sumptuous meal that only Lottie can make!"

Baking had always been a particular love of mine, and I constantly provided the church and local fête with cakes and flapjacks and so on. Annoyingly, my kitchen was always in a state of chaos when I had finished. I remember my mother constantly ticking me off for being an 'untidy cook'. Anyway, my kitchen looked marvellous now and I was determined to keep it that way.

I love my garden, and do what I can. It's so annoying now I am a geriatric 78 year-old, as I find I can do less and less of digging and weeding. I gather I can't even have old Fred to come every other week as before, as no one must come in, just as I am not supposed to go out. Well, I just have to do what I can, and if the weeds grow, so be it.

I have my favourite spot, just under the apple tree, and when the weather is fine I sit there admiring my sweet little garden, and listening to the birds and the bees, before often, I admit, drifting off into a gentle afternoon nap.

Lara was so clever. She organised a huge delivery of food for me just as lockdown started. Masses of ready-prepared frozen dishes for when I can't be bothered, and as many essential items as she thought I would need. She is such a good girl, and I am very lucky to have her. It is only sad she lives over two hours away. Her husband is a renowned vascular surgeon and is often away as he is in much demand as a lecturer at various medical establishments world wide.

After her father died, Lara wanted me to move nearer her. I was tempted, but in the end decided to stay where I was, close to my friends and continue the life I had made for myself, with the book club, church activities, and being a member of a group which organises excursions to various exhibitions, or theatrical performances in places I would never be able to go to on my own. No, I have a life here, and here I want to stay. I didn't reckon on Covid-19 raising its ugly head, though.

But I don't regret staying. This dear little house is my home, and Gerald and I spent many happy years here before that cruel disease took its toll.

My next job I decided was to tackle the large wardrobe in the spare bedroom. Such a useful space it had become over the years. "Where on earth shall I put this?" The answer always seemed to be in the wardrobe in the spare bedroom, and I would deal with it later. Try as I might to ignore it, I had to admit that finally 'later' had well and truly arrived.

It was raining – thankfully, as the garden needed it – so no more excuses. Upstairs I went and opened the doors of the wardrobe. Out came dresses, skirts, coats and jackets that somehow I never wear now.

"Charity pile," I said to myself firmly. "What's this?"

I struggled to release an unwieldy bag and as it pulled free of course I knew it was Gerald's golf bag and clubs. I had stuffed it there so it was out of sight, and not there to remind him he couldn't play any more.

I touched the clubs, and imagined his hands gripping them as he lined himself up for a stupendous shot. Dear Gerald. He loved his golf, although he was never terribly good. It was the life at the golf club that he really enjoyed.

"Charity pile," I said.

Next I found my old record player. Lara told me to throw it away as no one plays actual records any more. She keeps on talking about 'streaming'. What on earth is that? Still I know she manages to listen to music on her mobile telephone which is quite extraordinary. It is as much as I can do to talk on the wretched thing, but I *have* learnt how to ring people, *and* to accept her FaceTime calls. So all in all, I feel pretty *au fait* with mobiles.

I looked at the old machine and it brought back so many memories. How we loved to play and play again and again our favourite numbers. Pat Boone. Bing Crosby. *Darling* Frank Sinatra. And of course Elvis Presley. Great songs with words you could actually hear and had some meaning. I can still sing so many of them even now. Word for word.

I can't quite bring myself to give that away just yet. Who knows... one day it might be a valuable antique.

Before I put it back in the cupboard I saw the box.

"So that's where it is." I had over the years wondered where I had put it, and even once made a cursory look in the wardrobe, but not far enough as it was tucked right at the back and even now, hard to see.

As a box it is not particularly special as it is made out of sturdy cardboard, with a well fitted lid, and holes on either side for ease of carrying. A good size. I would say about 1½ feet all round, and don't ask me in centimetres as I haven't a clue.

I heaved the box out of the wardrobe and managed to carry it downstairs without falling over and breaking my neck. Making myself a small pot of tea, I settled down in my sitting room to discover the contents of the box.

I held in my hand a tiny cloth wristband with my name, Charlotte Deen, just decipherable written on the side. A little pink ribbon tied in a bow was attached to it, and hanging from the ribbon was a note written on a piece of card:

"Lottie's hospital band she wore when having her tonsils out aged 5."

I was transported......

I was sitting on the floor of our sitting room and Mummy, my Aunt, my big sister Emily and even Mrs Packard who helped Mummy in the house were all looking at me in a very strange way. Sort of smiley. Sort of sad, and altogether odd.

"Don't worry Lottie, you wont be there for long, (WHERE?) you will soon be home again."

"Of course you will have a bit of a sore throat, but you will get LOTS of ice cream, lucky you."

"I will come and see you every day," said Mummy, "and the nurses are very kind."

For the life of me I could not understand what they were all talking about. I sort of gathered they were trying to prepare me for something, but for what, I had no idea.

Next day Mummy amazed me by waving at a taxi. We never went anywhere by taxi. We always used a bus, and walked. Anyway – I didn't mind. It was fun in the taxi.

I wondered why Mummy was carrying my very own little pink suitcase. Where was hers?

The taxi stopped in front of a HUGE building. Miles bigger than our house. Then Mummy said, "Let's go into this shop first and I will buy you a present."

Another surprise, and it wasn't even my birthday. What a strange day this was turning out to be.

In the shop were masses of jars filled with lots of different coloured and delicious looking sweeties. Mummy bought me some pear drops. They were white, yellow, orange and red. She also bought me some barley sugar. I couldn't get over this. Were these all mine? I was used to picking two sweeties a day only and everything in the tin was shared with my sister and cousin.

"I will take two colouring books as well, and a small box of crayons," and then Mummy said, "Oh look, there is a torch just like the doctors use. I will buy it for you and you can have your very own, and use it to play doctors with Di-Dee Doll."

Di-Dee Doll was my very favourite. Once Mummy had been away for a very long time, and when she came back, she gave me Di-Dee Doll. I knew that was her name as it was written on the back of her neck. My big sister had read it for me.

Then Mummy took me into this huge building and we went inside a box which moved and when we got out again we looked out of the windows and we were up in the sky and could see the tops of other houses.

Suddenly I was in a very big room full of beds with children in them.

"Why are they all in bed?" I asked Mummy. "It's not bed time yet."

In one corner was a small table with chairs. Mummy and I sat down and she asked a nice lady who was dressed all in white, and had a funny shaped hat on her head which I thought was a paper boat, to please get us some sugar sandwiches. Mummy liked to give me sugar on bread and butter as she said sugar had been so hard to get in the War.

The white lady came back and told me she would show me my bed. It was right by a window and I could see lots of chimneys and roofs.

Mummy undressed me and put me to bed. It was nowhere near my bedtime and I did not like this.

The white lady came back and whispered to Mummy who then said to me, "I must go now. Be a good girl and be brave. I will come and see you tomorrow."

"Do I have to stay here?" I asked.

"Just for a little while," said Mummy.

"But I don't want to. I want to go home."

"Now now darling, the nice nurse will take you out on the balcony and you can wave to me."

Mummy looked very small. The white lady held me very tightly. I waved and I cried.

Once I was back in the bed I took Di-Dee Doll and hid under the bedclothes, shining the light from my torch onto her sweet face.

With a sudden movement, as a stern voice said, "Who have we here?" the sheets were roughly pulled back.

This lady was older, and dark blue and white. She had papers in her hand and she read out "Charlotte Deen. Tonsillitis. Operation tomorrow morning. Now – what's this?" she picked up my torch. "Where did you find this, you naughty girl? This is a doctor's torch and you have no business taking it."

I tried to cling on to it. "It's mine," I cried. "My mummy gave it to me."

"Lying as well," said the Blue and White One. "We do not tolerate lies or thieves here. Now hand it over."

Off she went with my special torch. I hugged Di-Dee Doll and cried myself to sleep.

———————

How strange that I should remember that all so clearly. It was the first time in my life I had been unjustly accused. However, the rest of my time in hospital obviously passed without any other major drama and once home and recovered, I was soon back to my mischievous childish ways.

Mummy had mentioned the War. Of course I knew about the War as we had all very nearly died in a bombing raid. I scrabbled about in the box as I knew that somewhere my mother had saved a memento. Ah yes, here it was. A piece of charred, black heavy metal. Part of the flying bomb that only missed us by pure good luck.

———————

We had a house in London. Mostly it was all right living there. In the sky you could see huge great grey things that Mummy said, or so I thought, were 'Garage Balloons'. How funny to think that people keep their cars up there. How do they get them inside? I spent quite a few minutes pondering on this.

I liked going for walks in the park. There were lots of brave soldiers and sailors everywhere, and even some poor wounded people. Mummy was running across the road one day pushing me in my pram (it was a long walk to the park), when one of the wheels came off. I was flung all over the place but luckily didn't quite fall out. A kind soldier found the wheel and put it back on again. I always liked soldiers.

One night I was in my bed when the horrid sirens started. I hated those. They were scary. Mummy rushed in and picked me up – I think I was nearly four – and took me downstairs. My aunt, sister and cousin were already there. We sat on chairs in a line close to the stair case.

"I think we had better go to the shelter," said Mummy, but then she said, "Shh." We were all quiet and we heard the noise of an aeroplane up in the sky. Suddenly we couldn't hear it any more. Mummy said, "Please God, help us," and then there was the biggest ever noise and I screamed as loudly as I could. Mummy held me tight. The noise went on and on. Our front door suddenly broke into pieces. When I opened my eyes the whole house was so full of dust it was hard to see.

It seemed ages before Mummy said, "Is everybody all right?" Then we picked our way over broken bits of wood and glass and went into the shelter.

I told Mummy my teeth were wobbling and someone gave me a glass of milk.

God had helped us, and He did again a short while later as once again we heard the aeroplane buzzing over head and it suddenly stopped. Everyone was very quiet and still as we waited for the big noise. It never came. Later on we heard the flying bomb had not exploded. If it had, we would have died.

"Well Mr Hitler," I said as I fingered the piece of metal that had started its journey in Germany on its way to kill us, "you didn't succeed with us. Here I am at 78 and still going strong."

My reverie was interrupted by the sound of a telephone ringing. Silly me – I had left my hands-free one in my bedroom. As I was extricating myself from the contents of the box I managed to drop the whole thing, upside down on the floor. Anyway I scurried to my bedroom and picked up the handset. "Hello? Hello?" – Nothing. No one there, just the dialling tone. How strange. The ringing started again. "Oh silly me – it's not the landline, but my mobile." Into the spare room and there it was on a table and I just got there in time, as Lara said, "Mum... the girls want to do FaceTime."

We had a lovely chat, and I heard all about their school day, including a science lesson on worms and spiders, and learning to sing 'Do-Re-Mi' from *Sound of Music*.

Back to the box and I looked in dismay at the conglomeration of insignificant stuff I had filled it with.

Was it me or my mother who had saved so much of my childish writings? I had always enjoyed writing stories, but was the story about a tramp's lost boot that was eventually found and rescued, entitled *The Old Boot*, really worth keeping?

Now this was more like it – my autograph book. I and my friends had always been dead keen on collecting autographs. I wrote to anybody famous I could think of and many of them sweetly replied. I even wrote to the English cricket team, and now I gazed at their signatures and realised my granddaughters would have no interest in these long-forgotten men at all.

Tucked into the back of the autograph book was a somewhat grubby, folded-up piece of paper.

'Top Secret. Look inside on pain of DEATH'.

I am thirteen years old. Minna and I have known each other since we were five years old. That is a seriously long time. I really, really do like Minna, though at times she can be jolly mean. Even a bit spiteful. When she is like that I tell her I will never be her friend again. After a bit we usually make it up and promise to be nice to each other.

The difference between Minna and me is that she cares awfully if she doesn't win at something. It doesn't matter what. A game of jacks, or cards or even me learning a new poem by heart before she does. It seems to worry her so much and it really doesn't bother me if she wins, which she often does.

Mummy says she just has a 'competitive spirit' and I don't. Mummy says Minna will probably go far in life as she is so determined.

Anyway two weeks ago we had a competition. It was rather fun. We had to rush around the school and grounds either collecting things or answering questions, like "Who painted the portrait of our Founder?"

We also had to do some arithmetic, French and spelling and then we had to write out a poem in our very best and neatest handwriting.

I was better at French but Minna was brilliant at arithmetic. I guessed we had been about the same with our collections and answering school questions, but when it came to handwriting, I knew I was best. Minna has dreadful writing, and I often get given good marks for mine. I wrote out the poem in my very best and neatest handwriting. Minna had already done hers.

I thought it was jolly nice of Minna to offer to hand in my pieces at the same time as hers. We skipped off happily to have a snack while we waited for the judgement.

"There are two girls who were way ahead of the others," said our Headmistress. "It was hard to judge until the last item, the poem. One looked as if it had been written in a dreadful hurry and was really quite hard to read, whilst the other had been painstakingly and beautifully written."

I know it is being a bit boastful, and Mummy says I must learn to be humble, but I just knew the Head was talking about my poem.

"So the winner of the prize is…" and I started to get up with a smile on my face, "Minna Wallace."

I have to admit I sat down with a bump and hated the giggles I heard from people around me. Minna came back triumphant. While everyone was congratulating her I snatched her box containing her collections and work, and saw MY poem amongst them.

"Minna – you CHEAT!" I shouted out. "You took MY poem."

"Charlotte Deen, sit down at once. No one likes a bad loser. Apologise to Minna at once."

Everyone was looking at me and I was crying. It was SO UNFAIR. I mumbled, "Sorry," and vowed never to be her friend again.

It was ages later that Minna came to me and said, "I am sorry Lottie. I did wrong. But you see my Daddy gets so angry with me if I don't win at things and I was scared he would beat me."

Then she put on her sweetest face, the one I adore, and said, "I promise I will never do anything like that again. PLEEESE forgive me."

So of course I did. Then we decided to declare our friendship for ever, and to sign our names in BLOOD!

I carefully unfolded the piece of paper in my hand, and read the somewhat faded, but well written by me, words.

We the undersigned do solemnly sware that from this day onwards we shall be

FRIENDS FOR LIFE

and no one shall come between us.

Signed and Sealed in our own blood

this day of 17 June 1953

Charlotte Deen   *Camilla Wallace*

(written in my own BLOOD)   *(This is MY own BLOOD)*

Pity I had to spoil it by spelling swear wrong!

Our friendship was good on the whole until we both fancied the same boy when we were fifteen, and he kissed me first! After that we began to drift apart, but I have kept an eye on her from a distance.

Minna ended up as head of a highly thought-of investment company in the City of London. She married at least twice, if not three times. She always seemed to have some extremely rich man on her arm. I don't think she had any children. I suddenly had an urge to speak to her again.

I telephoned an old school friend who had made it her business to keep in touch with all our year, and manfully organised a get-together when we all turned fifty. She gave me a number for Minna, although she said she could well have moved which was quite a regular activity.

To my amazement the telephone was answered after the second ring, and a voice said, "Hello – this is Minna Shively speaking."

"Minna – this is Lottie! How are you? I know I am a voice from the past but I had to ring as I have just come across our declaration of friendship signed in our blood. Do you remember?"

"Hello – this is Minna Shively speaking."

"Yes Minna, I know. This is Lottie. Lottie Deen that was. You remember me, I am sure."

"Hello – this is…" And then another voice: "Hello. Who is this, please?"

I explained who I was and why I had telephoned.

The new voice then told me she was a carer and that sadly Mrs Shively had advanced dementia and was about to be admitted to a nursing home.

"Oh dear, Minna," I said to myself. "I am so sorry."

I looked once more at our declaration of friendship, and then tore it into little pieces and threw it away.

I was having second thoughts about looking through this box as it was forcing me to relive some rather painful moments. I was just about to stuff everything back into it again when a brown envelope with my name and address typewritten on it fell out of a small bag. I instantly remembered what it was, and to my astonishment found my old heart beating in anticipation. Out of the envelope I pulled a single playing card, the queen of hearts. A typewritten note was attached to it.

———————————

"Will you be my Queen of Hearts this Valentine's Day?"

I looked and looked at the card and desperately tried to guess who it was from. I hoped against hope it was Charlie Peters.

I am now 19 and have just started a job in the local library. Charlie Peters is a regular customer. He takes out masses of books on history. He is somewhat dishevelled looking with rather long dark hair that flops over his face, and he is always pushing it out of his eyes. I wonder why he doesn't have it cut. He has the most gorgeous eyes. They are the clearest blue, and totally mesmerising. He often stays to chat to me when he is exchanging his books, and for this I get stern looks from Miss Godley the Librarian. A couple of weeks ago she actually 'tut-tutted' and Charlie and I had a sudden fit of the giggles which was even worse. Suddenly he scribbled something on a piece of paper, and he thrust this into my hand when he left with his pile of books on the Spanish Inquisition.

Charlie had asked me to meet him during my lunch hour. We went to a coffee shop and had a sandwich. I know I was awfully gauche, but he was totally gorgeous and soon we were laughing away as if we had known each other for yonks.

It turned out the card was from him. Charlie couldn't keep it a secret! After that he became my boyfriend, and we both fell head over heels in love with each other.

What a heady time that was. We did all the trad things like sitting in the back row of the cinema not watching the film at all, but holding hands and kissing.

One summer's day he took me out for the whole day. He had a car. Beat up and rather scruffy like him, but full of character. He even named his car 'Matilda'.

We had a picnic on top of a hill with heavenly views, and then he kissed me, really seriously, and for a moment he clambered on top of me, when suddenly, for some reason, he lost his balance, and both of us started to roll down the hill! We laughed until we cried. We were so happy. BUT we didn't go 'all the way' as of course I was far too frightened about getting pregnant.

We had a wonderful summer together, but when September arrived, Charlie told me he was going to Spain for a year to learn Spanish and really study Spanish history as he had decided this was to be his speciality.

I thought my heart would break. We swore undying love. Initially he wrote constantly but then his letters started to peter out. I suffered the agonies of torment and misery. I doubted I would ever recover. Then one day I received a letter in his writing, and my heart leapt for joy, only to discover that Charlie had fallen in love with a dark-haired señorita and had decided to live in Spain for the foreseeable future.

"What I need after all that is a good drink. I am feeling quite worn out with emotion."

I made myself a large gin and tonic and put one of Lara's frozen meals in the oven, and told myself I should just close that box up again and take it to the tip. Except of course I couldn't, due to Lockdown. So I resolved to shut it up and do something else.

Tiger Lily appeared and rubbed my legs, mewing softly for her food.

I put everything back in the box again, trying not to allow myself another peek, except at the snapshot of me and my father on a beach when I was about eight. I had to smile at what we were wearing. Me in one of those ghastly misshapen bobbly swimsuits and wearing a floppy sun hat, and my father – the grandchildren will laugh when I show them this – dressed for the beach in long trousers, turned up at the bottoms, bare feet, long-sleeved shirt and a rather smart trilby! We were both looking immensely pleased with ourselves having created a rather stupendous-looking sand castle.

I did mean to put it away. Really I did, but I then saw a bunch of letters in Gerald's handwriting. Dear Gerald. He was neither the most literate nor romantic.

"Gosh I think of you all the time. Hope you miss me? I jolly well miss you."

Also there was the menu from 'Le Petit Bijou' where we had our engagement meal.

There was our marriage service sheet with a sweet little painting of the church someone had done for us. Who?

I was returning them to the box when I saw the adorable little baby dress Lara had worn. I hugged and kissed it, and made myself remember the happy times.

Anyway, I was being firm with myself, so on went the lid and I put the box back in the wardrobe, promising to deal with it another day.

My determined mood disappeared as I watched the seven o'clock news. Covid-19 deaths are mounting up. The infection rate will soon be out of control. The most vulnerable in society are the elderly (just like me). Save the NHS, etc,. etc.

"Wash your hands. Do not go out of your house. Do not see anyone."

The messages were constantly dinned into us.

I was filled with longing to hug Lara and the girls. I wondered how much longer I could cope with this. I feared for the future my granddaughters would inherit. To be truthful, I also feared for my own future as well. I was beginning to feel desperate.

I rang Lara. I didn't say much. I was in danger of feeling very sorry for myself.

The next day I arose very early and went into the garden in my dressing gown and wandered around admiring the flowers, and enjoying the birdsong... The rising sun touched everything with its mellow glow and by 8 o'clock it was warm enough for me to take my breakfast outside and sit in its warmth, which Tiger Lily approved of as she jumped up onto my lap, causing me to very nearly spill the coffee.

I decided to ring Frances, my *New Best Friend*. That is, new for about three years! I told her about the box and its contents and she laughed as she said she had done almost the same thing with a chest of drawers, and had had the same reaction.

"Now listen old thing," she said. "We have got to get through this. Remember, we were War Babies and know how to cope with deprivation. Let's make a pact to call each other every day at this hour, and we *will* survive this beastly lockdown. And I for one am bound and determined not to get this disease, and I don't care how old and vulnerable I may appear because like you, inside I am full of grit."

I felt better at once. Good old Frances. I dressed and then decided to make my favourite chocolate cake for when I see the family again.

Just as I put the cake in the oven there was a loud knock on the front door.

Gingerly I opened it and there on the step outside was the most gorgeous bouquet of flowers.

A note attached read –

"I thought you seemed a bit sad today. This is just to let you know that Paul, the girls and I all love you very much."

I am a sentimental old fool, I know, but tears welled up and spilled over. As they poured unchecked down my cheeks, surprisingly my despair diminished. I looked out of the window at my sunny garden, and as I gazed at my beautiful bouquet I at last had a feeling of hope.

Now when I have my low moments about the future of our beautiful planet, I think of all the good people there are in the world who are working hard to clean our seas and save our animals, as well as those clever scientists who are striving to find a vaccine to beat this pandemic.

I just regret that I am too old to help. But like Frances, I am bound and determined to survive, and I know the day will come when once again I will hug my three girls.
